The Clothesline

EILEEN FINN LOVING

First Edition

PAGE PUBLISHING, INC.
New York, NY

First originally published by Page Publishing, Inc. 2019

ISBN 978-1-64424-764-8 (Paperback)
ISBN 978-1-64424-765-5 (Digital)

Printed in the United States of America

CHAPTER 1

It was Saturday morning in Baybridge. The sun had given notice that it was rising, by the glowing orange rim framing the horizon. Within seconds, the rays rose up and spread out behind the clouds, giving them the appearance of net curtains drawn over lamplight. Blink now and the miracle would escape you. In what seemed to be an instant, the curtains were drawn back, revealing the sun in all its glory. Fiona Hannon woke with a start and sat bold upright in bed. The room was lit by bright sunshine, and she could see it was 7 o'clock. She lay back on her pillows and took a few moments to compose herself. She had a feeling of apprehension settling under her ribs. She had no memory of a dream and knowing that nothing in particular was worrying her, she asked herself aloud, "What in the world is the matter with you?" Instead of answering herself, which would squarely fall into the category of talking to herself, she decided to get out of bed and start her day.

Her house was located on the outskirts of Baybridge, a small city on the west coast of Ireland. It was situated at the foot of Shadow Ridge Mountain to the east and Three Peaks to the north. Nestled in between lay Swan Lake, so named for the ballet of swans that called it home. The river that gracefully meandered through the city earned its name from these magnificent birds who used it as their main thoroughfare. Swan River was the focal point of the city.

"Tea is ready, want toast?" asked Mark, her husband, as he heard her at the top of the stairs. She could see his blond curls bob about through the banister as she came down.

"Good morning!" she replied. "Just tea." She debated whether to mention her odd feeling to him. She decided not to. If it didn't make any sense to her, how was it supposed to make sense to him? Anyway, it was fading. "What time are you heading over to the club?" she added as she noticed he was already dressed in khaki pants and a collared shirt sporting the Gaelic Football club logo.

"It's an early start to a long day," he replied, giving her a morning kiss. "Games all day, but look at the lovely weather we have.

"That's true," she said, "great walking day and great drying day too. Speaking of drying, let me get that load of jeans started and out on the line before my walk."

"Oh, by the way," Mark continued, "Conor has the last match today, so Brian will most likely drive in with Yvonne and little Lilly. Can't imagine his mam and dad missing a game, can you?"

"No way! They will be there. Our son, daughter-in-law, and granddaughter all cheering our grandson to victory. You will have to remain neutral though."

"Of course! The club manager will always remain neutral," he said with an exaggerated wink. Fiona, now bent over the washing machine, looked over her shoulder and returned the wink.

After Mark left, she sat a moment to finish her tea. The telephone caught her eye. Thinking about her son prompted her to call her daughter, Cate, who lived just two streets away. She got so excited at the thought of spending time with her and her two grandchildren, Cara, age five, and Mathew, age two, that you would think they lived across the country instead of two streets down.

"Granny," squealed Cara, "are you coming down?"

"Morning, Cara. Your voice matches the bright sunny day. Can you get Mammy for me?" asked Fiona.

"Such excitement around here!" said Cate as Cara reluctantly handed over the phone.

"I wish my clients greeted my like that!" said Fiona. She was a social worker, and not all her home visits generated such welcome.

"Well, you're very popular down our way, that's for sure! I understand the lack of enthusiasm with the clients, though," said Cate, "we teachers suffer the same fate on occasion."

"I was hoping you would be free this afternoon," said Fiona. "Wouldn't it be a great day for the beach?"

"Oh my gosh! I was just thinking exactly the same thing! Colm, the wonderful husband that he is, is already mowing the grass. He mentioned that he was going up to the club to give Dad a hand today. Games galore, all day, apparently."

"I heard! Are we on for the beach then?" asked Fiona.

"Absolutely! After nap?" asked Cate.

"Good. I'll get a good walk, a few loads on the line, a bit of tidying, and then we'll be off. Tell Cara."

"I will but I beat you. I have two loads out already!"

"Show off!" her mother said, laughing, and hung up.

Traditionally the washday was Monday, and Fiona wondered if that was because it was considered woman's work, and when everybody left for school or work, the women got on with washing the clothes. She remembered her own childhood ritual. Saturday nights, the whole house had their bath, and all clothes were changed from the skin out for Sunday Mass. That would generate a whole lot of washing! Time was marching on, so she jumped up, headed back up the stairs, and threw on her gym clothes.

Jeans were always washed separately, never mixed in with other clothes. It did not matter that they had been washed several times before; it was a long-held belief that if they were not washed separately, the dye would run into the water, rendering every other stitch of clothes a dirty gray color, and the jeans themselves would fade. Now, faded jeans were quite fashionable, but if that is what you were going for, you bought them that way. You did not rely on a laundry *mistake* to achieve the look. So in they went, by themselves, good and early because they took days to dry. Getting the clothes dry was an art in and of itself in this damp part of the world, and although most houses had dryers, no self-respecting lady of the house would use one. Fiona had to wait for the jeans to wash and get them out on the line before her walk. Timing was everything.

CHAPTER 2

It really was a beautiful, bright, sunny morning, a spritzing of dew reflecting on the grass in her neat front garden and an air of freshness and newness about the place. Her house was on Shadow Ridge Avenue, an ideal spot to start her walk. At the end of her driveway, she had two choices. Turning right, she faced Three Peaks, a spectacular mountain; turning left, she had a view of the town nestled below. Fiona liked loops for her walks rather than turning and retracing her steps. She didn't make a conscious decision to turn towards the town; it just happened. In Baybridge, everywhere you went involved a hill. Fiona lived halfway up one of these hills, and it was a workout just going out the front door, it seemed. The view was inspiring and took the edge off the hard work.

As she got into her stride, her mind wandered. She still had not completely shaken off that earlier feeling of anxiety. Despite that, she decided to put her best foot forward. As she picked up the pace, she began to miss her youngest daughter, Laura, who was married to Sean and had two little boys, Paul, four, and Caleb, everyone's favourite, who just turned nine months. They lived about three hours away, but even so, they saw a lot of each other. Laura worked part-time in a bank and was not averse to bundling the boys into the car and heading north at a moment's notice. Everybody loved these visits, which would prompt an invitation to come and see her next weekend, and someone always did. Fiona powered along, arms pumping, lost in thought, and almost bumped into Mr. Doherty. He was coming out of his gate, head down, and was suddenly right in front of her. "Good morning, Mr. Doherty, I didn't see you there," said Fiona.

"Right. Nice day," he replied and headed rapidly in the direction of the corner shop. Mr. Doherty was a man of few words with a reputation for knowing the hot favourites for every horse race run on Saturdays. He was on his way to pick up the newspaper. He would return home to a few hours of intense study then reappear at 10 o'clock as the bookies opened. This was serious business, not to be taken lightly.

Fiona silently wished him good luck, and almost immediately her thoughts were again invaded, this time by laughing, giggling, and clicking of heels as Carmel and Maura Murry came into view. Now there's a sight for sore eyes, thought Fiona, as she enjoyed the twin sisters clicking their way down the hill that led into town. They were simultaneously bumping into each other and pushing each other away in a fit of giggles. Fiona was not sure from behind, but it appeared Carmel was taking a bite out of something in Maura's hand when they bumped together. Granola bar? Breakfast on the go? Those two seemed to share everything! She enjoyed their antics and agreed with all and sundry that these were good kids. They were seventeen now and would be doing their Leaving Certificate Exam next year, a grueling two weeks of testing that would decide acceptance to a reputable university. No doubt they were on their way to their Saturday job at the most fashionable clothing store in town and enjoying having exchanged their school uniform for the latest trends.

It was time to make her turn to the left, heading away from the town and back up the hill towards home, bringing the second of the Baybridge mountains, Shadow Ridge, into view. This was Fiona's favourite part of her walk, and although it was a steep hill, she loved it. Once the hill was conquered, the view was spectacular. The few houses along the way were to be envied, old stately homes, built on many acres and had been there forever, it seemed. Mrs. Shiva, who lived in the last house on this road, was in her driveway buckling her baby in the push chair as Fiona got level with her house.

"Good morning, Mrs. Shiva!" she called, as she waved and slowed her pace. "Lovely morning, isn't it?" She did not know the lady very well but knew her husband and brother from her visits to the restaurant they owned in town.

"Don't stop, don't stop! Enjoy your walk," replied Mrs. Shiva. With another wave, Fiona moved on, thinking of the excellent food served at their restaurant, aptly named Pepper.

Pepper was an upscale restaurant located on the outskirts of town with a hilltop view of the mountains in the distance. It was a detached building boasting a garden area in the rear, beautifully appointed for outside dining, certainly a place to show off your best frock!

As Fiona continued her walk, two things were uppermost in her mind. First, how could she arrange a dinner date with Mark at Pepper? And should she stop at Mrs. Quigley's corner shop to pick up goodies for a picnic at the beach, which she decided, would be much more enjoyable than going into a café? Smiling, she increased her pace and continued the uphill climb. Arriving at the shop, she noticed that it was busier than usual, and she was surprised to see Mr. Doherty standing just inside the door. She had to manoeuvre around him just to get in and he seemed none too happy. As she entered the shop, she overheard Mrs. Quigley explain, "I'm very sorry, Mr. Doherty, but the papers have not yet been delivered. Jimmy, the van driver, just called to explain that he is stuck behind an accident about three miles away. He said he will be here as soon as he can. Would it not be better if you came back later?" Mrs. Quigley took a deep breath.

Mr. Doherty grunted and said, "I'll wait."

Mrs. Quigley was a tall, thin quiet lady who hadn't changed in all the years Fiona had been going in and out of her shop. She always seemed to be working and was sometimes helped by one or two of her children, or occasionally a local schoolgirl. She sold a spectacular array of individual pies, cakes, tarts, and breads that she herself made. The fresh smell alone was enough to bring in the customers. Two young girls, Amy and Angela, were in deep consultation at the sweets counter. They lived immediately next door to Mrs. Finnerty and were the surrogate caretakers of her cat, Mrs. Miller. Serious decisions had to be made about how to spend their pocket money, and they did not seem to be in agreement. Negotiations continued as Fiona moved on. Meanwhile, up at the counter, Mr. Doherty impatiently awaited the arrival of the paper. This delay might put his first bet of the day in jeopardy. Mrs. Quigley remained the same as she always did, tall, thin, and quiet—no doubt her mood honed after years of dealing with the Mr. Doherty's of this world.

There was a queue now forming at the counter, and Fiona went forward with her choices. She saw another of her neighbors standing in front of her and thought that that was the end of the queue but in fact as she got closer she realised it was not. Mrs. Finnerty was standing off to the side, empty basket in hand and a vacant, lost look on her face. In fact, Fiona had to call her name twice to get her attention.

"Mrs. Finnerty," she said, lightly touching her sleeve. "How are you?" The noise of the negotiations at the sweets counter had risen a decibel or two, but Mrs. Finnerty did not seem to notice. Normally, this kind of thing would have amused her greatly but not today.

"Oh, good morning, Fiona. I was away with the fairies there for a minute," said Mrs. Finnerty.

"Sure I'm often like that myself. I just popped in to get some of Mrs. Q's goodies. Cate and the kids are coming up later, and I thought it would do me no harm in the popularity department to have a few to take with us to the beach today," Fiona answered. "Not that I am conspiring or anything!" she added with an impish grin.

"Indeed," said Mrs. Finnerty listlessly. "I used to bake myself, once upon a time, but since Mr. Finnerty passed on, I just didn't see the point, just for one. It's been years now."

"My mother baked too, but I never got the hang of it. Maybe you can give me a few tips," Fiona replied lightheartedly. Mrs. Finnerty did not reply.

"How is Mrs. Miller?" Fiona asked, referring to Mrs. Finnerty's cat, the pride and joy of the street and the epitome of royalty. Mrs. Miller had fluffy long snow-white fur decorated with ginger patches. Her face was very small, and you always felt she should be wearing rimless reading glasses. She sat on the outside ledge of the bay window in the front of Mrs. Finnerty's house, and every man, woman, and child said hello to Mrs. Miller as they passed. Her reply was merely the slight raising of one eyebrow. Mrs. Miller was truly the cat's meow!

Mrs. Finnerty brightened a little at the mention of Mrs. Miller but did not recount any of the cat's goings-ons, as she usually did.

"Have you much shopping to do? I can give you a hand with some of the bags if you have anything heavy," offered Fiona.

Again, a vacant pause before she replied, "Just a few small items really. My usual order was brought up yesterday afternoon from town by young Finbar. I'm not sure really, so I might just look around."

"All right then. If we have time for a walk later when Cate comes, we will look out for Mrs. Miller."

Fiona joined the end of the queue and, looking over her shoulder, saw that Mrs. Finnerty was still standing where she left her. Once again, that feeling of apprehension started to creep in under her ribs. The two young girls were in front of her and had obviously agreed on the selection of sweets. As she got nearer to the counter, she noticed the absence of Mr. Doherty, which she took to mean that Jimmy had arrived with the papers. Mrs. Finnerty stayed a moment longer, put her empty basket on the floor right where she stood, and left the shop.

CHAPTER 3

Fiona stood on the top of the dunes, looking out at the ocean, and felt what she always felt every time she saw the waves break, a deep sense of peace. She felt as if the waves were taking her worries out to sea. She always came to the beach when she was troubled or had a major decision to make. It was therapeutic. She was born five miles from this very place and had been coming here all her life. Still, every time she saw the ocean, she was in awe of its grandeur. She felt it was a new discovery each time she came here. A few minutes earlier, when they had come over the hill that brought the vast expanse of water into view, they had all yelped with joy. It seemed that Fiona had passed her passion for the ocean on to her family. They parked, tumbled out of the car, grabbed their picnic basket, buckets, and spades, and then made a beeline for the sand dunes.

There were three beaches here, as if the ocean had taken three enormous hungry bites out of the land. They were known as First Strand, Second Strand, and Third Strand. As kids, they had always chosen Second Strand, and that habit continued. The sand was fine and white, and the dunes had settled into a selection of rooms sheltered by tall rushes. This is where they would have their picnic. The children would first play on the vast expanse of wet, darker, solid sand near the water, paddling at the water's edge, squealing when they got caught by the wave, running out of the water, returning to the water, and doing it all over again. The game was to challenge the wave, but the wave always won. Every family there played the same game with the wave and believed they were the first and only family to do it. You owned yourself and your thoughts completely when you were at the beach, no need of company. Little clumps of people sitting on towels, no matter how close to you, would never consider striking up a conversation. The sheer size and expanse of the space made you free.

"Granny, I'm starving!" said Cara as soon as they reached the sand.

Fiona, smiling, replied, "I know you are, pet!"

Everyone was always starving at the beach! It didn't matter that you had just eaten before you arrived; you would state loudly that you were starving. This would lead to a retreat from the wet beach back to the little sandy rooms protected by the rushes. It was as if you were going into your house, a returning home from a great adventure, and a quietness descended while you waited for that first sandwich.

In Fiona's family, a beach picnic had to have sandwiches. Tomato sandwiches, with or without ham, for the grownups, and for the little ones, banana sandwiches. This menu was laid down a long time ago when Fiona was a small child. She was transported back to another time as she sat there. Her father rented a wooden chalet for them every year, and they stayed for two whole weeks. It was a wondrous experience! The chalet was solid wood through and through, including built-in bunk beds and a veranda leading right out to a stony inlet. Everybody saw the chalet and admired it as they entered the village. It was a local landmark. As it was stony there, one had to walk a short distance to get to the beach proper. This was where they learned to pick perfectly flat stones and skim them on the top of the water. Her brother, Declan, considered himself the expert skimmer.

She could hear his voice clearly declaring, "Nona, flat stones, not fat stones!" as her choice of stone sank to join the others at the bottom of the ocean. Her brother always called her Nona. The skimming rivalry between Declan and his three sisters was fierce.

Her father usually booked the first two weeks after school closed for the summer holidays. They had what might be called a corner shop. He closed the shop at 7 in the evening during these two weeks. He would cycle out in the evenings to join them and bring chocolate bars.

He needed help for the rest of the summer, especially their mother's. The children had specific jobs to do and were an integral part of the workforce. Any maintenance that had to be done was done while the children were home. It was also cost-effective as they did not have to hire outside help.

The shop was not on a corner but rather halfway along the street that led from a residential area to a major road passing through town. It was a very successful enterprise since it was open from 8 o'clock in the morning to 11 o'clock at night. These hours accommodated the early and late shopper as well as the customers who shopped there on a regular basis.

Her father was meticulous about everything, from his own appearance to the way he maintained the shop—starting with how the shelves were stocked, how the white weighing scales were cleaned, and how the surgically carved bacon was placed on the white enamel tray. This tray became the centerpiece of the shop window and enticed many a customer. The plateglass window was cleaned at least twice daily, using water and newspaper. This attention to detail was given to everything that was sold in the shop. Display was everything! Despite his meticulous ways, they laughed a lot in the shop.

"Daddy had us all in stitches today!" was a common refrain. He was known for his quick wit and ability to see humour in the mundane. Customers came in just for the banter.

Her mother was the one with the sense of community. She knew her customers very well and the huge contribution they made to the economic success of the town. Baybridge was a port with a vibrant economy. The vast majority of the male customers worked on the docks unloading coal, timber, and dried goods from various parts of the world. Her mother understood that if there was no boat, there was no work and no wages. She developed a discreet and respectful system to enable the wives to provide for their families during the times when work was scarce. She had an understanding with her suppliers that informed her when certain goods were about to go on sale. She got first dibs on bananas about to be overripe or pastries a bit too beat up for display. She would send word that she had some specials, and the customers always knew what that meant. Her mother had bought these goods at a reduced cost and could sell them for mere pennies, and in so doing she allowed them to maintain their dignity as there was no charity involved. She would add a few loaves of bread from the shop for the ever-popular banana sandwiches.

Mothers often confided in her when one of their children was sick or having troubles at school. When first Holy Communion time came around, it would not be unusual for her mother to have a First Holy Communion dress or suit in just the right size. The choosing of the dress or suit in the elite clothing store in town was not taken lightly. Whoever was going to be wearing these clothes were well-known to her and deserving of the best. She took great care to match the outfit with each child's personality. On the day of the big event, the children came into the shop just to show off their outfits. Of course, she was completely surprised by how beautiful and handsome they all were.

Her mother was known as the good woman. Her father was the first to call her that. Fiona learned how to treat people with respect and dignity from her mother, who had instilled in them a clear understanding that no one was superior to anybody else. Fiona's oldest sister, Eiler, a director of nursing in America, always said that "Mammy was the first social worker I ever met." She was, in fact, an accountant. Fiona, of course, did become a social worker herself.

Some of the customers who came into the shop were local farmers. They grew potatoes, cabbage, carrots, and other produce and sold them to the shopkeepers in town. One such supplier was Mr. Feehily, who sold his produce to her dad. He came into town every Saturday morning in his van. Fiona and her siblings were always excited to see him. They liked his stories and because he gave them each a three-penny bit, a bronze, multisided coin discontinued long ago. This coin was used to buy the same packet of mints from their father's shop every single week. It was Mr. Feehily who would make a special trip on the first Sunday after school closed to take them to the chalet in his van. It required two trips to get to the chalet, one for the supplies and one for the family.

One of the more popular items sold in the shop was the loose-leaf tea. It came in a large wooden box called a tea chest and was weighed out by their father into pound bags. The smell was amazing. Two of these tea chests would be saved for the beach trip and filled with food supplies, cooking utensils, dishes, and bedding.

She could practically smell the tea as she remembered helping to unpack those tea chests. She told the story to her grandchildren, sitting there on the same sand dunes.

"When we were small, just like you are now, your great-grandparents took us to this beach every summer for two weeks. We thought it was so far away from our shop in Baybridge and so different, it was like we were in a different country altogether."

The children moved closer to their granny, wide-eyed. Each time Cate heard this story, she felt that somehow, she had missed out on something magical.

"Up closer to the road there was a wooden chalet like you see in pictures of places where it snows a lot. It had built-in wooden bunks and wooden benches to sit on. All the hot food was cooked outside on a Primus stove. That's a kind of camping oil stove that made great rashers and eggs and the best fried bread ever!

"Where is the wooden house now?" asked Cara.

"Somebody moved it to a safer place when they put in the new road," answered Fiona.

"I hope they still make fried bread," said Cara. Mathew wanted fried bread right then and there. He was placated by half of a banana sandwich.

"These are the exact kind of sandwiches my mother used to make for us to take to the beach. Somehow, we always got sand on them, but we didn't mind. Tomato sandwiches still remind me of sand," continued Fiona.

The kids giggled and Cara examined Mathew's sandwich from a distance. It looked a bit sandy to her! She resolved to be more careful with her own. Cate was so totally absorbed in her children's reaction to her mother's story that she had to be reminded to serve the remainder of the picnic.

As they sat in their sheltered little sand room, the children devoured their banana sandwiches, by now squashed and sandy. As Fiona watched Cara and Mathew polish off the last of Mrs. Quigley's treats, she felt a burst of energy and raced down to the water's edge, her turn to do battle with the waves. She left Cate and the children in their dune room.

CHAPTER 4

Mrs. Finnerty had a cheerful disposition. She was not peppy, by any means, but always seemed in good humour, interacting with her neighbours when she met them, either on her walks, in town, or in her driveway. Because of Mrs. Miller, her famous cat, there were lots of meetings in her driveway.

She did not favour one season over another but instead enjoyed the changes each of the four seasons brought. She was a teacher in India for many years. Her husband, who had been there two years before her, while showing her the ropes, had fallen madly in love with her and she with him. They married within a year, and that love flourished throughout their marriage. Although they had no children of their own, they cherished their pupils. Teaching these youngsters delighted Mrs. Finnerty, and she got as excited as they did when they learned something new. It was as if she herself just made a discovery. Sadly, six years into their marriage, Mr. Finnerty passed away. It was a devastating loss for her, and she had to reconsider her future without him. Supported by a genuine circle of friends, she decided to stay in India and remained there for over thirty years. She had begun to miss Ireland more and more and decided to return about seven years ago. She had traveled around Ireland when she first came back. As she had no living relatives remaining in her homeland; it was as if she was shopping around for just the right spot. She found it in Baybridge. She loved the scenery, and the people were kind and friendly. The town boasted a first-rate Indian restaurant that she discovered on her first day in Baybridge. She often remembered that day and how a chance encounter on the train had changed her life. She was traveling west on the 8:00 a.m. train from Dublin to Baybridge. She was engrossed in her book when she heard a voice.

"Excuse me, is this seat taken?" said a tall, handsome, impeccably dressed man. For a second or two she was disoriented. She hadn't noticed that the train had stopped and this man had just boarded. She did notice he spoke with a familiar Indian accent.

"No," she said as she sat up a little straighter, "it's free."

"Good! It's getting a bit crowded. Big turnout at the market here this morning."

"Market?" she asked.

"It was mostly for merchants at first, but it's grown so much over the past few years that now it is open to anyone."

"What kind of market?" she asked.

"They have the highest quality meats and locally grown produce. One particular supplier has the most comprehensive array of imported spices I have ever seen, a must-have for the dishes we serve in our restaurant, Pepper. It's in Baybridge," he explained.

The lilt of his accent was familiar.

"Baybridge! That's where I'm headed. In fact, I just moved back to Ireland from India. I spent over thirty years teaching in a village in Tamil Nadu State," she said.

She noticed him staring at her as he said, "I was born in Tamil Nadu."

Now it was her turn to stare at him.

"Forgive my rudeness!" he said, standing up as if to salute. "My name is Deva Shiva, and I am the proud owner of one of the finest Indian restaurants in Ireland. We would be honored if you would be our guest for lunch this coming Sunday." He ceremoniously bowed at the waist.

She accepted. They talked at length about his home and shared many memories.

As their destination approached, Mr. Shiva asked if anyone was meeting her.

"No," she replied, "I will take a taxi to the Glass Swan Hotel overlooking the river. I'm hoping to end my search for a home here in Baybridge. Oh my! Where are my manners!" she said, offering her hand. "I am Rebecca Finnerty."

His car was parked at Baybridge station. She accepted an offer of a lift to her hotel. She met the nicest people she had ever met in the next few days.

On Sunday, she took a taxi to Pepper where she met Mr. Shiva's brother, who helped run the restaurant. He led her to a table in an alcove that allowed her a clear view of the dining room and was spacious enough to accommodate guests. She was joined by Mr. Shiva's wife, Usha, and their two-year-old daughter, Anu. They became friends that, day and Mrs. Finnerty ate her lunch there every Sunday since. She had found her home, and now she needed a house.

There were lots of complaints about the weather in Baybridge. Too damp, too unpredictable, too windy, but Mrs. Finnerty always said, "This is the price you pay for this glorious land!" People had to agree with her. She was intrigued by the part the weather played in getting the washing dried. She remembered the extensive vocabulary that grew out of this all-consuming obsession when she was a child. The clothes could be either sopping wet, wringing wet, soaking wet, and dripping wet, well soaked, damp, stiff, bone-dry, or very dry. One had better know which word to choose when reporting the state of the washing on the line back to the person who sent you to check. The next move depended on which word you used; whether the clothes would stay on the line, rechecked later, or brought in to the inside line to be aired. No article of clothing *ever* went on an Irish body without it being *aired* first! "You could catch your death of cold" was the common belief. She loved to hang the washing on the line and compete with the elements to get it dried. It was a challenge!

She chose a house on the outskirts of Baybridge because of the view of the mountains from her bedroom window. It brightened her soul on rising every morning. The house looked the same as all the others on the street from the outside. The garage had been converted to a room in most houses, but in Mrs. Finnerty's house, the entire ground floor had been remodeled and was now a library. Books were housed in elegantly carved bookcases ceiling to floor on every wall. All the rooms on this floor had been made into one. As you entered the front door, which was flanked by a bay window on either side, no obstacle obstructed your view, and you could see through to the backyard. The once-big kitchen was now shrunk and a small vanity room had been discreetly added. Even the clothesline had been moved out of view. The most impressive feature of the room was the three-step library ladder that slid along the floor to make the higher shelves accessible. To one side of the room and facing one of the bay windows was a carved table in matching wood. Natural light flooded the library. Just inside the door to the right was a cozy corner with an armchair, reading lamp on a small side table.

Mrs. Finnerty always sat at the large table with her open book placed on top. Today she sat there after her return from Mrs. Quigley, just staring out of the bay window to the front of the house. This was how Mr. Doherty found her when he made his usual Saturday afternoon visit.

CHAPTER 5

The Saturday ritual between Mrs. Finnerty and Mr. Doherty started many years earlier and quite by chance. Mrs. Finnerty was out for an early morning walk one Saturday, and Mr. Doherty was in his front garden tending to his flowers. He was standing near his gate, examining a beautiful flowering plant, still in a pot. He was holding it on high, and Mrs. Finnerty stopped dead in her tracks and was held spellbound by the color and shape of the flowers. Still trying to decide the best spot in which to plant it, he noticed her standing there. He put the pot down on the paved driveway and walked over to her. After greeting each other, a lengthy conversation ensued about plants and flowers, both local and from many parts of the world. Mr. Doherty had been in the Merchant Navy and had traveled extensively. He had a green thumb since his childhood, and his travels had broadened his interest in more exotic plants. Today he was in a quandary about whether to transplant this beautiful specimen into the ground outside or leave it in the pot and bring it back indoors where it had been thriving but getting very big. Mrs. Finnerty recognised it as an exquisite bougainvillea. She herself did not have a green thumb and knew she could kill a dandelion just by looking at it. She had always loved a lush, beautiful garden. Her house in India boasted such a garden, colourful bougainvillea hedges everywhere, skillfully tended by the gardener. This was why she was so taken by Mr. Doherty's plant. She, of course, would not be of any use to him in his current dilemma as she had no instinct for actually growing anything. Mr. Doherty was to learn as they talked that though she did not grow any flowers, she had quite a collection of books about them, and she asked if he would like to borrow some. He said he would, and so it was that he agreed he would come to her house later that day, and she would have a book ready for him.

Somehow, while they were talking about their time abroad, she mentioned that she also loved horses and was quite a good rider in her younger days in India. Horse racing was a common event on Saturdays. It was something to look forward to, and she and her coworkers enjoyed the excitement of placing a small bet or flutter as they used to call it, on a certain horse. There would be such yelping as the race was being run, such clapping if they won, and feigned misery if they lost. It was now Mr. Doherty's turn to stare at her. He, of course, was a serious betting man and would be making his trip to the bookies as soon as he studied the racing pages of today's paper.

On an impulse, he said, "Mrs. Finnerty, as it happens, I place the odd flutter myself on Saturdays. I'll be going to do just that here shortly. By any chance would you like me to put a small bet on for you, so we can either clap or pretend to be miserable after the race?"

Mrs. Finnerty replied, "Mr. Doherty, that's the best idea I've heard in ages. I don't have a purse with me right now, though."

He stopped her with a wave of his hand and said, "If you let me take care of the betting, I'll let you take care of the books." A deal was made, and they kept to it every Saturday since.

CHAPTER 6

It was time for Mr. Doherty's visit. She dreaded it but needed him to come. She had thought about nothing else except Dr. Owens's words since leaving his office on Thursday afternoon. She had nobody. Was it selfish to involve him? What did she expect him to do? He was not family. They had kept their Saturday routine for over six years now, but was it a friendship? Did she have the right to burden him? Was it fair? One thing she knew for sure, she had to share her fear. She was terrified.

She opened the door to him and immediately he knew something was very wrong—she looked scared to death. He quickly scanned the room behind her, but nothing seemed amiss.

Mrs. Finnerty stepped back.

She told him.

He sat down.

Mr. Doherty never sat down in Mrs. Finnerty's house.

Cate parked the car outside her mam's house, unbuckled her seat belt, and stepped out. Fiona did the same on her side, and as she turned to open the car door to get Mathew out, she caught a glimpse of Mr. Doherty coming down Mrs. Finnerty's driveway. She vaguely thought it odd but continued to get Mathew out of the car. He was delighted to be free again and ran towards the house. By that time, Mr. Doherty had reached them.

"Mrs. Hannon," he said, addressing her formally, "you're back from the beach, I see."

"Hello there!" replied Fiona. "It was a great day for it!"

"Could I trouble you for a minute?"

"Of course," she said. "Let me get this lot into the house. Come on in!"

He patted Mathew on the head and followed her to the door. Cate had gone ahead with Cara and as Fiona drew level with her, she whispered, "Put the kettle on and keep these two with you for a minute." "I'll take him into the front room. Oh, would you ever check the line?" she added, as an afterthought.

"We'll go in here for a bit of quiet," she told Mr. Doherty as she led him into a bright, cheerful room. Comfortable chairs and some child-sized wooden furniture, made by her husband, Mark, gave the room a relaxed feel. Fiona did not want an office in her home but often sat in here to do paperwork or just have a think.

"You seem a bit troubled, Mr. Doherty," she said as she motioned for him to sit down.

He plopped down heavily, looked at her straight in the eye, and said, "Mrs. Finnerty is very sick. She has an awful lot to arrange, and I don't know what to do." Mr. Doherty was a single man. Having been a sailor for many years, he was uncomfortable with other people's personal issues, especially illness. At that very moment, a small knock on the door interrupted them, and Cate came in with two cups of strong tea in the best china on a small tray. No biscuits, she knew it was not an occasion for biscuits. Mr. Doherty took his cup straight off the tray and downed it in two gulps, no time to ask if he liked sugar. Cate left the room quietly—no need for words.

"That is very hard news to hear, very hard, indeed. I saw you come from her house. Did she just tell you now?" Fiona had to tread lightly here. She was a social worker and governed by all manner of patient privacy and confidentiality regulations.

"Just this minute. I had to sit down. I don't normally sit down or stay at all when I call on Saturdays. I just get a new book and tell her the results of her race. If there are any big winnings, I leave them with her. Usually I just place another bet for her the next week, but today it was a fierce shock, I just sat down. She sat at her table near the books. I left her still there. Mrs. Miller is outside on the windowsill."

Fiona was confused by Mr. Doherty's account. She really had no idea what the man was talking about between the books and the bets and the sitting down and the not sitting down and the cat! She was, however accustomed to this type of rambling when people got bad news. She did note that Mrs. Finnerty had told him about her illness but asked, "So she wanted you to talk to me?"

"Yes, yes, what else could she do?"

Fiona was satisfied that Mrs. Finnerty knew Mr. Doherty was sharing this information with her, and she really did need help.

"Thank you for coming in, Mr. Doherty. It's a big shock to you, I know. I will call down to talk to Mrs. Finnerty shortly. Maybe I can get a few more details from herself, and between us we will make a plan. After we talk, we can move forward fairly quickly. I can honestly say that she will get all the help and support she needs."

Mr. Doherty looked sad as he left.

Cate was in the kitchen when Fiona reappeared and shot her a glance over her shoulder. She knew immediately that this visit from Mr. Doherty involved something confidential and knew better than to ask questions. As a teacher herself and senior enough to have administrative responsibilities, this needed no explanation.

"I raided the fridge, Mam, and put the tea together. The kids are starving again. I put out Mrs. Quigley's bread—hope you were not saving it," Cara said, placing thick slices of Mrs. Quigley's brown bread on the table.

"No, no saving here, eat away," said Fiona. "Let's open the jam while we're at it. I'm starving again myself."

It was usual for the main meal in Ireland to be called dinner and eaten at midday. The evening meal was lighter and known as the tea. A more substantial tea was called for today because a beach picnic does not qualify as dinner. Fiona was looking forward to sharing hers with Cate and the grandchildren. It was all part of this day spent together.

After much persuasion to leave the toys for now, Cate managed to get faces and hands washed and two hungry children seated at the kitchen table. Fiona joined them and was just about to pour the freshly made tea when Cate jumped up from the table, exclaiming,

"The washing, I forgot to take it in!" And with that, she was out the back door.

Hovering above her chair for a moment, Fiona decided to sit back down. Cate would bring in the clothes. Minutes later, they were all back at the table together. Clothes in off the line, clothes dry, soon to be aired, day saved, whew!

During the meal, it was decided that they would take a walk up to the football club. Cara and Mathew clapped hands at this suggestion; they would see Grandad and maybe Conor and Lilly and certainly get a chance to see a match, great!

Fiona helped Cate spruce up the children before leaving. She said she would stay, tidy up, and walk up to join them later. Fiona needed a little time to gather her thoughts before going to see Mrs. Finnerty.

CHAPTER 7

Sitting in her comfortable front room, Fiona thought back on her visit with Mr. Doherty. She really wasn't sure what to think. He told her about Mrs. Finnerty's illness without any details. This could have been in part due to Fiona's reluctance to ask or Mr. Doherty just not knowing. The fact that Mr. Doherty was the one coming to her to ask for help was unexpected. The relationship, whatever it was, between these two neighbours was not known to her previously, and she was not sure how to proceed. From what she could gather, they met regularly on Saturdays for some time now, and it had to do with books and bets. There was obviously a level of trust between them as she sent him for help.

As a diversion, she went back to the airing line strategically placed in the small room just off the kitchen, which her mother would have called a scullery. The clothes were airing nicely. She snatched her handbag from the kitchen chair and headed out the front door. Checking on drying clothes can be a very focusing activity.

The chatter in Mrs. Finnerty's driveway could be heard a couple of doors away. Amy and Angela were sitting on the ground, deep in conversation with Mrs. Miller. It was not unusual for Mrs. Miller to have visitors. She really was the kind of cat that made people stop and visit. To Fiona's surprise, as she reached the driveway, she could see that they each had a slice of cake on a small colorful plastic plate. On the windowsill stood two matching plastic mugs. The surprise really was how little Fiona knew her neighbour. If Mrs. Finnerty had a set of children's dishes, this was probably not the first time Amy and

Angela had been given treats by her. Books, bets, and beakers! What other surprises could there be?

The library was the first thing Fiona saw as the door was opened. Evening sun lit the space from back door to front, and Fiona's jaw dropped in sheer amazement. Following Mrs. Finnerty into the house, she expected to see a replica of her own. Remembering this moment later, she was sure she appeared rude or stupid or both but not a professional woman coming to her aid. Luckily, everybody who came into the house for the first time had that same look and needed time to compose themselves. As Fiona was an avid reader since childhood and still went frequently to the local library, she took a little longer to recover. Looking back over her shoulder, Mrs. Finnerty said with a sweep of her hand, "I love books. I always said I would surround myself with them. I was lucky enough to meet an architect who knew a builder who also loved books. He took a chance and created this." Fiona remained speechless until Mrs. Finnerty led her back to the small kitchen area and offered her a cup of tea. Her recovery was slow as she sipped the hot tea and began to remember why she was there.

"Forgive me for staring, but I can't believe this is possible, our houses look the same from the street," whispered Fiona."

"Well, they are the same really, it's just the ground floor that was changed, and I didn't need all those separate rooms and that huge kitchen. There were a few hairy moments during the construction, but my good bookworm builder kept the faith, and here we are."

"Wow!" was all Fiona could manage.

"I hope you weren't alarmed when Mr. Doherty caught up with you when you came back from the beach. I told him you mentioned earlier at Quigley's that you were going with Cate and your grandchildren. I saw Dr. Owens on Thursday afternoon to discuss the results of some recent tests. One worried him and is now constantly on my mind. He ordered a colonoscopy for some time next week. I had just told Mr. Doherty about all this when we saw you at your house. It occurred to me that you might be the right person to advise me. He offered to go right away, as you were home, and I agreed." She stopped talking and took a short deep breath and then continued, "Fiona, let's go back into the library, I love to see the sun there in the evenings." They went into the front of the house, and Mrs. Finnerty motioned to Fiona to take a seat in the reading area. Fiona watched her, and just before sitting down, she said, "He suspects colon cancer."

Fiona stood, walked to her, and placed her hand on Mrs. Finnerty's shoulder.

As the details of the week ahead were being explained, Fiona expected some display of emotion, but there was none. The to-do list was quietly discussed. As Mrs. Finnerty was a patient of Dr. Owens, Fiona would be the assigned social worker. This elevated the relationship.

A biopsy was taken at the time of the colonoscopy, and the results would take a few weeks. The surgeon performing the colonoscopy would have a good idea of the diagnosis at that time but will await the official report. Other tests may be added when the biopsy results are known.

As a social worker, Fiona was aware of the procedures in such cases and was reassured that the patient had a good understanding of how things would proceed.

The sun continued to fill the library with light, and glancing out of the window at the street, Fiona asked on a whim, "Why don't you take a little walk with me up to the club? Cate has gone ahead with the children. It's still a lovely—"

"That's a great idea!" cut in Mrs. Finnerty. "Let's just do that," and immediately she stood, took her wool cardigan and small handbag from the back of her chair, and headed towards the door. Fiona followed in amazement.

Mrs. Finnerty told Amy and Angela to leave their plates on the windowsill. "Back soon!" she said over her shoulder. Fiona had to quicken her pace to keep up with her.

As Fiona walked with Mrs. Finnerty along the path to the football pitches, she found herself glancing over at her more than once. There had been a few surprises already today, but it seemed that more might be coming. The fact that Mrs. Finnerty was the one walking along beside her was surprise enough, but the pace and the vigor of each step were what kept Fiona stealing glances at this older woman. This was one strong lady, and in light of her current medical condition, Fiona was heartened to see her strength.

CHAPTER 8

It was obvious by the roar of the crowd that the last match of the day was a lively one. The twelve-year-olds were on the field and somebody had just scored. The spectators were on their feet. Fathers, mothers, brothers, sisters, grannies, and grandads were all screaming. It must be a close game, thought Fiona as they approached.

You had to pass the clubhouse on your right to get to the fields, and when you did, you were always amazed to see just how close to the farmlands and mountains you were. On your way to Quigley's shop or down the hill towards the town, this view was obstructed by the houses on either side of the road. Once you cut between the houses and passed the clubhouse and a white house standing alone, a spectacular view opened up to you. The first surprise was the size; there were at least six pitches marked out. The grass was green and lush with no sign of the clumping football boots can cause. When you looked beyond the green, it was breathtaking to be so close to the mountains. The sheep, cows, and little houses that dotted the landscape were the stuff of postcards. The sun was going down as she stood there. The mountains were encased in the red-gold glow of the evening, and Mrs. Finnerty scolded herself in no uncertain terms for not exploring this part of her neighbourhood sooner.

Her house was quite near to where they now found themselves, but having never ventured this far, she was taken aback. She often heard the sounds coming from the various games, but this was the first time she had crossed the street and wound her way behind the houses to this hidden treasure.

Cate saw Fiona arrive and had to look twice to see who was with her. It wasn't until they were quite close to the pitch that she realised that it was Mrs. Finnerty. Fiona noticed Cate looking at her quizzically and said, "Cate, you remember Mrs. Finnerty. She's been listening to the deafening roars from this place long enough! She thought it was time she found out what it was all about.

"Can be deafening all right, Mrs. Finnerty, especially when there is more than one game going on. This is the last match for today, though. Mam, Conor scored, but they're still down by one goal," said Cate as she ran away to retrieve Matthew from the side-line. Brian spotted them from the other side of the pitch and pointed out Lilly and Yvonne sitting behind him. Brian nodded towards the clubhouse, meaning they would meet there after the game. Fiona did not know how much time was left in the game, but as she turned around to ask someone, she noticed Mrs. Finnerty sitting on a bench flanked on either side by the twins, Carmel and Maura. Fiona had seen them that morning clicking their way down to the town, and now here they were with Mrs. Finnerty. She was more than a little surprised to see how familiar they were with each other.

It seemed that the twins were just happy as Larry sitting with Mrs. Finnerty. As the game neared its end, Fiona made her way towards where they were sitting. When she got closer, she heard Carmel say, "I'm on the last chapter, should finish tonight, I'll drop it off tomorrow. I have a lot of questions, though."

Mrs. Finnerty paused and, in a solemn tone, replied, "Girls, I don't want you to get all horrified like the character in the book. I want you to listen to me now." Mrs. Finnerty nodded at Fiona, indicating she was being included in this exchange. The girls leaned in towards her as if they were used to listening to her. "I have been attending the doctor, he ran some tests, and some of the results are not good." The girls looked at each other and moved in even closer.

"You both have been volunteering at the rehabilitation centre where your mother works and have both talked about becoming nurses. You are very smart young ladies. You know that some abnormal results require further testing and sometimes even an operation, and you also know that things can sometimes turn out very well.

Carmel, hold on to your book for now and read that last chapter with care. Maura, you still have a way to go yet with your book. Continue with your reading, and depending on the outcome of these tests, Mrs. Hannon can let you know when it will be a suitable time for you to come and see me. Off you go now, back to your friends. No squawking or moping about the place. Be happy. See you both soon!"

Fiona took Mrs. Finnerty's hand and said with a smile, "Nicely done! Nicely done! I do believe there's a couple of drinks in that clubhouse with our names on them."

They sat at a corner table. Mark was behind the bar checking stock. When he saw them come in, he raised one questioning eyebrow, and Fiona returned it with a smile. Mark put his papers down and came over to their table. "Mrs. Finnerty, I wondered if you would ever grace us with your presence. I know, she made you come, didn't she?" Mark said, nodding towards Fiona.

"Dragged me, actually and now she's making me drink!" replied Mrs. Finnerty.

"Oh, that's her all right. So what will you have?" he asked.

"Your best brandy, if you please, Mark." And they all burst out laughing. That was the scene that greeted the rest of the family when they came to join them. If they were surprised at Mrs. Finnerty's presence, they did not show it. All attention was on Conor as he explained the technical details of the game and why they lost. Soon bedtimes were announced, and they all made their separate ways home. As they left the clubhouse, the sun was already swallowed by the mountains, and the moon had taken over. It occurred to Mrs. Finnerty that by now the same sun that just set was rising in a part of the world she knew well. People would be waking up in joy to share their new day.

By the time, they had reached Mrs. Finnerty's gate, she had invited Fiona and Cate to Sunday lunch at Pepper

Last surprise of the day!

CHAPTER 9

As Mrs. Finnerty rested on her soft pillows, she found herself thinking back on the events of the day. She noticed that she was more at ease than she had been for days, relaxed even. She remembered how she had stood in Quigley's shop that morning as if in a trance. She wondered how she made it home safely. Meeting Fiona in the shop had no special significance at that time. As the morning wore on, however, a thought began to form in her mind, and soon it became apparent that Fiona would be able to help her. By the time Mr. Doherty arrived, she knew what she needed to do. Before becoming ill, she was comfortable with her life in Baybridge. She felt at home here. It was her *home*! Significant relationships had been formed between her and Mr. Doherty, the twins, and the members of the Mrs. Miller Fan Club. Sharing her books brought her joy and coaching Carmel and Maura in the year leading up to their Leaving Certificate had real meaning. They had met quite by chance one day when the girls were much younger. It was an unusually hot, sunny day, and her front door was open. She heard them chatting with the cat and was amused by the conversation. She went to the open door to greet them and saw that they were staring past her into her front room. "You have a lot of books, Mrs. Finnerty!" said Maura, leaning further in.

"Would you like to come in and look at them?" asked Mrs. Finnerty.

"Could we?" asked Carmel.

"Of course, of course, come in. See if you find one you would like to borrow," Mrs. Finnerty answered, smiling.

They were delighted with this; they told her that they loved to read and to her great delight returned a few days later and asked if they could borrow another book. The impromptu book club started that day. Now Amy and Angela were also members. What a joy for her to have these youngsters sharing her passion for books.

This day started out with real anxiety for her. Lying there in bed, it dawned on her that she was part of this community. She had not thought of herself in that way before. Yet surprisingly, she felt comfortable enough to ask Fiona for help. An added bonus to discover she worked with Dr. Owens. Even more surprising was the fact that she had invited Fiona and her daughter, Cate, to lunch at Pepper. This was something she had never done before. She loved having her Sunday lunch at Pepper but was quite excited about having guests with her tomorrow. Won't that surprise Mr. Shiva!

As she drifted off to sleep, images of the football fields and the white house came into her mind. She remembered the clear view of the mountains on all sides of the football fields, and it seemed to her in her drowsy state that they formed a protective ring around the players. She was amazed that such beauty was so close to her, and she was not aware of it, even after all these years. If she hadn't been so sleepy, she might have berated herself for not knowing.

Fiona was still reeling from the events of the day. Mark would not be home for quite a while yet. After her bath, she sat in silence in the front room where she had met with Mr. Doherty earlier. Her first thought was, poor man to be given such a task today. He was in a state of shock. However, fair play to him, he did what he was sent to do. He was genuinely concerned about Mrs. Finnerty and not just a messenger. The thought occurred to her that they were good friends. She knew that her own role would be formalised on Monday by Dr. Owens. She would be assigned to the multidisciplinary team that would be responsible for Mrs. Finnerty's treatment. The thing that unsettled her about Mrs. Finnerty's case was how her previous assumptions about her neighbour had not been correct. She often met her while on her daily walks, brushed shoulders in Quigley's or in Baybridge itself. They would exchange pleasantries but never engaged in a deep conversation. Fiona had assumed that this friendly, fit lady elected to keep to herself socially and did not want to build any deeper relationships. Their conversations were general and superficial in nature.

This day and all the surprises it revealed astonished her. It occurred to her that a day in a life was like an empty clothesline. One did not know at the start what items would be hung out or in what order. No two clotheslines were ever the same, not even your own. The common myth that living in a close-knit community meant that everybody knew your business was definitely dispelled today. Fiona realised that she knew little or nothing about her neighbours and questioned the reason for it. She had thought of herself as being much more involved in her neighbourhood, but apparently that was not so. There was a fine line between being nosey and being helpful, and who decided when that line was crossed?

CHAPTER 10

Mark had made his way from the kitchen to the dining room in the front of the house by the time Fiona opened her eyes. Mug of tea in hand, he savoured the early-morning sunlight streaming in through the bay window. The kitchen was large, and they ate most of their meals there, but the front of the house always beckoned them in the mornings. Fiona's quiet room was on the opposite side of the hallway, but Mark favoured the dining room for his thinking place. In fact, it did not go unnoticed by Fiona that the dining table was beginning to resemble a desk.

He had just started to remember Mrs. Finnerty's appearance at the club when he spotted his wife in the doorway. He greeted her with a broad smile, and she in turn raised one eyebrow just as he had done at the club the previous evening and said, "Cheeky!"

He got up, gave her a peck on the cheek, and said, "There's cheeky for ya! Sit down, I'll bring you a mug of my best. Strong and sweet!"

Her reply, "No sugar, Mark, just milk."

He returned quickly with the tea, and they both sat in silence enjoying each other's company and the warmth of the early sun.

"I have an unexpected lunch date today, and unfortunately you can't come," said Fiona.

Mark did the raised-eyebrow thing and said, "Really now, and why might that be?"

"Well, because you have games, but mostly because you are not invited," Fiona replied.

Mark asked, "Where is this grand luncheon to take place?"

Fiona struck a very hoity-toity pose and, in the most snobbish accent she could muster, said, "Our daughter Cate and I will be lunching at Pepper as guests of Mrs. Finnerty."

Mark stared at her, then recovering in the nick of time stood up, tightened the belt of his well-worn dressing gown, stuck his nose in the air, and said, "Very well then, I shall be at my country club!"

Their laughter could be heard for miles.

Fiona went back upstairs to get the basket of laundry she had sorted before coming down earlier. The weather was still glorious, so, as was her habit, she put in a load of washing before her walk. By the time she returned, this load would be ready for the line. She checked the clothes on the airing line from the previous evening. Perfect! It was all in the timing!

As Fiona reached the end of her driveway, the decision to turn right was made easy for her by the clear view of Three Peaks. She delighted in that view and started her early-morning walk with enthusiasm.

Little did she know when she was walking yesterday how differently she would feel today about her avenue and the people living there. Knowing Mrs. Finnerty's story and her interactions with the neighbours still baffled her. She was excited about going to lunch at Pepper albeit without Mark. Poor Mark! She would have to make it up to him. She was almost at the top of Carter Hill without realizing it, so preoccupied was she with what she would wear to lunch. In no time, it seemed, she was back at home, clothes on the line and aired clothes put away. Mark had made breakfast with no mention of Pepper except to say with feigned reluctance that he hoped she enjoyed it. With a kiss and a wave, he was out the door.

The prearranged plan was that Fiona would call up to Mrs. Finnerty's house, and they would walk to the restaurant, picking up Cate on the way. Mrs. Finnerty had mentioned that she would enjoy the walk, and Fiona took this to mean that so far, she was feeling well enough to do so.

Fiona still could not get over the fact that they were having Sunday lunch with Mrs. Finnerty, at Pepper, of all places. She would not have imagined Mrs. Finnerty enjoying Indian food, not in a million years! Cate was still in the dark about the whole affair but did not raise any questions with her mother. After a pleasant walk, they arrived.

Mrs. Finnerty was welcomed at Pepper like a visiting dignitary, and she responded in kind. Cate and Fiona had no time to take in their exotic surroundings before being ushered by Mr. Shiva to what was being referred to as "Mrs. Finnerty's regular table." Fiona stole a glance around them and tried not to gape as he and Mrs. Finnerty exchanged personal greetings, family inquiries, and other such pleasantries. Clearly, they knew each other well, and most definitely this was not Mrs. Finnerty's first visit to Pepper.

Mr. Shiva then turned to Fiona and Cate as Mrs. Finnerty introduced them. She referred to them as neighbours and friends. "How lucky am I to have both of these beautiful ladies, mother and daughter, join me today?" she said.

"Delighted to see you back again," said Mr. Shiva, astonishing them that he remembered their last visit. It was several months ago on the occasion of Cate's birthday.

Just then, an impeccably dressed waiter arrived with the menus. Unlike others they had seen, these menus were slender and tall with few pages. They were made of very sturdy cardboard covered in burgundy silk. The front cover had a cutout into which a clear glass panel had been inserted. The border was studded with small glittering stones. A perfect *P* was etched on the glass. When the diner opened the menu, it revealed secrets from the Pepper kitchen. Within were four inserts of equally sturdy cardboard, one green, one blue, one yellow, and one pink. On each, the chef had a description of the dishes being served today. This included the meat, vegetables, sauces, cooking method, and spices that were used to create the dish. It was as if he was writing a short letter in gold ink to each individual patron inviting them to partake of the sensual taste of coriander, cardamom, cumin, and many other exotic spices. Fiona was sure that whoever said you eat first with your eyes was not referring to a menu. This menu was the exception.

A comfortable silence prevailed while they each studied the tantalizing dishes until Cate asked Mrs. Finnerty if she had any recommendations.

"Not really, Cate. It's a matter of personal taste," she replied. "For myself today, I've decided on some of these vegetable dishes. We can share and try each other's, though. That's always an enjoyable way to settle on a favourite for next time. What about some chutney for a little sweet and some raita, a mixture of yogurt and cucumber, to cool the palate? Let's have a taste adventure. They are very good at that here."

They all agreed with anticipation. The waiter appeared as if from thin air and took their orders. While they waited, they sipped the lemon ice water they had ordered when they first arrived. Mrs. Finnerty began to speak. She explained how she had been a teacher in India and how she had met Mr. Shiva on her first day in Baybridge and discovered he had been born in the same area where she had been teaching. She went on to tell them about Mr. Doherty and his love of books and plants and the little flutter on a Saturday. Knowing Mr. Doherty's reputation, they understood that "the little flutter" was a reference to Mrs. Finnerty's bet. Fiona and Cate smothered a chuckle.

"I was surprised to see that you knew the twins so well," said Fiona.

"Carmel and Maura, just like Amy and Angela, first made friends with Mrs. Miller and still are members of 'Mrs. Miller Fan Club.' Carmel and Maura, however, discovered the library and their loyalties switched a bit," explained Mrs. Finnerty.

"They began borrowing books, and after reading them, we have a discussion. Not unlike a book club. Amy and Angela are now showing interest in the books as well, and I look forward to continuing the tradition."

Cate leaned forward in her chair. "Mrs. Finnerty, at five years old, is Cara old enough for your book club?" she asked.

"Absolutely!" beamed Mrs. Finnerty. The future looked bright!

All during lunch, the ladies listened to her and were enthralled. Mrs. Finnerty managed to tell them things about themselves and their families. She knew quite a lot but at no time, over many tantalizing dishes, did she ever cross the line. Fiona found the answer to her question of the night before; who decided when the line was crossed? The listener did!

The conversation then changed to Mrs. Finnerty's health. It was reaffirmed that Fiona would talk to Dr. Owens the next morning and officially become part of the care team. As Mrs. Finnerty spoke freely in Cate's presence, Fiona thought it best to address the confidentiality issue. "You seem quite open with Cate, Mrs. Finnerty," she said.

"Fiona, I understand that you have certain professional restrictions and are bound to stay within these parameters. I, on the other hand, am free from all that!" said Mrs. Finnerty with a wink and a nod towards Cate.

She then excused herself and left the table, and they noticed that many of the other patrons greeted her. She passed from table to table, and Fiona and Cate were again surprised at Mrs. Finnerty's popularity and standing in the community. They were also both wondering silently about the bill. Mrs. Finnerty returned to the table accompanied by Mr. Shiva. He bowed and said, "It was a delight having you both here today as our guests. Mrs. Finnerty has expressed a wish that when the current situation is resolved, we will all meet here again and rejoice in her good health."

Mr. Shiva and the waiter helped with the chairs as they stood up. He accompanied them through the garden exit and stood with them as they all enjoyed the vista. He was finding it hard to digest the news Mrs. Finnerty had given him when she went back to his office earlier. He watched her as she walked, keeping pace with the two younger women as they made their way down the steep hill.

They walked home and were delighted to see Mr. Doherty tending to his bougainvillea in his front garden. Nobody was more delighted than himself, seeing these three ladies together. He asked how Mrs. Finnerty was feeling and then looked directly at Fiona.

She understood that look to be a question, and she answered reassuringly, "We have decided on a plan starting tomorrow, and between the two of us, we will keep you well informed." He, in his usual manner, smiled and nodded.

Cate busied herself admiring Mr. Doherty's flowers while the others finished their conversation. Soon all three fell in step as they continued their journey. As they neared Cate's street, Mrs. Finnerty said, "Cate, we will meet soon to select a book for Cara. I usually meet with Amy and Angela on Sundays when I get back from Pepper. I am later than usual today, so I hope they waited for me. Depending on what happens this week, maybe Cara could come and meet the girls next Sunday."

"Oh, she would love that!" answered Cate. "If it's okay, I'll check with Mam later in the week. I won't say anything to Cara until we know more. Thank you again for a wonderful lunch."

"Best not make any promises to Cara," replied Mrs. Finnerty as they hugged and said goodbye. "I enjoyed your company very much today."

"I will give you a call tomorrow evening, Cate," said Fiona as they, too, embraced.

Fiona walked Mrs. Finnerty to her gate and explained that she had three patients already scheduled for Monday morning. She would see them first and planned to be at Dr. Owens's office just after his last morning patient. They agreed then that Fiona would call to see her in the afternoon. If Dr. Owens's office needed to talk to her, they would call her directly. Mrs. Finnerty thanked her with a rather tight hug that conveyed some of the anxiety and fear that had been evident when they met the previous day.

Before Fiona could do any reassuring, a squeal of delight echoed in their ears as Amy and Angela came running towards Mrs. Finnerty. They were both waving books, and for the moment, Mrs. Miller was forgotten. Fiona smiled as Mrs. Finnerty greeted the girls with great delight as her mood was instantly lifted. As she turned towards her own house, she saw Mrs. Finnerty take a small box from her handbag. She opened it, and the girls peeped in.

"Laddu! You brought us laddu!" sang Angela. "We love laddu!"

Unbeknownst to Fiona, Mrs. Finnerty had ordered extra dessert to take back to Amy and Angela. They had enjoyed the sugar-dipped doughballs after lunch themselves. What an amazing woman to have thought of bringing these treats to the girls considering the uncertainty of the next few weeks.

"Let's go inside, and you can have them after we discuss your books, and you each have chosen another. Say goodbye to Mrs. Hannon," said Mrs. Finnerty.

Mrs. Finnerty's generosity had touched Fiona deeply and sparked a self-awareness in her that had not been there before. It was certainly giving her food for thought.

The last item to be hung on today's clothesline was the sweetest of all!

CHAPTER 11

Dr. Owens was a very popular doctor. He was tall with a mop of dark curls, aqua-blue eyes, a square strong jawline, and a good sense of humour. His colleagues liked him because he was a good doctor. His paediatric patients liked him because he made them laugh and put them at ease. Their parents liked him because he looked like he could be James Bond. The elderly patients thought he *was* James Bond! Dr. Owens himself was a hardworking, caring general practitioner and didn't spend any time thinking about his reputation.

He was at his desk early on Monday morning. Ask any health-care provider about Monday mornings, and you would need to sit down for ten minutes to hear the reply. This particular Monday morning was hard for Dr. Owens. Two patients were weighing heavily on his mind. On Friday, he had reason to discuss his findings on both with specialists. The conclusion reached was that his suspicions were well-founded. He needed to proceed with further testing and referrals.

Fiona arrived at Dr. Owens's office just before noon. Her Monday morning had gone relatively smoothly for a change, and she was in good spirits. That changed quickly as she knew it would when she tried to find a parking space. There were two spaces reserved for social services at this very busy practice, but they were both taken. She was about to start the dizzying drive around the car park when to her utter amazement one of the other social workers leapt into her parked car and reversing out indicated to Fiona that the space was hers. Fiona responded with an appreciative smile. Spirits restored, she parked and made her way into the building.

Brenda, the receptionist, was smiling from ear to ear, as usual. This never ceased to amaze Fiona. She could not recall ever going into this waiting room and finding Brenda in a bad mood. The medical staff were equally pleasant. They were all just happy caring for their patients. This positive, pleasant attitude was infectious, no pun intended.

"Morning, Fiona," said Brenda as she shut her computer down for the lunch break. She had already activated the answering service. "Last morning patient is in right now. Go on back to your desk, and I'll buzz you when they are done."

"Thanks, Brenda," replied Fiona as she made her way to the space that was allocated to the social workers. Four doctors worked in this practice, and social services was a big part of the multidisciplinary team.

No sooner had Fiona placed the briefcase on the small desk when Dr. Owens popped his head around the corner. "I heard you were in, how was the morning?" he said with a lopsided grin. "Home visits on a Monday morning can be treacherous."

"No treachery today, Dr. Owens," answered Fiona. "Not even in the car park."

"Good job then," he replied. "I have a female patient from your neck of the woods, Fiona that I'd like you to follow. It's a Mrs. Finnerty."

"Actually, Dr. Owens, she sent a neighbor to my house on Saturday. He was very concerned about her. After I clarified with him that Mrs. Finnerty had asked him to come and get me, I did pay her a call." Dr. Owens nodded as Fiona continued, "I gathered from her that she had some positive tests recently, and you suspect colon cancer. She asked me to talk to you. She will need support going forward. She has no living relatives at all. I'm glad she contacted me."

"Great! That's a good start. I talked to Dr. O'Connor, the gastroenterologist, on Friday and he agreed to go ahead with the colonoscopy. They can fit her in at 11 o'clock on Thursday. Brenda called and got her to come in at two o'clock today," explained Dr. Owens.

"She seems to have a good grasp on how all this will proceed," said Fiona. "She was quite calm when we spoke, but according to Mr.

Doherty, the neighbour who came to ask for help in the first place, she was very scared. I was surprised to learn that they even know each other."

"We often think we know people and then find we don't at all. It happens a lot with patients, especially as they age. We make assumptions and really don't have meaningful conversations when we do talk. Our major downfall is that more often than not, we aren't really listening. Fiona, are you free to be here for the two o'clock appointment?" Dr. Owens asked. "She may need help on Thursday with transportation and support afterwards."

"Certainly. Lots of paperwork to keep me going till then," agreed Fiona.

"Best get the afternoon show on the road, then! Brenda will give you the nod around two," said Dr. Owens with his usual smile.

Fiona sat down and, for the first time, tried to anticipate what exactly Mrs. Finnerty's needs might be.

Mr. Doherty picked Mrs. Finnerty up for her two o'clock appointment with Dr. Owens. He was a punctual man. They had spoken earlier in the morning as he was coming home from Quigley's shop. Mrs. Finnerty was in her doorway calling out for Mrs. Miller. After they greeted each other he asked, "Any news from Mrs. Hannon or the doctor?"

"Yes, they called from Dr. Owens's office a little while ago. They said the colonoscopy was scheduled for Thursday morning. I'm to go in at two o'clock today to get instructions," she answered.

"Oh," he said, trying to keep the worry out of his voice. "Well, I'll give you a lift down then, since it looks like we are in for some rain later today."

She accepted his offer without hesitation, surprising herself. He said he would be back at one o'clock and, with his usual nod, continued on his way.

Fiona did not expect to see Mr. Doherty with Mrs. Finnerty at two o'clock. Neither did she expect to hear him say he would take his friend to the hospital on Thursday. He also planned to bring her home and stay with her.

"Thank you, Mr. Doherty. I'll check in later in the afternoon," turning to Mrs. Finnerty, adding, "just to make sure the sedation has worn off and you are back to yourself." Dr. Owens accepted this, and so it was settled. Mrs. Finnerty, it seemed, was not alone.

Later, on their way out, Mrs. Finnerty heard a familiar voice and turned to see Mrs. Coughlan and Angela checking in with Brenda at the reception desk.

CHAPTER 12

Mrs. Coughlan's heart was beating rapidly in her chest, and a faint wave of nausea gripped her periodically. Angela had gone over to the Kids' Korner of the waiting room. This was the third visit to Dr. Owens in as many weeks. Angela had complained of a painful spot on her upper shin for a couple of weeks prior to the first visit.

The little wooden step stool Angela used when she was younger was still kept in the kitchen. She liked to use it occasionally to reach the higher cupboards even though she was quite tall. At first, they dismissed the painful shin, thinking that she had banged it on one of the stool's steps. It was when her mother discovered a lump in that area that they decided to see the doctor.

Dr. Owens sat at his desk for a minute or two before going into the examination room to see Angela and her mother. Angela was the second of the two patients that were of concern to him this morning and that he had consulted on last Friday.

As he entered the room, Angela returned his broad smile. He shook hands with Mrs. Coughlan, took a seat on the exam stool, and wheeled himself over to Angela. She was sitting on the exam table but was not swinging her legs as she had always done before. Dr. Owens noticed this. Angela was an energetic girl and a vigorous leg swinger. It was known as her highland fling, and she would deliberately exaggerate it as he came into the room. The still legs were a significant sign today, and Dr. Owens attributed this change to pain. She was known for her deep, full-bodied laugh. Hers was the kind that just hearing it made others laugh without ever knowing why they were laughing. Amy, her younger sister, spent a lot of time laughing. Nobody was laughing today. Angela already knew that the lump was bad. "Back again to see me?" he asked. "Let's have another look at that leg, then. Anything new with it?"

She looked over at her mother, who answered, "Much the same, really, Doctor. It still hurts."

As Dr. Owens continued the examination, he noticed that Angela flinched in anticipation as his hand neared the painful area. He stopped the examination there and spoke directly to Angela in a matter-of-fact tone. "Angela, the results of those x-rays we did are back. They do show that there is a little lump on the bone just below your left knee. Now bones below knees don't like lumps on them, so we are going to do something about it. First thing I did was tell my friend, the bone doctor, about this lump and he agreed we must do something about it. His name is Alan Moran and all he does all day long is do something about bones. Imagine that!" He glanced over at Angela's mother, and she was smiling. "So my bone doctor friend, who likes to be called Dr. Alan, wants more pictures of your bone. I told you he loves bones. This picture is a bit fancier than an ordinary x-ray. It's called an MRI. If you and Mam agree, I will get Brenda to make that appointment, then Dr. Alan himself would like to see you and your bone. What do you think of that plan?"

Angela nodded and looked at her mother. Mrs. Coughlin nodded too and tried to smile.

"Good," said Dr. Owens, "Mrs. Coughlan can you take Angela to the Kids' Korner and pop back in for us to choose a good day for that appointment. Won't take long, Angela!"

Dr. Owens and Mrs. Coughlan spoke openly. He explained that this lump could be serious. He was ordering an urgent MRI. He spoke highly of the orthopaedic surgeon, Dr. Moran. Though trained in Dublin and London he was based here at Baybridge Medical Centre avoiding the need to travel for specialised procedures.

Mrs. Coughlan left his office with only a slight improvement in her heart rate and nausea, but oh, how she loved the way Dr. Owens spoke to Angela!

Fiona was still at her desk in Dr. Owens's office when he appeared again in the doorway. She was mulling over Mr. Doherty's generous offer to help Mrs. Finnerty when she saw the expression on the doctor's face. She knew instinctively that he was going to refer a new case and it was serious.

"Me again," he said. They tell me at the desk that you are on call for paediatrics."

"Yes, it's me," she answered, her heart sinking.

"Fiona, this could be a case that brings us all to our knees. I just saw Mrs. Coughlan and her ten-year-old daughter, Angela. I hear they are also your neighbours so you probably know Angela already. I saw her a few weeks ago with a painful lump just below her left knee. Her x-ray results came back on Friday, and there is a clearly defined lesion on the bone."

It was difficult for Fiona to breathe normally as the doctor continued to give her a summary of the case to date.

He continued. "I've already spoken with Alan Moran in orthopaedics. We are lucky to have him here in town with his experience. I ordered an urgent MRI at his request and then he will see her himself. He agrees that we are probably looking at a malignancy. As I said, this is going to be a tough case. If it is as we suspect, there will be long-term support needed for Angela and for the family," said Dr. Owens.

Fiona responded as professionally as she could, but in truth, her heart was aching.

"I do know the family. They live a few doors down from me but right next door to Mrs. Finnerty. I saw them together on Sunday. Angela and her younger sister, Amy, are great friends with her cat. Mrs. Finnerty has an extensive library in her house, and she lends the girls a book each week. They have formed a book club, and she leads a discussion on the books. This news could have a devastating effect on her and how well she does with her own situation right now."

"I did not expect to hear that the two patients that are of most concern to me are connected like that. It is inevitable that they will both know about each other. Mrs. Finnerty may need more support with little Angela's condition than her own. Fiona, sorry to give you this, but I'm glad it's you. This case needs your touch."

"Our case management meeting is tomorrow morning, so it will help to have input from the team. If necessary, I can move things around and be there for the MRI. I'll talk to Brenda about the details. It's sad, sad news about Angela. I agree, Dr. Owens, this could bring us all to our knees," said Fiona and sincerely wished she did not have to hang this item on today's clothesline.

Mrs. Coughlan told Mr. Coughlan about today's conversation with Dr. Owens and expected "ructions," a word her father used to describe a reaction to unwelcome news.

Mr. Coughlan was a sergeant in the Garda, the Irish police force. A tall, lean man with a reputation for favouring fair but swift justice. As a police officer, he was no stranger to shocking news, but this was entirely different. He was quieter than his wife had ever seen him, and her heart ached for him.

"We will be together in this, Caroline, all the way," he whispered as they stepped into each other's arms.

Angela had her MRI on the next day. Dr. Alan Moran spoke to the family after he reviewed the results. It was agreed to proceed with a bone biopsy. The doctor explained the procedure. He would insert a fine needle into her leg and take out a tiny bit of the lump and send it to the laboratory to be tested. He explained that as soon as he knew what the lump was made of, they would all get together—Mammy, Daddy, Amy, and Mrs. Hannon—to make a plan. With an impish grin, Dr. Alan told Angela, "We are going to assemble an army to do battle with this lump!"

A chuckle escaped from Angela, and they all heard it.

Mrs. Finnerty tolerated her colonoscopy well on Thursday. The surgeon told her when she woke up that her colon looked good except for one area. He explained that he took a biopsy and sent it to be tested. He would call her for follow-up when the results came back. Mr. Doherty took her home as planned and stayed until Fiona gave the all clear later in the day.

Mrs. Finnerty and Angela Coughlan would learn within days of each other that they both had cancer.

CHAPTER 13

Fiona sat in her thinking room at the front of the house. She was looking out of the window but couldn't see anything except sheets of rain running down the glass panes. The sound of drumming on the window was soothing. There would be no walking or laundry done this day! Ordinarily, she would be disappointed about that, but this morning, she was quite pleased the weather was forcing her to stay put. Mark was forced to stay put too because the football pitches were saturated, and all matches were cancelled until it was possible to inspect the field.

As she sat there, the oddest thought came to her: how did Mrs. Finnerty get upstairs? In all the wonder and intrigue of the remodeled house, she could not recall seeing a staircase. It certainly wasn't where hers was.

"Are you in your sanctuary?" called Mark.

"I am indeed, and if you are bearing gifts of tea and toast, enter!" came the command.

"Bearing same with marmalade," replied Mark.

He came around the corner carrying a tray with enough toast and marmalade to feed a small army. The teapot looked big enough for afternoon tea at a boys' boarding school. "Does this have to last us until the rain stops?" inquired Fiona, snatching a slice of toast in the most unladylike manner.

"Not if you keep grabbing like that," he said, also helping himself to a slice.

"Boy, oh boy, this is the life!" they both said at once.

After much licking of lips and fingertips, Fiona said, "You'll never guess what I was just thinking."

"How great a husband I am and how much you love my toast?" he said.

"That too, of course." She turned to face him and said, "Where is Mrs. Finnerty's staircase?" How does she get upstairs?" she asked.

"What!" he gasped.

"Well, it isn't where ours is. I've been in her little kitchen area—no room there. So how does she get to her bedroom? Where does she sleep?"

Mark shrugged his shoulders and took a gulp of tea and answered. "I've never been in Mrs. Finnerty's, Fiona."

"Oh," she said.

At that precise moment, Mrs. Finnerty was returning to her bedroom with a cup of tea and a slice of toast. She pressed the button on the wood paneling that looked like the back wall of her kitchenette. She stepped into the small lift, pressed the inside button, and ascended to the next floor. The lift opened into the small room beside her bedroom.

Resisting the urge to grab another piece of toast, Fiona took her cup of tea with her, kissed her husband on the forehead, and ascended her stairs. She changed into gym clothes and went into the small room next to her bedroom. In Fiona's house, it was a gym. In Mrs. Finnerty's house, it was a lift.

It was hard to get started. Earlier she was happy to be inside, but now she was restless. She knew that the now-familiar feeling of foreboding had started its upward journey towards her ribs. Suddenly she had to see her children and grandchildren.

Subconsciously, she knew the source of the fearful apprehension. She was not yet ready to assign words to it.

She went out to the landing and leaning over the banister called Mark. He appeared at the foot of the stairs and looking up at her said, "Figured out where the stairs are in Mrs. Finnerty's?"

"Mark, stop it!" she said. Too late, she realised that her tone was sharper than she intended. She continued, without apology, in a softer tone, "It would be great to get everyone together tomorrow.

The fields are bound to be closed again, and you could be home. What do you think?"

"If you are talking about endless food, drink, and grandkids, I'm in," came the reply. "Only one snag, we have no food or drink."

"We do have raincoats," she yelped. "Give me thirty minutes, make a list and call everyone."

The rain had let up somewhat by the time the calls were made, lists checked, shopping bags assembled, and Mark and Fiona were heading out the door. A huddled figure was passing the end of their driveway, and Fiona said aloud, "There goes Mr. Doherty to get the paper!" Too late she realised that Mark had not yet come out of the house. This meant that once again she was talking to herself. Mark soon appeared, sat in the car, and turned on the engine. They headed down the hill towards town, and Fiona confessed to Mark that she had been talking to herself.

Mark said with a chuckle, "Didn't your mother talk to herself all the time!"

"No, only on special occasions," she answered, swiping him on the arm.

"Every day," he said.

Fiona was quiet for a while. She remembered clearly how this habit of her mother's worried her father. He thought it was a sign of stress or overwork. The rest of them thought it was comical. She always mumbled when she hung out the washing. They could see her through the bay window. It looked as if she was talking to the clothes. She explained when they were older that it was a time when she was uninterrupted, could ponder, and problem solve. She was merely thinking out loud. Fiona wondered if she ever explained that to Daddy. Turning towards her husband, she asked, "Do you remember one Christmas when Eiler and her family were here? We were all talking about the kids, and she said her Aiden talked to himself all the time. As a small boy, he said he wasn't talking to himself, just thinking out loud to himself. That was Mammy's explanation too!" She smiled to herself, thinking of Aiden, now fully grown and a successful artist.

"Well, how do you explain all the shushing she did during the one o'clock news?" Mark continued. The whole family made fun of this in her presence as they grew up. Mammy loved to join in with louder shushing.

"It wasn't the news, it was the stock market report that followed. We were all home for lunch from school eating away like starving urchins. Nobody was talking, ever! Mammy uttered her first shush as soon as the report started. Still nobody talking, Mammy still shushing, and by now all of us trying not to choke as we stifled the giggles."

"Did she shush the giggles?" asked her husband. He was also trying to stifle a giggle, but Fiona caught him.

"Don't mock my mother!" she said, giving him another slap on the arm. "I don't think she even noticed, at the time." Remember how she used to remind us that those investments didn't do any of us any harm.

"Very true, very true," Mark added wistfully. "Mammy was a wise, generous woman."

The rain had stopped by the time they reached the car park, and it seemed that the entire population of Baybridge took that as a signal to go shopping. There were people milling about everywhere. Fiona thought of the scenes you see on television when a snowstorm is forecast in America. She hoped that she hadn't missed some news flash that had awakened the survival instinct of the locals. Would the shelves be bare of bread, milk, and toilet paper?

Three times around the car park revealed an empty spot.

"I'm going to run across to the hardware shop, Fiona," said Mark. "I'll catch up with you in a few minutes."

"Okay," agreed Fiona as she stuffed all the shopping bags into one. She removed her raincoat, threw it on the back seat, and stepping over a puddle, headed for the shop. "I'll probably still be at the deli counter," she added over her shoulder.

The shop was packed, but luckily there was still food visible on the shelves. The deli department was on the right immediately inside the door. No doubt this was to accommodate the lunch crowd from the nearby businesses, thought Fiona. No sooner had she formed that thought when she heard her name.

"Mrs. Hannon!"

She turned to see Carmel and Maura Murry standing at the counter, each holding a cup and a sandwich.

"Hello, girls, lunch break? I hope that's hot tea you've got there," said Fiona, indicating the cups. "Awful day!"

"Better now," said Carmel. "Mam gave us a lift down this morning. It was bucketing down!" After a slight hesitation and a glance at her sister, she continued, "We were going to call down to you, but we weren't sure if that was okay. We're anxious to hear about Mrs. Finnerty."

"It's okay to call down, but I have no news yet." She nudged them into a quiet corner as she continued, "She did have the colonoscopy. The results take a while, but we should know something by the end of this coming week. I am planning to call down to her this afternoon. I will tell her you are anxious. I am sure from your conversation at the match last week that she wants you close. Is that okay for now, girls?"

"Yeah, just tell her we were asking about her. Don't worry her at all," answered Maura.

"Good. Drink that tea now before it gets any colder. Stay dry," added Fiona.

As Carmel and Maura headed for the shop door, that now-familiar tinge of apprehension began to gnaw deeper under her ribs.

Mark caught up with her as she admired a head of cabbage, and seeing him wrinkle his nose, she put it back. Instead she dispatched him to the wine department while she examined every cut of meat with a critical eye. She traveled every aisle with determination and confidence. By the time she had finished, the shopping trolley was brimming over with all manner of provisions, some of which Mark had never seen before, and her heart was brimming over with love.

CHAPTER 14

Mr. Doherty was glad he got the fine hour to make his way downtown to Flynn's bookies. As he studied the paper earlier, he felt that his heart was not in it today. In fact, if it weren't for Mrs. Finnerty's flutter, he probably wouldn't have bothered at all. Things had to continue as normal, so he went. As luck would have it, Mrs. Finnerty had big winnings today, which would be something cheerful, at least, to talk about this afternoon.

The Coughlan family was on hold as they waited. Mrs. Coughlan waited as thoughts swirled around in her head. She imagined herself talking to Angela.

"Am I being your normal mammy? Can you tell that I am out of my mind with worry? Do you know that I can't even think about your pain, or I will fall down? Your daddy is melting. He is hiding inside his uniform. My pain for you is not in my thoughts, it is nowhere near my head. It is a feeling under my breasts that comes in waves and takes away my breath. I want to be wrapped around you. I don't know what you are thinking. Amy is quiet and I want to wrap myself around her. Maybe she talks to you."

Mrs. Coughlan made the dinner. While straining peas, she remembered Mrs. Finnerty. The girls always went next door on Sunday afternoon. Tomorrow. She doesn't know!

Mrs. Finnerty had decided that as far as her colonoscopy was concerned, her mantra would be "No news was good news." When she got the results that might change, "Cross the bridge when you come to it" was another good saying… As yet, nobody mentioned any bridge.

Mr. Doherty had been and gone today. He was clutching a tidy sum of money for her. She offered to share; he said it wasn't necessary. He had been equally lucky. He hoped the luck would extend to the colonoscopy results. She promised to tell him herself.

Mrs. Coughlan slipped from her house. She went next door. As soon after she saw Mrs. Coughlan approach, saw how she stroked Mrs. Miller, sitting on the windowsill, Mrs. Finnerty knew. She reached the door before Mrs. Coughlan rang the doorbell. Mrs. Coughlan was in deep pain. Mrs. Finnerty opened her arms to the other woman. Eventually when all was told, when all was said, when all was shared, the two women parted. It was settled that Amy and Angela would come to book club tomorrow. Mrs. Finnerty would go to Pepper, come home laden with laddu, and they would read together. The girls would save some laddu for their mam. Long after Mrs. Coughlan had gone through the front door, petted Mrs. Miller, and entered her own home, Mrs. Finnerty sat looking out the bay window as tears rolled down her cheeks.

When Fiona arrived to check on her later in the afternoon, it was obvious that things were not okay.

"Have you had news from Dr. Owens?" asked Fiona as she stepped into the library. It was too soon for a colonoscopy result.

"Mrs. Coughlan, Angela's mother came over earlier, and the poor woman is beside herself with worry about Angela's leg. Fiona, all I can think of is, what if I am not well enough to be there for them? What if I can't help Angela?" said Mrs. Finnerty.

While acknowledging the concern, she did not know the extent of the information exchanged between the two women, so she asked, "Isn't tomorrow book club day? It hasn't been canceled, has it? I didn't make any plans yet with Cara.

"No, they are coming over, and I decided to go to lunch at Pepper, as usual. Mrs. Coughlan suggested that we keep to our routine, but I agree, we should wait to include Cara."

"That's great that you are going to lunch," said Fiona. "Oh, by the way, I ran into Carmel and Maura today while I was out. They both send their love and are anxious to know how you are though they gave strict instructions not to worry you."

"Those girls are so kind, and I really do miss them. Fiona, thanks for helping me to keep in touch with them for now."

Staring off into the distance, she simply said, "Darling Angela."

This selfless lady was tortured with worry about the little girl and her family next door. There was no mention of her own colonoscopy.

Fiona sat in her thinking room that evening. A brief encounter with this amazing woman had left her stunned once more.

Sometimes there is an item that is best discarded rather than hung on the clothesline. In life, we do not have that choice.

CHAPTER 15

By 11 o'clock Sunday morning, the Hannon house smelled like Christmas. Two beautiful, free-range chickens were roasting away. The occasional spatter could be heard from the oven, causing Fiona to look towards the stove and nod her approval. Those chickens were doing what they were supposed to do.

She was surprised she had slept so well the previous night. She got up earlier than usual and was halfway through her walk before the rest of the household awoke. Laura and her family had arrived the night before. It was late, and the boys were tired and a bit cranky. Traffic was heavy, Sean, her son-in-law, explained. Four-year-old Paul and nine-month-old Caleb were not impressed with all the stopping and starting. Quick hug, quick snack, and bed were the only cure. Apparently, they slept well too.

Earlier, when Fiona had turned into the driveway from her walk, she was greeted by two bobbing heads, waving hands, and broad smiles visible through the bay window. She had a reception committee in her thinking room. They looked like they were going to come out through the glass in their excitement. This is what she had been longing for, aching for, in fact. She opened the door to shouts of "Granny!" from Paul and some similar squeals from Caleb.

"Oh my gosh, look at how big you both are! Stand back and let me have a good look at the two of ye!" she had asked. Paul obliged, but Caleb came closer and was soon scooped up by Granny. They all ate an easy breakfast together.

"Mam, it feels like Christmas!" said Laura as she came into the kitchen from the backyard.

"Do you think so?" asked Fiona. "I had that feeling earlier when the chicken started spattering in the oven."

"It kind of reminds me of Granny's too, when they had the shop. Do you remember?" Laura asked.

Fiona stopped what she was doing at the kitchen counter and turned to face her daughter. "I remember it well. You know how the shop and the house were on Maple Street? Then you went out the back door beside the big window, walked down the concrete path, and into a smaller building. Remember it had a loft and a garage? That was on another street, we had two addresses."

"That's right, Grandad kept his car there. It was a Morris Minor, wasn't it? He loved that car! We were warned against going up into the loft, we were a bit scared of it, actually," Laura answered.

"I only ever went up there once, and your Grandad was with me. It was nice and neat up there, like all his things. I was amazed to find a wooden rocking horse. He made it himself. It was painted red and in perfect condition."

"What! Whatever happened to it?" asked Laura.

"I really don't know, but speaking of Christmas, I remember our Christmases very well. The huge turkey was stuffed the night before. The range was stacked to keep hot all night, and of course, the turkey was in the oven for hours. The shop was closed except for one hour in the morning. Your grandmother gave out milk and bread to those who may have run out and always added something sweet. Then they closed for the rest of the day. Grandad took us kids to the beach after mass, so we could work up a good appetite. What we could never figure out was, how did Granny know the exact moment we would be coming up the yard from the garage? We always, I mean always, saw her lift the turkey from the oven at that precise moment. We wondered as we got older if she took it out several times thinking that she heard us. She claimed she just knew we were back. It was the highlight of our Christmas Day," Fiona answered.

"Wow! You never told us that before!" said Laura. "We need to start making memories for our boys at home too."

"Laura, you don't plan them. What happens just become memories."

"It is a daunting responsibility," said Laura wistfully.

Crossing the kitchen and giving her a hug, Fiona whispered into her daughter's black shiny hair, "It is, pet, it is."

Brian, Cate, and their families soon arrived. Brian joined Mark and Sean somewhere down the backyard. The kids made a beeline for the toy box in the thinking room after first jumping all over their granny. Cate announced that the table was set in the dining room. That pleased Fiona. She hated setting tables; she always forgot something. "Thanks, Mark," she said aloud.

"Mam's talking to herself!" the sisters said simultaneously.

She swiped them with the tea towel.

Hunger got the better of everybody, and soon they were all seated at the dining table. The usual pandemonium of a family Sunday lunch ensued. A chorus of "Pass me this, pass me that," "Would you like some of this, some of that," "No, thank yous," and "Yes, pleases" echoed around the room. The conversation was sprinkled with outbursts of laughter, gasps, and the occasional cry. One thing was certain; Mark got his wish—endless food, drink, and grandkids.

Fiona was very happy to hang this item on today's clothesline.

Meanwhile, Angela and Amy were having a great time at Mrs. Finnerty's. She had brought them their usual laddu, but this time they got a lovely little gold-and-cream box with four more in it to take home.

"One each, for another time," said Mrs. Finnerty. "Don't forget Mammy and Daddy."

Angela was ahead with last week's book. "I was off school a few days this week. I had tests on my legs, so I spent a lot of time in waiting rooms. I didn't mind, I read all the time," explained Angela.

"That's a great way to pass the time," answered Mrs. Finnerty.

"Dr. Alan is very funny." Angela continued, "He has another name, but he likes Dr. Alan best, and he likes bones. He is going to get rid of the lump on my bone. That's what he does. Dr. Owens says he looks at bones all day long. He's his friend. He calls him the bone doctor."

"Good to have a bone doctor if you have a lump on your bone, especially a funny one. Oh my! Not a funny bone, I mean a funny doctor!" Mrs. Finnerty chuckled.

"A funny bone?" squealed the girls.

"We have two of them, you know, in our elbows, better not bang them!" said Mrs. Finnerty.

More squealing from the girls, and Mrs. Finnerty was loving it. Angela had more to tell so she continued, "One day, Dr. Alan wanted to borrow a book, but I said sorry, he couldn't, it's from the book club. Instead, he let me borrow one of his. *Make Way for Ducklings*, it's called, it's an American book, and it has lovely drawings. Will I show it to you next week, Mrs. Finnerty?"

"Oh, you are lucky! Did you have a look at it, Amy," asked Mrs. Finnerty.

"It is lovely, the drawings are kind of old-fashioned," answered Amy.

"Well then," announced Mrs. Finnerty, "let's make that our book for next week. You can each take a book today, but we will talk about *Make Way for Ducklings* next week. Agreed?" It was agreed.

Mrs. Finnerty was astonished at the simplicity of Angela's explanation of her condition. She was soothed by the matter-of-fact way she spoke, even in front of Amy. A lot to be learned from these two young girls.

CHAPTER 16

"Good morning, Brenda," said Fiona as she put her mug of tea on the kitchen table. It was past 8 and she was dressed and ready to leave the house as soon as she finished her tea.

"Hi, Fiona, glad I caught you at home. I was in two minds whether to page or phone," added Brenda.

"Still here, just gulping down the last drop of tea. What's the latest?" asked Fiona. She did not get early-morning calls very often, but when she did, it usually meant that the schedule for the day was changed.

"Don't gulp, you've got time. Mrs. Connolly is being discharged from the centre earlier than planned. I see she is on your list for a visit tomorrow. Her daughter arrived last night and can stay for the whole week, so she is going home today. Dr. Owens wants to take advantage of the help in the home, so he's agreed to let her go early. Can you fit her in first thing this morning?" asked Brenda.

"That's great news for the patient. I saw her midweek, and there was a question about her daughter getting time off. The staff at the rehabilitation centre feel she will do very well at home with her daughter's support. As it's just a couple of miles farther from my house it makes sense to go there first," explained Fiona.

"I love it there," said Brenda. "We are so lucky in Baybridge to have that option between hospital and home, especially for those who live alone."

"I agree with you, Brenda, I love it too. Whenever I see their big ornate sign, I get a nice warm feeling. It is a very happy place, and they have positive outcomes with their patients. What about that view, Brenda? And those grounds?" added Fiona.

"I know! I often think I could do with a stint there myself," Brenda said wistfully.

"It's not a hotel!" yelped Fiona, and they both had a good laugh.

"Behave yourself, Mrs. Hannon!" said Brenda. The laughter stopped when Brenda added, "On a much more serious note, Dr. Owens wants me to let him know as soon as you come in today. He's expecting Angela's biopsy results. Oh, Fiona, is anybody ready for this?"

"Nobody, Brenda, nobody. I gathered all my lot yesterday for lunch just to have them with me. We all need to send every ounce of energy, love, and prayer that we can muster, to this little girl and her family. But as of yet, we do not have the result. Not knowing is all we have for the next few hours," said Fiona. "Let me go now and rejoice with Mrs. Connolly on her going home early. I should be in by late morning," she added.

"Drive safely, see you later," replied Brenda.

Fiona turned towards the mountains and the beach when she left her driveway. Very soon she arrived at the entrance marked by the big sign. The drive from the road to the building was impressive. What you saw was a seamless joining of the old and the new. The original property had been one of those stately manors Fiona passed on her walks. The main entrance, reception area, sitting rooms, and dining rooms were part of the old house. The bedrooms upstairs were remodeled to accommodate medical equipment, but the main structure remained. A stately carpeted hallway led to the new building.

The extension rivaled any modern gymnasium. If you entered the building via the side door, you were greeted by an open-plan exercise paradise. This was the Physiotherapy, Speech, and Occupational Therapy Unit. The unit was the reason for their success rate. Two sides of the area had ceiling to floor windows, and the mountain was visible from every corner. Little areas of blue peeped beyond the grounds, revealing patches of the Atlantic Ocean. On the second floor of this building were the rooms assigned to new admissions.

They more closely resembled a hospital room than those above the old house.

One incentive to comply with the rehabilitation plan was to gain enough independence to move into a room in the manor, as it was called. A degree of artificial snobbery was encouraged by the therapists. "Just a few more steps now, and you will be that much closer to the royal suite" was a common instruction. Peals of laughter often followed. Those extra steps were always willingly taken!

Brenda was right; it could have been a luxury hotel.

Mrs. Connolly was in her room in the new wing. She greeted Fiona with a smile.

"Well done, Mrs. Connolly, well done! I hear your daughter did get the time off to be with you, so now you can go home earlier than planned," Fiona said as she walked into the room.

"Yes, she did," she replied, "and I'm so relieved. I was a little apprehensive about going home, but this way, I will have a chance to settle in before Marian has to go back. Thank you, Mrs. Hannon, for coming out this morning at short notice."

"Do you still have any concerns or questions about going home?" asked Fiona.

"No, I don't think so," replied the patient.

"The discharge plan is tailored to your needs. If you have any questions while I'm explaining, just stop me. Would you like to wait until your daughter gets here before we do that?" asked Fiona.

"As a matter of fact, I expected her before now. Ah, here she is!" said Mrs. Connolly as Marian appeared in the doorway.

After the introductions, Fiona reviewed the discharge plan with mother and daughter and was satisfied the plan the team had put together did suit this family well and it was a safe discharge.

As she continued her rounds, she found herself wishing that she could prolong the morning. That gnawing feeling had crept under her ribs again, and she knew that no amount of dallying would change what lay ahead of her this day.

CHAPTER 17

At ten past 11, Dr. Owens received a phone call. He waited a moment while a written report appeared on his computer screen. He read it. He got up from his chair and went out to his car through the staff door. He sat into the driver's seat. He retrieved a day planner from the passenger's seat. He looked up one name and telephone number. He got out of his car. He returned to his office. He placed the unopened planner on his desk. He leaned back in his chair. He turned to face Brenda as she stood in the doorway. All this, he did in slow motion.

Brenda knew but did not speak. She put a yellow sticky note on his desk saying Fiona was in. She closed the door as she left. She told the eleven-thirty patient that Dr. Owens would be a few more minutes. She went to the ladies.

Angela and Amy were both at school. Mr. Coughlan was at the Garda station. Mrs. Coughlan was at home. She was staring at the clothes being swished around in sudsy water in the washing machine. She found it soothing.

Dr. Owens went in search of Fiona when he finished with the last morning patient. She saw him approach and braced herself.

"Angela's report is back, Fiona, it's as we feared. The biopsy showed osteosarcoma. I just got off the phone with Alan Moran, who did the biopsy and it was not an easy conversation. He has grown very fond of her. Noticing how much she reads, he let her take a book home from the office." Dr. Owens paused a moment before continuing, "The first thing we need to do is establish if there is any metastatic disease. We need to know if there is any spread. He recommended we consult Dr. Gwendoline Myers in Dublin. He worked on her team when he was there, and he says you couldn't get better. He called her already. She was with a patient, so he left a message asking her to call me. I am not sure how her day is, but I expect a call some time later today."

"I am really sorry to hear this news, Dr. Owens. How are you, yourself?" asked Fiona.

"Thanks for asking about me. There is no softening this. I have one hope and one dilemma, the hope is that it is nonmetastatic, no spread, nothing else, just the one area. I'm hoping you can help me with my dilemma. I have seen Angela and her sister in their home a couple of times when they were younger. I saw their grandfather there once when he was visiting. My question is, should I call to the house to give them the news? I need to go to the rehab centre later today anyway. I will be passing their door. Or should we ask them to come to the office? I don't want to alarm them any more than I have to."

Fiona replied, "You're good at this, Dr. Owens. You know this family well. Should the whole family be told together? What do you think is best?"

"It would be a bit awkward to have everybody coming all the way up here," Dr. Owens said. "Mr. Coughlan would likely be in uniform and the girls just in from school. I could get Brenda to call around four thirty or so. She could explain I need to go to the centre anyway and ask if I could call in on my way there. I think it would work better. If Brenda calls at the end of the day, they won't have too long to wait and worry."

"I think you are right, Dr. Owens. You probably will have heard from Dublin by then, and you will have more concrete information. Maybe some tests can be done in Baybridge. The need to go to Dublin can be introduced without urgency. It's the right approach, I'm sure," said Fiona.

It was agreed. Now they just had to wait to hear from Dr. Myers.

The pressure under Fiona's ribs was squeezing the breath from her. There was only one item for her clothesline today, a big sopping wet blanket that took up the whole line. She couldn't imagine ever being able to lift it.

CHAPTER 18

Dr. Gwendoline Myers was walking down the hall just outside the oncology suite when her mobile phone buzzed. Glancing at the screen, she recognised Alan Moran's name immediately. She remembered him well and the memory brought a smile to her face. He was one of the best orthopaedic surgeons and the funniest currently in practice. They had worked together in Dublin before he moved to Baybridge. His message asked her to call a Dr. Owens in Baybridge. A ten-year-old girl had just presented with osteosarcoma. Alan had done the biopsy himself. The message was left a few hours earlier, but she did not have access to this phone until now. She quickened her pace and soon was at her desk.

"Good afternoon, Dr. Owens," she said when the number given to her was answered. "This is Gwen Myers in Dublin, I understand you have a newly diagnosed little girl, not good news under any circumstances."

"Dr. Myers, it's good to hear from you so soon, thank you," said Dr. Owens. "Yes, Angela Coughlan is a ten-year-old complaining of a painful swollen area just below the left knee. She first came to see me over a month ago. She thought she had banged her shin on some steps a couple of weeks earlier, but now it was painful and limiting enough to bring her in. I ordered an x-ray and then talked to Alan Moran. He saw her immediately and ordered an MRI. Following that, he decided to proceed with a biopsy. I just got the report late this morning."

"You're certainly moving along at the appropriate pace, which is vital," said Dr. Myers.

"The family is very easy to work with," continued Dr. Owens. "The dad is a sergeant in the Gardaí here in town. Amy is her eight-year-old sister. Angela is a delight, and she and Alan are getting along like a house on fire. He noticed how much she reads between tests, and I understand he's lending her books now. She calls him the bone doctor. I may have said something to that effect when I referred her."

"Oh, he is a bone doctor all right, and no better man for the job. I'm assuming he will continue with the orthopaedic side of things. Where possible, it is best for the same surgeon to do the biopsy and the subsequent surgery. The medication and chemotherapy management would be my side of things," said Dr. Myers, "and more importantly, we do have beds. Is that the plan you had in mind, Dr. Owens?"

"Yes, yes, that is what I am asking. Obviously, I have not spoken yet to the family, but that is what I will recommend," cut in Dr. Owens.

"Good, good," replied Dr. Myers. "Now, as you know, we have a few more steps before treatment begins. Angela could be admitted within the next few days. If you think the family would agree, we could continue the groundwork here and then start the chemo. We have to establish first if this is nonmetastatic, no other lesion anywhere in the body. Otherwise, Alan can do the bone scan in the next few days and complete the rest of the workup there. Then she will need to come to Dublin and prepare for the first chemo cycle. It's a grueling regimen, on a tolerance scale of one to ten, it's a fifteen. It's a thirty-five-day cycle, and she may need two cycles prior to the removal of the tumour. It all depends on the result of the bone scan. She can be home from around day three up to day twenty-two if the side effects are manageable. We could team tag during that period if you feel comfortable. First, we need the bone scan, chest x-rays, and more labs."

"If it's at all possible, clinically, and it's what the family wants, then I'm willing to manage the symptoms and blood tests here. I will work closely with Alan and you and your team. We have an excellent social worker here at this practice. In fact, she is a neighbour of the family and knows them well. She's has been assigned to Angela's case," said Dr. Owens.

"That's a great asset. This family is going to need a *lot* of support. Let's leave it like that for now. Do you plan on seeing them today?" asked Dr. Myers.

"Yes, this evening, on my way to our rehab centre to see another patient. It's near their house and shouldn't seem too out of the ordinary. Fiona, our social worker, thought so too," explained Dr. Owens.

"Now that's the sort of personal touch that will make a big difference. We don't have a chance for much of that in the big city. We do, however, have accommodations for the family. We can get into all that with our admissions team when they make their choice. You have my number. Thank you, Dr. Owens. We will talk soon," she concluded.

Dr. Myers was a lady in her early forties. She had beautiful, wild, curly red hair. She realised when she finished her phone call that she was still wearing her bright colorful turban. While on duty, she always covered her hair with the most exotic headwear. The daily fashion show made for a much better conversation than the alternative in a paediatric oncology unit.

CHAPTER 19

It was around twenty past five when Dr. Owens rang the Coughlans' doorbell. A stampede followed as Amy and Angela made it to the door ahead of their father. Angela limped a bit. "It's Dr. Owens!" they hollered and made their way back to the kitchen.

"These long legs of mine are of little use in this house," Mr. Coughlan said, shaking hands with the doctor and ushering him in.

"I see," replied Dr. Owens over his shoulder as he continued down the hall. "Is it safe?" he added as they both peered around the kitchen door.

"Not always! Too early to say," replied Mr. Coughlan.

He did, indeed, have long legs and today they were clad in smart khaki slacks. The royal blue V-necked sweater gave him the look of a businessman awaiting a cocktail rather than an off-duty, hard-hitting police sergeant.

They made their way to the kitchen, which boasted a large circular wooden table. This area had been extended since his last visit, thus the space for the table. Mrs. Coughlan greeted him and, per usual Irish tradition, invited him to sit and offered him a cup of tea.

"A mug, please, Mrs. Coughlan. The tea is not the best at work. You know what it's like when the water is not boiling!"

"I do, indeed!" she replied, "I just scalded the pot too when I heard the doorbell. No lukewarm tea in this house. Right, Tony?"

"Oh God forbid!" answered her husband.

Dr. Owens was seated by this time. Tony took the chair opposite him. The girls changed where they were sitting a few times but then settled beside each other and close to the doctor. Mrs. Coughlan stood and placed a basket of scones on the table. Dr. Owens's eyes widened as he said, "These are huge, Mrs. Coughlan, did you bake them?"

She hesitated for a moment and said, "It's not recommended that you lie to the police or your doctor, so I will have to give the credit to Mrs. Quigley."

He looked confused and Mr. Coughlan saved him by adding, "Corner shop."

"Oh well, they look delicious. Want to share one with me, girls?" he asked. They nodded, and Dr. Owens cut one in three. He took a small bite of his piece, drank some tea, swallowed, looked at the girl's parents, and said what he came to say. "Angela, Dr. Alan and myself had a chat today. He got the results of that biopsy he did on your lump. He was right about it not being a good lump. It definitely has to be removed. How has the pain been, since last week?" Dr. Owens paused and looked at the mother and father.

They showed no sign of alarm. Angela looked at her mother, then back at the doctor, and said, "It hurts more at night now."

"Are you able to sleep?" the doctor asked.

Angela replied, "Sometimes."

"It's not a good thing to be kept awake because of pain. Angela, now that we know what this lump is made of, we know what needs to be done. The question is, where are we going to do it? Some of the answers to these questions must come from your mammy and daddy. We also must tell Amy here what is going on. You probably have a load of questions already. I have a few more bits of news first, and then you can fire away, okay?"

They all nodded.

"Dr. Alan came to Baybridge from Dublin. He worked in a special unit there. As you know, with him, it's all about bones." Dr. Owens stopped for a second because Angela and Amy started to squirm, and it looked as if they were trying not to laugh. "One of the doctors he worked with is called Gwendoline Myers. She still works in that unit. She's actually the boss and very famous. Dr. Alan called her on the phone this morning and told her all about your lump. She then called me. She wants to help us get rid of this lump once and for all. She said she never knew a better bone doctor than Dr. Alan."

A loud spluttery outburst of wet laughter exploded from the two girls. They *had* been suppressing a laugh earlier. The parents gaped at them, but their faces wore a complicit grin. Angela nudged Amy and managed to say, "You tell them I can't!" as she covered her mouth with the palm of her hand and spoke through spread fingers.

"Mrs. Finnerty, she's our friend," began Amy, "she made a mistake. Angela told her about Dr. Alan and how you said he loved bones and that he is funny and that he is going to get rid of the lump and Mrs. Finnerty said it was good to have a bone doctor if you had a lump on your bone especially a funny one then she made the mistake and said not a funny bone a funny doctor!" All this, Amy said without taking a breath. By now both the parents, the girls, and even Dr. Owens were in convulsive laughter.

Gasping for breath, Angela added, "She said we had two funny bones, one on each elbow, and we better not bang them!" Angela Coughlan had the gift of laughter.

Angela left the room for a moment while they composed themselves and returned with Dr. Alan's book. She opened it at the last page and placed it on the table in front of Dr. Owens. She read aloud, "And when night falls, they swim to their little island and go to sleep."

She had given them her answer. Whatever plan was made, home would be the foundation. Dr. Myers would cleanse her body. Dr. Alan would remove the lump. Dr. Owens would be the link. Mrs. Finnerty would be her friend forever.

Thirty-five minutes after entering the Coughlan family home, Dr. Owens left a changed man. In that short time, he saw love at its truest. What had worried him for days had been neutralised by this love. The joyful respect and honor exchanged in his presence astounded him. The unconditional acceptance of the simplicity of their young daughters by Mr. and Mrs. Coughlan left him speechless. Angela had, in her own way, chosen home, and he had no doubt, when possible, that that was where she would be cared for.

Dr. Owens's clothesline of life was sporting cashmere today, and he would wear it proudly forever.

CHAPTER 20

Dr. Alan answered his phone on the first ring. He knew that Dr. Seth Owens was visiting Angela and her family this evening. He had been on tenterhooks since he got the biopsy report this morning. It might well have been him who was telling them the news, but they both agreed that Seth would be the one. He was the family doctor and knew them well.

"How are they, Seth?" His anxiety showed in his tone.

"Alan," Dr. Owens said, "I have never met a family like them. I can't get over the experience. We sat at the kitchen table, shared a currant bun the size of a boulder, drank tea, and ended up laughing hysterically about you."

"Me? You were making fun of me? Well, that's nice," replied Alan Moran.

Dr. Owens continued, "Some story about their neighbour and you being the funny-bone doctor but not a funny bone, a funny doctor. Anyway, the laughing started, and you know when Angela laughs, everybody laughs! The ice was well broken by then. We started to go over the options and what Angela did next is going to blow you away. The results did not seem to faze them. They didn't react at all. Then Angela went to another room and came back with the book you lent her, the duckling one."

"What? *Make Way for Ducklings*? You're joking, it's as old as the hills!" said Dr. Alan.

"Well, just wait," Seth continued, "she placed it on the table right in front of *me* and just as if she were on stage, she read the last line loud and clear."

"And when night falls, they swim to their little island and go to sleep."

"Alan, she chose home and she chose you."

A long silence followed. Dr. Alan Moran said softly, "I will do all in my power to make that happen, Seth, all in my power."

He sat for a long time after the phone call and decided to make another.

Tony Coughlan answered. They had met once before when Angela had the MRI. Tony knew who he was when he introduced himself. "Dr. Owens and I were just talking, and it seems you would like us to do as much as possible of Angela's treatment here in Baybridge."

"Yes, it's what she asked for, and we do feel its best. Is there any problem with it doctor? If it's not—"

"No, no," cut in Dr. Alan, "none at all. I'm in agreement with it. However, we have a lot to plan going forward. It may seem that we are moving fast, and we are. The sooner we act, the better. I know it's short notice, but I would like to meet with Angela, Mrs. Coughlan, and yourself, tomorrow, maybe while Amy is in school? We need to talk about things in more detail and more frankly. I don't wish to alarm anyone, but now we have to get down to brass tacks. We have to avoid assuming that Angela understands what's involved. We have to be sure we don't overwhelm her or Mrs. Coughlan. Each phase of the treatment needs to be explained ahead of time."

"I understand, Dr. Alan. We knew this time would come. We noticed how you and Dr. Owens speak to Angela, at her own level, and we like that. It helps her feel in control. She used your book to make her wish to be at home where possible known," said Angela's dad.

"I heard about that and together with Dr. Owens, we will do our best to make that happen. She is a remarkable young lady, and I do enjoy her. I don't have any idea yet of a time for tomorrow morning. Is it okay for you to get a call first thing to set it up?" asked Dr. Alan.

"They persuaded me at the station to take a bit of time off. Between Caroline and myself, we've got it covered."

"Great! We're off to a good start now. Oh! My offices are at the hospital—near the action, eh? We might get lucky with the bone scan, too. One of the staff will call you early to give you time. Good evening now, Mr. Coughlan," concluded the doctor.

"And to you, Doctor," said Mr. Coughlan as he switched off his phone.

CHAPTER 21

Angela led the way down the corridor to Dr. Alan's office. She remembered seeing his name on the glass door as she passed by when he did the biopsy. It was done in a different area. They checked in at the reception desk and then sat down. Angela got up immediately and moved towards the books. Her name was called before she got there. All three of the Coughlans were ushered into the examination room. Angela had her temperature taken by a nurse called Kathleen. She asked, "What's that book you have there, Angela? Is it a favourite?"

"Yes," she answered, placing the flat of her hand protectively on the book. "Dr. Alan let me borrow it," she continued and pulled the book a little closer to her on the exam table.

"Did he, now!" replied Nurse Kathleen with the twinkling blue eyes and the freckles. "I've never known him to lend a book to anyone else. You must be a favourite yourself. As a matter of fact, he made a point of telling me first thing this morning that you were coming in. I'm getting the feeling that you are a celebrity."

"No, I just have a bad lump on my bone," Angela explained as she pointed to her left shin.

"A bad lump on your bone, you say?" questioned Nurse Kathleen, and her eyes twinkled all the more. "Well! You have certainly come to the right place! Dr. Alan spends the whole day dealing with just such a thing. All day long, bones, some broken, some with lumps, all sorts of bone problems. I would say he is a bone celebrity."

"I think he is. He's friends with Dr. Owens and a famous lady doctor in Dublin too," whispered Angela, leaning closer to the nurse.

"Isn't that just great for your lump. I know that lady doctor in Dublin quite well. Her name is Gwendoline Myers, you are right, she is indeed famous and she's lovely. Her name is known far and wide, even as far as Baybridge. She is the *best* at getting rid of any bad lumps inside the body. Big or small, it doesn't bother her, not one bit! Dr. Alan and myself worked with her in Dublin, and she and the staff there helped us develop our own unit here in Baybridge. When we were good and ready to leave, they gave us a very special gift to take with us. Would you like to see?"

Nurse Kathleen paused and, when Angela nodded, took a few steps away from the exam table and pulled back a curtain revealing a skeleton fixed to a wooden plinth. It was anatomically perfect and attached in such a way that, unlike most clinical skeletons, it did not dangle. The feet were firmly placed on the wooden base and its head, torso, and limbs were discreetly supported. The bones had a peachy hue, giving it a lifelike appearance.

She scooted her bottom to the very edge of the exam table and leaned forward to get a better look. "It's a child's skeleton! She's the same size as Amy!" Angela exclaimed, addressing her parents, laughter in her voice.

"You're right, she is," answered her dad, "all she needs is that wool hat of hers."

"Well, let me introduce you to Nora. Angela, this is Nora. Nora loves hats. She has a box full of hats, as it happens. Would you like to take a look?" offered Nurse Kathleen, helping Angela down to the floor.

She pulled out a canvas storage bin and invited Mrs. Coughlan to join in the rummaging. "You can try them on yourself or on Nora, she doesn't mind."

Mrs. Coughlan picked one out and raised it up to show Mr. Coughlan. His eyes widened. He usually didn't spend much time noticing the girl's hats, but this one he recognised. Amy had one just like it.

"That's a nice one," said Nurse Kathleen, "let's see how it looks on Nora. You can give her a middle name if you like, maybe Angela?

She doesn't mind when we give her a new middle name. Nora Angela sounds posh, what do you think?"

So Angela and her mother set about dressing and naming the child skeleton that stood in Dr. Alan's office.

"Perfect!' said Nurse Kathleen, eyes twinkling more than ever. "Let me help you back on the exam table now, and I will go and inform Dr. Alan that Nora Angela is ready. Okay?"

Everybody nodded. The atmosphere in the exam room was playful, with all anxiety dispelled. Nurse Kathleen had done her job.

After Mr. Coughlan responded to the gentle tap on the door, Dr. Alan entered. He was a big man, broad shouldered and fit. As an orthopaedic surgeon, he was the consultant to many local sports teams, and he played on the Baybridge Rugby Team since moving there. He was known as a team player both on and off the field. He was dressed in teal scrubs with a hint of white undershirt at the neck. His hair was covered with a matching scrub cap, though wisps of dark hair could be seen on his forehead. Today he wore glasses.

Glancing to his left as he entered, he said, "Good morning, Nora, nice hat," and walking towards Angela, he continued, "I see Kathleen got you to dress her for the day, stylish." He detoured to shake hands with her parents. Mr. Coughlan stood up and remained standing. Mrs. Coughlan smiled. The doctor turned his attention back to Angela and asked, "Did you give her a middle name?"

"Yes," she answered, "Angela."

"Well, I could do with two of you, but I hope she doesn't start laughing at my funny bone like some Angela's I know."

"It was Mrs. Finnerty—she made the mistake!" pleaded Angela.

"All right, all right, it was Mrs. Finnerty!" interrupted the doctor. "I hear that's your next door neighbour with the huge library. I don't want to upset her. I might need to borrow a book someday. Speaking of books, I also hear you want to stay home for as much of this lump treatment as you can. You want to sleep on your own little island like the ducklings. Am I right?"

"Yes, I would. Can I do that, Dr. Alan? I brought the book back today, but Mrs. Finnerty wants to read it on Sunday with Amy for our book club, so can I do that too, can I?"

"Angela, poor Dr. Alan, all the 'can I's,'" her mother interjected.

"Oh, that's okay, Mrs. Coughlan, I'll just have to tell Mrs. Finnerty if she keeps up the nagging," replied Dr. Alan. Contagious giggles from Angela.

"Down you come now, from your high horse, missy, Nora wants to show you something." As he spoke, he helped her down from the exam table and led her across the room. He positioned himself so that the parents could see what was happening. He took a small magnet, resembling a tumour from his pocket, handed it to Angela, and said, "Put this on Nora's leg exactly where your leg hurts." She glanced at her parents and then confidently placed it just below Nora's left knee. She was surprised that it attached itself so easily as if it were part of Nora's bone. "Good job, Angela, now Nora has a lump like you. She is going to help me explain what we must do to get rid of it. Everything that happens to you, Angela, will first happen to Nora. She will let us see inside her body so that you can understand what is happening inside yours. You sit on that little chair there and keep this stool for me. I asked Mrs. Hannon to join us this morning. I'll just go check to see if she has arrived. This is our planning place, we call it Nora's Nook."

CHAPTER 22

Fiona was out walking when the phone rang. She expected it to be Brenda. One of the patients on today's home-visit list had not returned her call yesterday, so she was unable to set a time. She was hoping that Brenda had reached her. Instead, Fiona found herself talking to Robert, one of Dr. Alan's schedulers. "That you, Fiona?" he asked a bit briskly. She forgave him. He was a busy man.

"It's me, Robert," she replied, "early bird catching the worm?"

"Don't talk to me about birds, Fiona Hannon, you with your lovely fit self, wandering the streets at all hours of the morning with nothing better to—"

"Robert! Robert!" soothed Fiona, "you should join me. I'm just attacking Carter Hill right now, should be a snap for a big, burly rugby player such as yourself."

"Don't 'burly rugby player' me at this hour! Himself, the good doctor, played like a brute on Saturday. It'll be days before any of us can walk. Anyway, he needs you to come in at ten this morning. It's the big meeting with the Coughlans. He said if you can, I said of course she can, can you?" pleaded Robert, breathless by now.

"I can, Robert," replied Fiona.

"Oh, thank God!" and then Robert was gone.

Fiona stared at the blank phone and smiled.

Mrs. Finnerty was walking from Quigley's when she spotted Fiona coming up Carter Hill on her left. She lingered to allow her to catch up. Fiona saw Mrs. Finnerty dallying and picked up her pace. Soon they were side by side.

"Anything good in the bag there, Mrs. Finnerty?" asked Fiona, sniffing as the aroma of freshly baked goods wafted towards her.

"Oh, Fiona, you know already it's a pastry bag from Mrs. Quigley's!" Mrs. Finnerty scolded good-naturedly. "Angela and her parents are meeting with the orthopaedic surgeon this morning. I'm on standby for Amy in case they are delayed. Just like you say yourself, you can't go wrong with Mrs. Q's treats!"

"Never let me down yet!" answered Fiona.

It was easy to forget that Mrs. Finnerty was awaiting her own results. She was so absorbed with Angela and her family. Fiona decided to ask her if she had heard from Dr. O'Connor. "Not yet, towards the end of the week most likely. I'm just anxious to hear what news Angela has. Apparently, the whole long-term plan is being explained today," answered Mrs. Finnerty.

Fiona's heart leapt in her chest at the mention of Angela, and the anxiety started to gnaw under her ribs remembering that she, too, would be at this meeting. Careful not to disclose any information about another patient, Fiona asked, "Is Mrs. Coughlan keeping you up-to-date on things then?"

"Well, yes, but they won't know much until after today," explained Mrs. Finnerty. "She did say that the biopsy result was not good. Oh, she also said Angela was hoping to be able to stay in Baybridge for some of the treatment. A specialist in Dublin was also mentioned. Apparently, it's all going to be decided today. I hope and pray that any stay in Dublin will be a short one."

"So do I, Mrs. Finnerty, so do I," answered Fiona.

A change of subject seemed to be what Mrs. Finnerty needed. As they got closer to her house, Fiona said, "I saw Mr. Doherty at his front door as I passed. We didn't get to speak though."

"I might walk down that way later. Mrs. Miller is giving me fits over her food. She's just not eating. Do you think she knows?" asked Mrs. Finnerty.

"Animals do sense when things go awry. Mr. Doherty is a good one to ask. Maybe she needs a little treat too," added Fiona. Mrs. Miller, sitting on her windowsill, raised one eyebrow in agreement.

The meeting! thought Fiona, in a panic. "What time is it?" she asked herself aloud as she scurried away from Mrs. Finnerty and Mrs. Miller.

Try as she may, she failed yet again to lift that heavy, wet blanket onto today's clothesline.

CHAPTER 23

It was just minutes to ten when Fiona arrived. She saw Dr. Moran at his office door. She clicked her way towards him, waved, smiled, and hoped to God he didn't notice the state she was in. He returned her smile and indicated for her to slow down. She immediately obeyed and was now walking in slow motion. It felt like she was watching herself in a movie, knees up high, shoes paused in midair, briefcase held aloft, hair blowing in the wind, then she was at his side. The doctor was still smiling and didn't seem to notice anything amiss. He simply said, "Good timing, we're all here," as he led her in to join the others.

Fiona was sure she was going to faint when she saw Angela sitting in Nora's nook. She didn't faint, but instead her heart slowed, and her breathing settled. Her well-trained, professional self returned. Bending down, she gave the little girl a hug, greeted her parents, and paid attention to every word Dr. Moran had to say.

"Thank you for making it in on such short notice," he started, addressing Fiona. "We were just talking about Mrs. Finnerty and her book club." He sat on his stool before starting his explanation. "As you can see, Nora is all gussied up, thanks to Angela. She, too, has a lump on her left shin."

"I see," said Fiona, "great hat too."

Mrs. Coughlan nodded in appreciation towards Fiona.

"Angela," said Dr. Alan, "we have some heavy work to do. Can you persuade Daddy to come over here and help us? He is just the right height."

She walked over and, taking her father by the hand, led him back to Nora's Nook.

"Mr. Coughlan, we need that case on the table there, open, so Angela can see inside. Gather around now, ladies, it's showtime!" Silent stares as Dr. Alan removed a set of small lungs from the foam lined case. He asked Angela to sit down and then he placed the lungs on her lap. "These are Nora's lungs, and Daddy is going to help you put them inside her chest. They will fit perfectly, just like yours," he continued. "If you please, Sargent, lift Angela up so she can reach." And with that, she slid the lungs into Nora's chest cavity with ease. The doctor and Angela resumed their seats as he continued his explanation.

"Angela, there are two tests required to make sure, absolutely sure, that the lump on the shin is the only one. In the first test, we're going to take a close look at the lungs. I arranged for that to be done at half past eleven today. It's called a CT scan. It does not hurt and takes about thirty minutes. Next is a bigger test. It's called a bone scan, not one bone, every single bone in your body, head-to-toe bone scan. Do you know the song 'Dem Bones'? It's my favourite song. Well, we have to see all them bones." He looked at her parents; they nodded. He continued, "Now ladies and gentlemen, Act II. Lights, please, Mrs. Hannon."

Fiona turned the office lights off and motioned everyone to come closer.

"Ms. Angela, if you please, press the red button," instructed the doctor. To everyone's amazement, Nora lit up to reveal pathways through her bones to simulate blood vessels not unlike a plate of well-organised strands of spaghetti with a purpose. When the skeleton returned to its unlit state, Angela and her parents remained staring at Nora. As everybody returned to their seats, Fiona switched on the lights. "When you have the bone scan, the doctor will put a small amount of dye into a vein at your elbow. It's just like when you have a blood test, but no blood comes out. A small amount of dye goes in and highlights your bones, making them easier to see on the test. If there is the smallest, tiniest bit of bad lump, it won't escape the dye. No pain at all, except the little pinprick at the start. That's a lot of information I know, Angela. Take a little rest now." Fiona gave her some water and sat with her.

Dr. Alan asked Angela if she had any questions or worries before she went down for her chest CT. "What about the famous doctor in Dublin?" That's what Angela wanted to know.

"Dr. Gwen," replied Dr. Alan, "that's a great question. No matter what the tests show, you will be going to Dublin to see her. I know her and her team. They are the best but, their job is to totally destroy the lump that you do have. The only way they can do that is with some powerful medicine. These medicines will make your stomach upset and make you feel very tired at the very least. That much we know right now. Very soon we will know exactly what we are dealing with. If we do not find any more bad lumps, less of the powerful medicine will be needed. That's where all our hopes lie. Before I let you go now, do you have anything else you want to ask or say?"

Angela looked up at Nora, now unlit and peachy: "I love you, Nora," she whispered, and taking her mother's hand on one side and Fiona's on the other, they hobbled down to radiology singing, *Dem bones, Dem bones.*

Sargent Coughlan and Dr. Moran continued to talk. The phone rang. The bone scan would be done at three o'clock today. In a few hours, they would know the extent of Angela's cancer.

CHAPTER 24

"No problem at all, Mrs. Coughlan, it's a pleasure." Mrs. Finnerty anticipated this phone call all morning. "We will have a good time."

"I would really like you to call me Caroline, you're such a good friend to the girls and now to me, please!"

"Okay, I would like that very much," agreed Mrs. Finnerty. "Being your friend is the easiest thing in the world. I'm anxious to know how the day is going, but that can wait. It's a gift that you got both the tests on the same day. Do not waste a single minute worrying about us. Amy knows I'll be collecting her, and the school has been informed. We're all set. I have to confess to picking up a few treats from Mrs. Quigley's this morning. We won't overdo it, I promise."

"Mrs. Finnerty, you spoil those girls! They love the spoiling, and you are good for them. Thank you very much. Angela is bubbling over with news. Please, God, when the test results are through, it will be good news," said Caroline Coughlan.

"Please God, indeed!" replied Mrs. Finnerty. "How are you and Mr. Coughlan holding up?"

"The doctors are amazing! We learn so much from the simplicity of Dr. Moran's explanation to Angela. One way or the other, we will have to take her to Dublin to start chemotherapy in a few days. She is so calm, she had us singing 'Dem Bones' on the way down to radiology. She is keeping Tony and myself grounded. Fiona Hannon is a godsend! All of you are just a blessing to us, that's all I can say! Thank you, again."

"Hush now, Caroline, off you go back to the others. If there are any hiccups or delays, do not worry. Do what you have to do with ease. Amy and myself will be fine here. God bless for now," comforted Mrs. Finnerty.

Anybody observing the scene on the playground could be forgiven for thinking that Mrs. Finnerty was a proud grandmother picking up her grandchild. The frequent up on the toes, peering left and right, fidgeting with her handbag, more peering, more up on the toes were all telltale signs. The woman couldn't wait for the school doors to open and Amy to come running out. As a teacher, she knew the anticipation and excitement of home time, but never experienced it from the outside looking in. It was such a thrill. She worried that it might rain. She checked her handbag again and reassured herself that she had not forgotten the little umbrella. All her book-club girls, both big and small, admired the decorative bright umbrella that lived in the stand just inside her door. It could be mistaken for a parasol but was quite sturdy and waterproof. Carmel and Maura had their eye on it too. At the slightest hint of rain today, Amy would get to use it.

On cue, the school doors opened. It started to rain. Children spilled out. Mrs. Finnerty was up on her toes again, scanning left and right. Amy spotted her first and waved. Mrs. Finnerty held her parasol/umbrella on high, which brought a bright smile to both their faces. Soon they were huddled tight under its shelter and made their way between the bouncing children to Mrs. Finnerty's home. Amy's foray into her neighbour's house had not extended beyond the street side of the library in the past. The books that were suitable for the younger readers were strategically placed there. Today, Amy would need to go upstairs, wash her hands, and change out of her school uniform. When Mrs. Finnerty suggested this, Amy looked a little lost and it took a few seconds for her hostess to realise the reason. The child did not know how to get upstairs.

"Oh, Amy! You don't know how to get upstairs. How could you, it's different from your house," said Mrs. Finnerty as she led her towards the kitchen. "It's a surprise!"

Amy was not sure how to react; she merely did as she was told, but her eyes lit up when the realization dawned that she was in a lift. She was tickled pink that Mrs. Finnerty had a lift in her house; she had never heard of such a thing.

While Amy was changing, Mrs. Finnerty was rummaging in the next room. She was looking for something in particular, but as always happens at times like this, she came across other items that piqued her interest. When Amy joined her, she hesitated at the door.

"Come on in, Amy," said Mrs. Finnerty. "I was looking in this drawer for something else. Look what I found." She held up some beautiful colorful fabric. Amy reached out and took one end.

"This is beautiful," said Amy and suggested, "it would make a lovely headscarf or hat."

Mrs. Finnerty took a closer look, and an idea was born. "Amy," she said, "you are a genius." Amy was not sure why.

They continued going through some more drawers, and finally Mrs. Finnerty exclaimed, "Here it is, I knew it was here somewhere! What do you think of this?" as she handed her find to Amy. "Take a look inside."

Amy was holding a decorative cloth bag. It was made of different-coloured squares, some bright yellow, red, purple, and blue, sewn together and randomly sprinkled with tiny gemstones. It reminded Mrs. Finnerty of the decorations on the menu at Pepper. Its base was reinforced to enable the bag to stand upright. In the middle, it was divided into three pouches, each large enough to hold two books. Along the length of the pouches on either side, enough space had been left to hold at least one large book. It was round bellied like a doctor's bag and snapped shut at the top with a magnetic clasp. One simple carved wood handle sat atop. It was a handmade valise fashioned as a book bag and given to her as a gift by the principal on her first day in school in India. She had treasured it all these years.

"It's a book bag, Amy. Do you like it?" asked Mrs. Finnerty. "I know it's very old."

"Is it? It's sparkly," answered Amy. "It doesn't look old. I like the different shades."

"It's colorful all right," Mrs. Finnerty added. "The people of India love bright colours. They mix them well and stitch them together with gold thread and add sparkling stones. It does brighten things up. Let's take it downstairs and see if we can find a use for it later."

When they got out of the lift, Mrs. Finnerty invited Amy to sit in the little kitchen area. She had already sat out cheese, ham, and Mrs. Quigley's treats. Amy had not noticed them earlier; so taken was she by the excursion in the lift. She was ready to eat now, and so was Mrs. Finnerty.

Between bites, she told Amy that her mother had telephoned earlier. Dr. Alan had been lucky enough to get the tests done in one day. Angela was in good spirits and had loads of news for them. She continued, "She even had them singing some song about bones in the corridor. That sounds like fun! Oh, I wonder if there was a bit in the song about the funny bone." That started the two of them laughing. Amy's laugh was pretty infectious too. When they stopped laughing enough to finish eating, it was time for homework. After a quick clearing of the little table and an even quicker check of the Coughlans' take-home platter in the fridge, they made their way to Mrs. Finnerty's big carved reading table. Amy was invited to sit on the second chair at the table and, retrieving her modern book bag, took her place beside her friend. She thought, of all the things that ever happened to me, this is the *best!* Mrs. Finnerty had exactly the same thought.

CHAPTER 25

It was ten minutes to seven when the Coughlans pulled into the driveway. It would be an understatement to say that they were tired. Mr. Coughlan went into their house to turn on lights, check the heating, close the curtains, and generally make the place welcoming. Mrs. Coughlan and Angela made their way into Mrs. Finnerty's. She and Amy were still sitting at the big table. Homework now finished, they were reading a book together. Amy opened the door to her mother and sister. Unaware of the nature of today's visit to Dr. Alan, she bombarded them with her own news. They let her tell them about the lift, the lovely food, and sitting at the big table on her own chair and choosing an extra book to read and about the laughing again at the mention of the funny bone.

Then she suddenly stopped and simply said, "Howya, Angela?"

They hugged and went over to their usual corner, and Angela bombarded her equally with her own news. She told her about Nora and how she lived in a nook and was Amy's size and had peachy pink bones and they lit up when you pressed the red button and daddy had lifted her up, so she could put her lungs in her chest and how Nurse Kathleen with the freckles had let her put a hat just like hers on Nora's head and how Dr. Alan said Nora was all gussied up. Now the two children burst out laughing while the adults in the room stared at them. Angela concluded by saying, "And I only have one lump."

Mrs. Finnerty had to be steadied.

"Well, Angela," prompted Mrs. Coughlan, "tell her about the trip."

"I was saving that part for you to tell, Mammy," replied Angela.

"No, you go ahead—"

Before her mother could say another word, Angela blurted out, "We're going to Dublin on Sunday!"

Mrs. Finnerty had to be resteadied.

Amy had to be told to stop jumping up and down.

By now, both Mrs. Finnerty and the girls' mother had migrated towards their space and simultaneously opened their arms to gather them in. It was the proverbial group hug with more meaning and emotion than any words could have conveyed.

"Going to Dublin on Sunday, is it?" said Mrs. Finnerty, releasing her neighbours from her tight grip. "I'm wondering if we could have book club on Saturday afternoon instead," she continued, casting a questioning glance at Mrs. Coughlan.

"I think that could be arranged," came the reply. Mrs. Coughlan's eyes were smiling. "Dr. Alan has extended the loan of the book indefinitely."

"Yes, yes! He said I could take it to Dublin with me," interrupted Angela with equally smiling eyes.

"Smart man, your Dr. Alan," said Mrs. Finnerty. "Seems like a few more books might be called for. What do you think, Amy?"

Amy seemed distracted and kept looking around the room. Finally, she saw what she was looking for. Standing on her tippy-toes, cupping her hand in typical secret fashion, she whispered into Mrs. Finnerty's ear. Angela and her mother looked at each other questioningly. Amy was about to be scolded for her rudeness when Mrs. Finnerty smiled and nodded. Amy ran to the back of the library and returned carrying the book bag they had found upstairs earlier. She carried it with both hands, and it glistened in the evening light as it bounced against her legs. When she arrived level with Mrs. Finnerty, she hesitated. Then urged on by this kind, generous lady, her friend, she handed the valise to her sister.

"It's from India, it's for you, open it," the little girl said quietly.

Angela took the bag and, admiring it, handed it to her mother. Mrs. Coughlan ran her hand over the surface of the bag and handed it back to Angela.

"It's very beautiful, go ahead and open it," urged her mother.

Angela's eyes widened as she saw compartments in the centre of the bag. She knew instantly, they were made to hold books. She had been given an exquisite book bag. Then she saw an actual book nestled in a larger section farthest away from her. Casting a glance at her mother and Mrs. Finnerty, she put the bag on the little table by the lamp and lifted the book out. She was holding a copy of *The Wonderful Things You Will Be.* She read the title in a soft whisper. She turned it over and read the back cover clearly and loudly:

This is the first time
There's ever been you,
So I wonder what wonderful things
You will do

Amy applauded her sister's performance without understanding its significance. The adults were grateful for the interruption as they steadied each other. Amy bounded over to her sister to see the book for herself.

Mrs. Coughlan began her protest against giving Angela the book bag. She was quickly silenced both by the look in Mrs. Finnerty's eyes and the vision of the two young sisters reading such a book together in the lamplight.

Mrs. Finnerty was first to speak. "Let them come Saturday around three o'clock. Amy can help Angela choose some books to take to Dublin. No doubt, *'Duckling'* will be going."

"More than likely," replied Caroline, having reminded her friend once more to please call her by her first name.

"Its great news about today's tests," beamed Mrs. Finnerty.

"What about your own result, any word?" asked Caroline.

"Oh no, maybe tomorrow" came the reply as if it was of no consequence at all.

"Mrs. Finnerty, please call Dr. Owens in the morning," urged Caroline. "For my sake, I would like to know before Dublin. Will you please?" She was successful in exacting a promise that Dr. Owens would be called. "Tony will think we've taken up lodgings with you if we don't go home," exclaimed Caroline, hearing the clock chime. "The girls will go to school as normal tomorrow. You will see them Saturday afternoon, and we will go to Dublin on the first train on Sunday. A trip, like Angela said. Lots of distractions on the train and a bit of reading, I'm sure. Amy needs to see the unit and meet the people that Angela will be with next week. The chemotherapy starts Monday. It's a tough, tough regimen but only one round needed before the operation. How Angela's body tolerates the drugs will determine how soon that will be and how long she will stay in Dublin. Dr. Owens has agreed to monitor all the blood tests, as you know. There is a good chance her hair will be affected, certainly by the time all is said and done. Dr. Myers is very aware of that, apparently. Tony and Amy will be back on the evening train on Sunday, and I will stay with Angela."

"Caroline, I have an idea about the hair-loss situation. Actually, it was Amy's. It's just a whim at the moment. Is it okay if I mention Angela's condition to the Shivas because I might be needing their help?" asked Mrs. Finnerty.

"Oh, by all means," Caroline replied. "Not just the Shivas, we will need all the support and prayers we can get. There's going to be an announcement at school on Monday and a school mass for her on Wednesday at the cathedral. People mean well at a time like this, the more goodwill, the better. There's plenty of support and prayers coming in from the Gardaí already.

"I applaud your attitude. Being open is best for all of you. Speaking of best, it's best you get those children home. I almost forgot, come with me." They walked together back to the little fridge, and Mrs. Finnerty said as she handed her a platter, "Take this with you. It should tide you over for a while." The platter was graciously accepted without protest. In truth they needed the food this evening.

Remembering Amy's earlier comment, Caroline said, "That's the *lift*! It's genius!"

"A stroke of genius on the part of the designers all right. I just needed to get up to bed!" quipped Mrs. Finnerty. A good chuckle escaped them both.

Mrs. Coughlan and her daughters went next door bearing gifts and food. The items on their clothesline of life were light and silky and swayed gently in the late evening breeze.

CHAPTER 26

As she sat facing the back window, Mrs. Finnerty could not recall ever sitting in this chair before. She eased back into its soft comfort and relaxed. The sun was still competing with the moon, and the spoils of battle were evident in the fiery red of the sky. The colors of the late evening cast a warm glow upon the room and reminded her that the days were getting longer, and summer would soon be upon them.

Sitting there bathed in the soothing light, she recalled the events of the day. First thing this morning she was so full of vim and vigour, she could have skipped down the stairs, that is if she had any. She remembered making a mental list of things to get at Quigley's for Amy's tea.

She was not surprised when Mrs. Quigley herself served her and said, "Very big day today, Mrs. Finnerty," as she smiled at her knowingly. "Extra treat in the bag for later."

Mrs. Finnerty's reply was as discreet as Mrs. Quigley's remark and her smile demure.

Meeting Fiona reminded her of her own pending result, which paled in comparison to Angela's. Today was not about her, today was about the Coughlan family, and the youngest member of the family had emerged as the star. Sharing the colorful umbrella with Amy on the way home from school, seeing her surprise when she discovered the lift, the mature way she sat at the big table to do her homework delighted her. The generosity she showed in giving the book bag to her sister was way beyond her years and was not lost on her mother. Most amazingly, her simple admiration of a piece of fabric had sparked a thought that was destined to become a movement. She was developing this idea further when her thoughts were interrupted by the ringing of the telephone.

"My apologies, Mrs. Finnerty, for the late hour," said Dr. Owens.

"Oh, Dr. Owens, not too late, not too late at all," she answered. Truthfully, her heart skipped a beat at the sound of his voice.

"Dr. O'Connor called just now. He had an emergency this afternoon and was unable to call earlier. He wanted you to know that the biopsy he did during the colonoscopy shows the small area of change in the bowel is cancerous. It may sound bad when you say it like that. It's good news. It's limited in size and may be a simple problem to solve. The reason for the late call is due to today's emergency, a slot has opened tomorrow for a CT scan. Dr. O'Connor wants you to take that appointment. It will give us a better look at the belly making sure that nothing is being missed. It's unusual to get an appointment at such short notice unless the situation is dire. Come to think of it, you got a colonoscopy due to a cancelation too," said Dr. Owens.

"I did, and I'm thankful for this one too. Anything is better than your situation being *dire*."

Dr. Owens could hear the humour in Mrs. Finnerty's voice as she spoke, and it pleased him. "That description doesn't quite fit you, Mrs. Finnerty, I must say. They need you at Radiology by eight tomorrow morning. I have a good feeling about this. As it's being done first thing, it's possible we will have results in the afternoon. Dr. O'Connor will most likely chase this result down himself. One way or the other either you will get a call tomorrow. Are you all right with all that?" asked the doctor.

"Yes, I am. I've actually not been giving it much thought. I don't want to put you on the spot, Dr. Owens, I really don't, but it's Angela next door that has me far more concerned than myself," she added. "If it's a simple cure and I can be well soon for her and her family, then I couldn't ask for more. I will be there in the morning, bright and early."

"I do know about your connection with the Coughlans and how close you are. For now, think positive thoughts and sleep! As my mother used to tell us, "The morning won't be long coming."

Mrs. Finnerty was smiling as she replaced the receiver, remembering her mother saying those very same words to her when she was a child. As the doctor had said she had positive thoughts and slept. She was tranquil and at peace as she readied herself for the arrival of the taxi. She reflected on how differently she felt today in comparison to the time she asked Mr. Doherty to go to Fiona Hannon for help. She was gripped by fear then. She couldn't explain now why her fear had left her. Mrs. Hannon went above and beyond in helping her. She was her friend and neighbour. Mr. Doherty had astonished her with his attention without being personal. She recalled his part in caring for her when she had the colonoscopy. Even the teenage twins, Maura and Carmel, had missed her and sent a message. Mr. and Mrs. Shiva showered her with friendship and support. Despite all that, Angela's health concerns had left her adrift. She'd been like an old balloon long escaped from a birthday party unable to land. She was lost to herself.

This morning was different. She knew that she would be fine. She knew now why she was destined to settle in Baybridge. She knew she was also destined to live in this particular house. She was absolutely certain that her future was tied to Angela. Of this, she had no doubt.

The unwavering belief that she held in her future showed in the way she closed her front door, jaunted down the driveway, and slid into the waiting taxi.

Jimmy, the driver, tipped the peak of his cap and, looking in the rearview mirror, asked, "We're off to the hospital, right?"

"Yes, indeed, Jimmy. The main entrance will do nicely, thank you."

"Right then," he replied, stealing another glance at his fare. He knew her well, so he continued bravely, "Are you sure it's not a dance or something we're off to?"

She caught a glimpse of his twinkling eyes in the mirror, and just for his benefit, she waved her gloved hand in royal fashion and said, “We might as well be, Jimmy, we might as well!”

When the scan was finished, she was delighted to see how early it was. It was a beautiful, sunny, warm morning. She made up her mind quickly not to call Jimmy to pick her up. Instead, she decided to walk across the bridge to the other side of the river, have a freshly made scone and a steaming mug of tea in Kelly’s. She loved the quaint ambiance in Kelly’s and the scones were out of this world. She reprimanded herself for not doing something like this more often. She used to be out and about all the time. Had she become an “auld fuddy duddy” with her books and her cat? No disrespect to the books or indeed to Mrs. Miller intended.

A gentle but cheerful voice interrupted her thoughts. “Lovely morning, ma’am,” said a beautiful dark-haired young lady. Her dark-blue eyes and porcelain skin were remarkable.

“Absolutely lovely, Grainne!” replied Mrs. Finnerty, leaning in slightly to read the young woman’s name badge. “One of your raisin scones and a mug of tea would make it perfect.”

“Coming right out” came the reply. “Would you like today’s paper?”

“Grainne, I’m just going to sit here, pay no attention to the world’s problems, and study the swans.” She had settled in the bay window alcove, giving her a clear view of the river just a few feet away. “I don’t remember when I last saw a swan,” she added.

“Were you over at the hospital, then? Are you sick?” inquired Grainne, genuinely concerned.

Mrs. Finnerty was impressed by Grainne’s astute observations and answered, “I am not sick in a way that keeps me away from the swans. No excuses there, I’m afraid.” She paused briefly then decided to tell her about the CAT scan.

“A lot of people come into Kelly’s on the way to and from the hospital. You can’t always tell the state of their health by their looks. You, ma’am, you are going to get good news today,” announced Grainne, and off she went to get the tea and scone.

Mrs. Finnerty did get good news from Dr. O'Connor, and he would tell her about the simple operation needed when he saw her at quarter past eleven on Monday morning.

CHAPTER 27

Mr. Doherty was out at first light puttering in his backyard. It was literally a jungle. This was his space for experiments, randomly taking a cutting from here, planting it there, joining this with that, some in pots, but mostly in the ground. If asked about the science behind all this, he would have no answer. He had an idea at any given time, and either it worked or it didn't. A lot worked.

This morning he was interested in the progress of a particular plant he had played around with. He had Mrs. Finnerty in mind when he started this project. She had often claimed that she could kill a weed just by looking at it, a claim he didn't accept. His dilemma was not whether she would kill it, rather would she want the bother of it. He had all but decided to leave it where it was when he found himself talking to a magpie in the tree above his head. He looked around for a second bird because according to the children's nursery rhyme:

One for sorrow
Two for joy
Three for a girl
Four for a boy…

Sure enough, he spotted the partner on a branch higher up and took it as a sign. "This little plant is for Mrs. Finnerty and it will bring her joy. Your fault if it doesn't, you two," he informed the pair of magpies. All he got back was their familiar throaty rattle!

He took the plant into the house, wiped the earth from the pot, washed his hands, and headed to Quigley's for the paper. On the way there, he started to have doubts again about the plant. Would it be seen as too forward, too familiar, misunderstood? He stopped himself by saying aloud, "It's in the hands of the magpies." A young lad, flying by on his bike, open jacket wafting in the wind, waved at him. Was he talking out loud? He grunted and kept on walking.

At the usual time, he arrived at Mrs. Finnerty's. The plant was in a plastic bag, within a bag, within a bag. God forbid he'd arrive looking like a suitor. He scanned the treetops. Not a bird in sight. He was on his own. Mrs. Miller cast one eye in his direction from her usual spot; she knew. As soon as she opened the door, he sensed a change in her. Smiling she ushered him in and asked, "Is that a bag of money?"

He wasn't sure what she was referring to at first. Then, remembering the plant he said, "Modest winnings, today, Mrs. Finnerty, but I believe what I have here is a winner for you." Having indicated that he needed to use the kitchen table, they both moved to the back of the house. Unceremoniously, he opened the outer bags. When he got to the bag containing the plant, he opened it as if it contained fine china. She witnessed the bag deliver an ode to all life, a plant. Its red petals fading to orange and back to a different shade of red to almost a deep pink dazzled her. She had never seen such colours on anything before.

"It's a celebration!" she announced as she gently touched the soft, velvety bright-green leaves. A green unusually bright for a plant. "Please put it on the ledge below the window, so I can see it from all angles. It's perfect!"

Mr. Doherty did as he was told. Now he was just standing there in a daze.

"As we are here in the kitchen, wouldn't a cup of tea be lovely?" She plugged in the electric kettle and produced two dainty sausage rolls, courtesy of Mrs. Quigley. "Please sit down, Mr. Doherty, it's just a wee treat." As she saw his hesitation, she added, "Won't take too long," They sat together like two old friends. She told him about the CT scan, meeting Grainne in Kelly's and what she predicted about her getting good news, the call from Dr. O'Connor, and the appointment on Monday. Most importantly, she told him without a doubt, that she was all right. "That's enough of that," she said and instead proceeded to tell him all about Angela.

Mr. Doherty did not say one word through it all. Mrs. Finnerty did not seem to notice that. Finally, she asked him, "What do you think of maybe making a sort of mobile library? Maybe it could be called 'books on wheels.' I don't know. I have this notion that getting Amy involved in choosing the books and wheeling them next door would be good for her. It would be fun too, especially if any fell off. Angela would get a great laugh out of that. Is it a mad idea?"

Now this was more in his line, not one for the philosophical or the medical, mobile bookshelves were right up his alley. "Not at all," he answered confidently. "How many books do you want to wheel, and will they be different heights?" She had no answer to that.

"Can you, can you make it, Mr. Doherty?" she squealed as she slid the sausage rolls across the table in his direction. He did not seem to notice.

"I can," he replied, sadness in his voice. "It's a terrible thing that this little girl has to go through all that, a terrible thing altogether. It's an easy enough job to make the bookshelves."

He slowly stood up and just nodded. "I'll leave the winnings on the table and take today's book. I'm glad about your good news. You are the best person for that family, next door. I'll collect you at half past ten on Monday morning, and after the doctor we'll walk over to Kelly's and have a chat with the swans on the way." pronounced Mr. Doherty. With that, he went out the front door. He winked at the cat and continued on his journey.

"I love the plant," said Mrs. Finnerty to the back of his head.

No tea had been made, no sausage roll eaten, no magpies in the sky, but today was a good drying day.

CHAPTER 28

Mrs. Miller was feeling neglected. People were in and out of the house at a great rate. Something was happening next door, something big. Mrs. Miller had a nose for this kind of thing. She resolved to be alert because at any moment the skills that only she possessed could be called for. As if on cue, she heard the rattle of the gate, and Amy and Angela appeared. "I knew it!" she meowed to herself. With that, the girls were upon her and the fussing started. Amy was carrying a book, and as she placed it on the doorstep for later, Mrs. Finnerty appeared.

"Good afternoon, ladies!" she said, noticing that Mrs. Miller was down from her perch, and Angela was shamelessly stroking the long, soft fur on her tummy.

Oh, I do have my uses, thought the cat, all feelings of neglect vanished.

Eventually they went inside, and the book club was called to order. All three were aware that today's book had deep personal significance for them. Reading it had the potential to evoke sadness and apprehension. Should a passerby stop and look in the window, they would not know that. Instead, they would see two young girls sitting close to each other, a large book spread across their laps. Sitting nearby an older woman, possibly their grandmother, intently listening. The last thing the observer would glean from this tableau was a young girl with bone cancer starting chemotherapy in forty-eight hours. Her younger sister, who was well aware of this, was about to help pack a book bag for her to take to the hospital. The older woman, not the grandmother, not a relative at all, had just been diagnosed with colon cancer. What the observer would be certain of was that all three shared a deep love, a love so true, it transcended all else.

When the book was read, all questions answered, explanations accepted and understood, Mrs. Finnerty declared, "Teatime, girls!" in her fake teacher's voice. The girls giggled and jumped up assuming the student's straight-line position and followed her to a wooden table on her back porch. "Picnic," she said in the same voice as before as she indicated the basket already on the table.

"Thank you, Mrs. Finnerty!" came the singsong reply all too familiar in schoolchildren. None of them could keep from laughing any longer. Teacher heaped praise on them for their acting skills, causing more laughter. Mrs. Miller crept around the side of the house to see what all the fuss was about, just in case she was needed.

Mrs. Coughlan's kitchen window and back door were open on this late spring day. From the sounds coming from the backyard next door, she guessed the book club was finished. She popped her head over the hedge dividing her backyard from Mrs. Finnerty's and got the nod to join them. As had been decided the previous evening, Mrs. Coughlan was the bearer of the book bag, just in case the girls got carried away and chose a few tomes. You never knew with those two.

Mrs. Miller gave her a questioning look when she appeared and thought, *Aha, something* is *going on!*

"Mammy!" squealed the girls and went to her.

"Picnic, is it? Isn't it well for ye and me slaving away next door!" teased Mrs. Coughlan.

"Aw, Mammy," said the girls in unison.

"All right, all right, I wasn't really slaving. I was enjoying hearing your laughter over here." She hugged her daughters closer. She wondered, not for the first time, what in the world she had ever done to deserve this neighbour? The love Mrs. Finnerty had for her girls was spilling over and filling her heart too. She was sure, as sure as she had ever been about anything in her life, this love would carry her and her family through the terrible ordeal that was about to start. She looked over at Mrs. Finnerty, now sitting at the picnic table, and seeing the expression in those eyes, she felt strength and confidence flow through her.

While the girls were choosing the books, no mean task as was expected, Mrs. Coughlan was relieved to get the update on Mrs. Finnerty's CT scan and her appointment on Monday with Dr. O'Connor. She was also surprised and happy that Mr. Doherty was taking her.

"Oh, I almost forgot, Finbar brought my usual grocery order up yesterday," cut in Mrs. Finnerty. "To tell you the truth, I think I order too much at the best of times, but if Dr. O'Connor goes ahead with the operation this week, it will spoil. Do you think Mr. Coughlan and Amy could help me out and take some? They would be doing me a great favour."

Now it was Mrs. Coughlan's turn to cut in: "Oh my gosh, we couldn't do that! Take your food!"

"Caroline," continued Mrs. Finnerty quietly, "you're not taking my food. I don't have freezer space or storage space. Have you seen the size of that kitchen?" She continued with a chuckle. "It's for a leprechaun. It might save Mr. Coughlan a trip or two to the shops while you are away." With a bit more haggling, it was decided that transferring the food next door made sense. The girls continued with their book selection, and to everyone's amazement, it was light enough for either of them to carry.

The goodbyes and well wishes had the potential to be emotional, but once again the belief that all would be well prevailed. Mr. Coughlan made a few trips back and forth and confessed that he was relieved not to have to go food shopping.

He had no complaints about the quality of the selection either!

CHAPTER 29

The path between the houses seemed so familiar. Her confidence in her decision to come here evident in her every step. Cardigan placed loosely on her shoulders, handbag swinging, and with a smile on her face she approached the bench and, without seeking a familiar face in the crowd, sat down. Placing her handbag beside her, she eased back and relaxed. An innocent onlooker would assume that this was her regular Saturday evening spot, reverently reserved for an avid supporter of the football club. However, this was Mrs. Finnerty, who had made a brief appearance on one occasion only prior to this, and until that moment, despite hearing the roar of the crowd regularly, had no idea how to trace it to its source. This evening she sat in their midst absorbed in their cheers and boos and felt like a loyal fan. They were her team and she was their supporter. To her, they were all winners.

The sun was high in the sky for a little longer. The mountains stood tall and craggy against the subtle changing light as evening approached. Mrs. Finnerty thought how she loved the changing seasons in this part of the world and the miracles each had to offer. The sky on the other hand had her spellbound throughout the day. The sun, it seemed, played an endless game of hide-and-seek. Sometimes in full view, then totally hidden behind a cloud, then a tiny peek and gone again, only to reappear in all its splendour. This sun was a rascal and played havoc with the nerves of many trying to dry clothes on a line. She attributed the antics of the sun to the proximity of the ocean. "It's just over there," she said aloud, nodding her head towards its blue in the distance, visible now and then through the trees.

"What's just over there?" asked a gentle, familiar voice.

"The sea," she answered, shielding her eyes from the late sun as she looked up into the handsome face of Mr. Shiva. Neither showed any surprise at seeing the other. They continued their conversation in a casual tone that conveyed it was the most natural place in the world for them to meet, at a children's Gaelic football game.

"My cousin's boy, Previn, is playing for one of the visiting teams. He's twelve now and showing some serious promise," said Mr. Shiva.

"Twelve is a great age for showing serious promise, in many areas," she replied with a smile. Spoken like a true teacher.

She moved her handbag to her other side subconsciously extending an invitation to Mr. Shiva to sit with her. His response was as spontaneous as hers. He sat close as if replacing the handbag and quietly inquired about her health. Her update was brief and light and ended with a comment stated as fact: "By this time next week, it will all be behind me." He believed her wholeheartedly and smiled.

"Mr. Shiva, you know Sergeant Coughlan and his family, I believe. My young book-club members and your biggest laddu fans," she continued in the same light tone without missing a beat.

"I do," he replied. "I know the sergeant well, both as a patron at Pepper and from various civic events in the county. An officer and a gentleman, I would venture to say."

"His wife, Caroline, and I have been visiting this week. I've been getting to know their girls, Amy and Angela, a bit more intimately. It's a big day for them tomorrow," she paused before continuing, "They are taking their ten-year-old daughter, Angela, to Dublin to start chemotherapy for a cancerous area on her leg. While her younger sister, Amy, was staying with me after school one day she saw some fabrics I brought from India. We were going through some drawers upstairs when we came across these lovely pieces. Her simple comment at the time was that they would make a lovely hat or scarf. I immediately thought of the hair loss her sister will inevitably endure. An idea came to me through Amy's comment. We need to make turbans and hats and all sorts of beautiful things, not just for Angela, but for the other children in similar circumstances in other units across the country." Mrs. Finnerty took a deep breath and looked at her friend sitting beside her. "Caroline, their mother is okay with us talking about Angela," she reassured him.

Mr. Shiva was looking straight ahead, his eyes wandering back and forth as he focused on the legs and feet of the young football players. He watched the skill of the toe work around the ball when an opponent threatened to kick it away, the speed of the legs as the challenging journey up the field began, and the sheer strength and force as the kick was taken in an attempt to score. As he watched the scene play out over and over, he thought of his little daughter, his cousin's son, and what yet might befall Angela's leg. He did not recognise that he was crying! Silence prevailed for an unmeasured length of time, then Mrs. Finnerty spoke, "I believe the usual place for a planning committee to meet is in a boardroom. Football fields can be far more inspirational." She cast a twinkling glance in Mr. Shiva's direction and saw that the hint of humour in her remark had broken the spell and he returned her smile. "Mr. Shiva, I am utterly devoid of the skill needed to even get this project started. The fabric I have at home is just enough to have something special made for Amy to give Angela, as this was initially her idea. I wonder if you can help me with the name of a seamstress and a fabric supplier for a much larger undertaking."

"Mrs. Finnerty," he answered, "there are those that would say, our meeting here was meant to be. They would say that Previn playing here today was preordained. Some would even say that you have special powers. I don't have an opinion on any of that. I do know that Previn's mother is a skilled maker of all things Indian in ladies' clothing. She imports the fabrics from Tamil Nadu and has an exotic booth at the market I was returning from on the day we met. The family is staying with us until tomorrow evening you would be most welcome to meet her tomorrow at our home."

She nodded her head in agreement, and so it was that the foundation known as Angela's Tresses and Turbans was born!

Her clothesline for today was light and colorful, draped with silks so fine they could easily pass through the centre of a wedding band.

CHAPTER 30

Angela knew it was right time to go to Dublin. The pain in her leg had intensified recently, especially at night. Tonight was the worst. She awoke just before 2 o'clock in the morning, and her mother was at her bedside before she had whispered "Mammy." Mother and daughter lay side by side for a while to let the pain medication do its job. The nightlight plugged into the wall at the foot of the bed cast a comforting glow. Angela knew her shell was cracking, but her core was intact. Emboldened by this awareness, she tried to comfort her mother. Her gentle but firm whisper broke the silence, "Mammy, the time is right for me to go to the hospital in Dublin. I know that the strong medicines will make me sick, but it's only the medicines, not the lump. I have to take them so that Dr. Alan can get rid of the bad part of my leg. That's all. I'm not sad. Will you not be sad so?"

Caroline, smothered in pain and anguish, sought her daughter's hand resting on the bedclothes, and with every ounce of strength she possessed, replied, "Not at all then, not at all." The gentle squeeze of her mother's hand sent Angela to sleep. Caroline dared not move a single muscle nor take a deep breath for fear her pain might explode into the night.

Her husband lay in similar paralysis in the room next to Angela's. Neither of them longed for morning.

Daybreak came, as it always does, and chaos erupted in the Coughlan household. Everything had been readied the night before. When was the last time that ever worked? Minds were changed, things packed were unpacked, and things not packed were now packed, pounding up the stairs, running down the stairs. After about three cycles of this mayhem, they found themselves sitting in their car in the driveway.

It had been decided that they would drive their own car and park at the station, despite many offers from the Gardaí to drop them off and pick Tony and Amy up that night. Tony started the car, daring to take one last questioning look at them. When no objections were raised, he eased out to the road that lead to Baybridge Railway Station. As always, it was very busy. Students sporting backpacks returning to university after the weekend at home. Grandparents visiting family, laden down with parcels. Businessmen with their suits and briefcases getting a head start on the workweek. Suitcases on wheels being dragged in all directions, and of course, the holiday makers heading for parts unknown with that look of excitement and fear blended on their faces. Who decided that it was necessary to check the whereabouts of their passports so often!

The Coughlans avoided the crush, as they had reserved seats and boarded the train without further ado. Tony Coughlan could be forgiven for assuming that reserved seats meant that nobody would be sitting in the seat that your ticket clearly stated was assigned to you. Wrong! For there, large as life, puffing on an unlit pipe and proudly wearing a trilby hat, sat one of the oldest and most elegant of men. As the whole family hovered in the aisle, Tony, towering above the guest in his seat, realised that they were obstructing the other passengers. He indicated to Caroline to sit at the table opposite to the one they had booked. It would all sort itself out. It did.

The train soon started to move. The Coughlans sat at the table on the other side of the aisle. The trilby-hat man sat alone and paid a lot of attention to his newspaper.

As each station approached, a recorded message, first in Gaelic, then in English announced each station's name, all the remaining stations, and ended with a request not to put your feet on the seats, please.

Amy and Angela sat quietly for a while, stealing glances at the trilby-hat man. Angela asked her dad if he was allowed to smoke a pipe. Tony just shrugged. He was enjoying the novelty of this eccentric man.

The modern trains did not have dining carriages, which was always a disappointment to Caroline. That was the highlight of a train trip when she was growing up. Lunch would be announced, and the passengers unhurriedly made their way to the dining carriage. Starched white tablecloths covered the tables, and the uniformed waiter placed linen napkins on their laps. The challenge, Caroline remembered, was to avoid spilling anything or dropping anything on all that starched white as the train lunged forward.

Nowadays, the highlight was the arrival of the catering trolley. Amy and Angela ordered a mini apple tart each and a small carton of milk. They chose some sweets to share later. Caroline and Tony did not eat. Neither did the trilby-hat man. As the girl unlocked the wheels on the catering trolley and started to move down the aisle, the trilby-hat man asked for a cup of tea. Tony shifted his position to allow her to reverse, giving him a more direct view of the man. Their eyes met. "May I offer you a cup of tea?" the trilby-hat man asked.

Tony hesitated for just an instant and said, "Yes, that would be nice."

"And the good lady?" continued the gentleman. Caroline agreed to tea, and so it was that the conversation started.

No names were exchanged, no personal information disclosed, all general niceties until the trilby-hat man said to Tony, "It would be nice if your little girl could rest her leg, stretch out a bit. You are welcome to join me here to make more room for her." He took the last sip from his paper teacup as he spoke. Caroline spread a cardigan on the seat and Angela stretched her leg.

The journey continued. More passengers boarded the train, some got off. The conductor checked the tickets with the same machine hanging around his neck as Caroline remembered as a child. It must be computerised by now, she thought. It looked the same to her. No questions were asked about the tickets, nobody claimed the seat they were sitting in, no comment from the conductor about Angela's leg on the seat. Tony sat with the trilby-hat man for the remainder of the trip into Dublin.

He could not have known that he was traveling with Sir James Butler, renowned paediatric oncologist. If he did, it would have answered his own question: how did the trilby-hat man know that Angela needed to stretch her leg?

CHAPTER 31

Park Edge Hospital was an impressive structure. From its humble beginnings as a cottage hospital at the edge of the park, it had grown to be one of the most prestigious medical centre in the world. Even today, one had the feeling of entering a stately home as you passed through the massive black and gold wrought iron gates and viewed the building in the distance. High above your head, spanning their width, arched a banner declaring *Park Edge Hospital* in enormous gold letters. It was necessary to step back, with care, to the very edge of the curb to read the banner. Thus instead, the gates became the landmark. Many explanations were given as to why the gates were closed at 10 o'clock every night for half an hour only. They were banged shut at 10 o'clock exactly and ceremoniously reopened at precisely half past 10. This was a joint task carried out by the senior porter from the day shift and the senior porter from the night shift. Each pushing one half to meet in the center. It was thought by some that the safety of the patients was being symbolically handed off to the oncoming night shift. No such ceremony took place in the morning. One old local man explained it by saying, "Sure, why would you need all that pallava when it's daylight." Point taken.

One way or another, the gates were a most distinctive feature and most often used when giving directions to the building. Gates such as these warranted a tree-lined avenue, and the Ladies Guild was more than happy to oblige. The avenue lay like a wide ribbon on a velvet blanket from the gold embossed gates to the white marble portico at the entrance. It was no secret that the gardening club, a subcommittee of the Ladies Guild, was indeed generous and so were its patrons.

The transition from stately manor to hospital, though subtle, was in evidence immediately upon leaving the grand foyer. It was then that the reality of today's excursion hit the Coughlan family. The girls thought the ride on the brightly painted golf cart from the gate along the avenue was great fun. They waved at their parents walking behind them and giggled at whatever the young uniformed driver was saying. Once inside, their demeanor changed. Despite its outward appearance this was a hospital; this was the place where Angela was going to be very sick. Amy and her dad would go back to Baybridge later today to worry themselves silly without Angela. Her mother would see her sickness firsthand and worry herself silly right there at her bedside. This was the beginning.

Another young, uniformed man appeared from nowhere pushing a vehicle that vaguely resembled a wheelchair. It had a second seat at the back. It was painted bright yellow.

"Your chariot awaits, ladies!" he announced with an exaggerated bow and a click of the heels. Angela was ushered into the front seat, and Amy took her place behind her. He placed the small suitcase on a luggage rack underneath the back seat and allowed Angela to keep the book bag on the seat beside her. "All aboard!" was declared as they began their journey. "Our guests are very independent here," this remark thrown over his shoulder to Caroline and Tony with a nod and a smile. The porter's words reassured them that Angela's independence would not be stifled here but nurtured and encouraged. They held hands as they followed their young daughters down the hall of the Dublin hospital.

Arriving at the paediatric oncology unit, the young porter punched in a number on the code pad on the wall and announced, "Ms. Angela Coughlan from Baybridge!" The door automatically opened. They were met by a nurse who introduced herself as Ellen. The porter handed over his charges to Nurse Ellen. He did not enter the unit and neither did his vehicle.

The family was escorted to a seating area immediately to the right inside the door. The furniture intrigued Caroline. Instead of a traditional armchair, Angela was shown to a child-sized chaise lounge, which automatically enabled her to elevate her leg without drawing attention to it. Several of these in various shades of blue were randomly placed about the area. Amy shared Angela's and sat at her feet. Caroline sat on another, her feet resting on the floor. Tony remained standing, declining the offer of a regular chair. Above Angela's chaise hung a painting of a seashore depicting a mountain in the distance, a thatched cottage, and two fishing boats moored in a sandy cove in the foreground. The space, as they sat there, had a nautical feel and coming as they did from Baybridge, so close to the ocean, it was indeed comforting. A lady approached from somewhere unseen and took Tony and Caroline into an office to complete the admissions paperwork. The package containing all the papers from Baybridge was duly handed over. "You can see the girls through this window," offered Mrs. Mitchell, whose name tag declared "Senior Admissions Officer, Oncology." Caroline tried not to see the word oncology pinned to Mrs. Mitchell's lapel. The process was relatively quick since Fiona had prepared all the relevant documents prior to them leaving Baybridge.

"Time for the tour now," came the voice of Nurse Ellen from the doorway. The unit had ten inpatient beds, all in separate rooms, five on either side as you entered the unit. Caroline noticed several chaise lounges grouped together at various intervals as they walked through the ward. Angela was leading the pack, walking slowly, and setting the pace when she suddenly stopped.

"Look," she said, "it's a pirate ship."

Her mother had been correct in detecting a nautical theme for there, straight ahead, just beyond the lounge area, loomed the rigging, skull-and-crossbones flag, mast and figurehead of a pirate ship. The wall behind was a painted seascape. Various people seemed to be walking about on board the ship. "It's the nurse's station," explained Nurse Ellen. It was hard to believe this until they got close enough to see all the trappings of a busy nurses' station hidden from the children's view.

If it were possible to put one at ease in such a place, Park Edge had given this their best shot, thought Tony as he lifted the girls up in turn to get a better look.

Off to the left of the pirate ship, sitting on the edge of an aqua-blue chaise, sat a lady wearing an extraordinary headdress. She was deep in conversation with a little girl, and the odd chuckle could be heard passing between them. Amy, drawn to the woman, could not look away. Soon the lady got up and spent—what seemed to Amy—a long, long time washing her hands and even longer time drying them. It struck her how each finger seemed to be washed and dried separately. It was more like finger than handwashing. Amy had never seen anyone wash and dry her hands like that before. The lady noticed Amy watching her and beckoned her to join her at the sink. Amy stepped in her direction, noticing her headdress instantly, reminding her of the fabric she had seen in Mrs. Finnerty's upstairs drawer. Amy was the first of the Coughlan family to meet Dr. Gwendoline Myers as she showed her how to wash her hands.

CHAPTER 32

They knew that parking was going to be a problem. Dr. O'Connor saw his presurgical patients in Baybridge Medical Centre. Realizing that preparing for an operation was traumatic enough, he made this arrangement to accommodate the complete process in one visit. Other doctors had followed his lead. Despite the popularity of the centre, and the continual praise heaped upon its staff, parking was a major bone of contention among the people of Baybridge. Whenever there were two or three gathered, the topic always raised its ugly head. No county council meeting or civic gathering was safe. "What about the church?" Mrs. Finnerty offered in reply to Mr. Doherty's mention of the parking.

Just before the medical centre on the opposite side of the road sat an old church. It stood high on the main road, its back to the river below, its face to the hospital and its ancient walls crumbling. The spire could be seen from any point as you approached the town. It was the most-talked-about church for miles for a completely different reason. The most popular feature of the old church was the four parking spaces it boasted out front on the main road. Every driver who had occasion to go to the medical centre/hospital, as it was often called, started his or her plea to their god way before leaving home, that one of the four spaces would be vacant. Most were disappointed. "I think we're in luck," he replied as he noticed the empty space from the corner of Maple Street. A prayer on his lips and his fingers crossed on the steering wheel, he deftly manoeuvred into the last remaining spot. Looking up at the spire, he said aloud, "Thank you." Mrs. Finnerty smiled in response.

With help from Mr. Doherty, she navigated the busy road and made her way via the side entrance to the outpatient department.

Knowing he had time on his hands, he made his way down the steep, narrow, cobbled lane alongside the church to the river. Years ago, when he first moved to Baybridge from his hometown on the banks of the Shannon River, it wasn't possible to walk along the length of Swan River. The only view you had was from the bridge spanning the salmon leap where crowds gathered in excitement in the hopes of catching a glimpse of the silvery scales glimmering momentarily in midair. A local Garda was sometimes in the mix to deter illicit fishing. If you walked in the opposite direction along the footpath away from the bay, the river did eventually come back in view. Fishing boats bobbed lazily here and there, their lapping sound getting your attention. If you stood still and looked deep, you had another chance to see a salmon making its way back up the river to spawn. None of this seemed to interest the swans. They were about their own business, quiet until you reached the lake. There, a raucous and sometimes violent outburst erupted between swan and duck over a crust of bread. Human intervention strongly discouraged.

In recent years, the promenade had been created, giving Baybridge a continental flare. *Good for business,* he thought as he took in the curve of the widening river. Restaurants and boutiques had sprung up all around. Old warehouses and factories now sported fancy names. Some original structures had been preserved and repurposed. Others defaced or demolished. Sad. A history of settlements in Baybridge going back to the Mesolithic era had been recorded. Old buildings, new uses. Respect for the city and its history often in question. Nostalgia, history, beauty and modernization forever conflict.

He looked at his watch and started to climb back up the steep lane towards the car. At about the halfway mark he turned and went back to where he had been standing on the bridge. An older man passed by greeting him with a tip of his hat. A middle-aged woman with a shopping bag was approaching from the town side of the bridge, followed by two school-uniformed girls on their lunch break from class. Mrs. Finnerty had crossed here the morning she ate the fresh scone at Kelly's.

Grainne, the waitress, was setting the table in the bay-window alcove, the same table where Mrs. Finnerty had sat. Looking out the window, she saw a man on the bridge, his hands slowly sliding down the railings as he fell to the ground. She stumbled through the door, bumping into others on the way. She was the first to reach him. To Grainne the world had stopped, the silence of it ringing in her ears. Slow, slow, everything was so slow. She tried to rouse him. She checked his pulse, none, no breathing, she opened his shirt collar, so slow. It only seemed that way because the schoolgirls had already begun resuscitation on hearing her words. The shopping-bag lady called the ambulance. The spectators cleared a path for the emergency-response team. The schoolgirls continued their work counting aloud to each other until the crew took over. The manager from Kelly's went to the girls. "Come on over with me, there's tea already made," she soothed, "you two were great, just great." Grainne was still crouched on the ground, her world suspended when a pair of ladies' shoes caught her eye. She followed the pair of legs upwards, passed the skirt hem, higher along the floral cardigan, until her eyes rested on the face of Mrs. Finnerty. She stumbled to a standing position and made her way around the commotion to her side. "Is this your friend?" she asked. The dazed woman nodded. "Were you at your appointment?" Another nod. Grainne's world started to spin again. "It's best to go back to the hospital," she explained, "they will take him there. Are you able to walk up the lane?" More nodding.

Behind them, Grainne could see the patient was on his way to the ambulance, cardiac compressions still in progress. Along the banks of the river, onlookers stood in stunned silence. Was that rosary beads in the hands of the shopping bag lady? As Grainne and Mrs. Finnerty were about to cross the road at the top of the lane, an ambulance sped past, siren blazing. Neither of them made any comment. Moments later, Mr. Doherty was pronounced dead on arrival.

As always happens, word had reached Dr. O'Connor's clinic that somebody had collapsed on the bridge. Now seeing Mrs. Finnerty returned to them begged the question of a connection. One of the nurses was promptly dispatched to casualty for a report when Grainne hurriedly explained that the man who collapsed was Mrs. Finnerty's friend. They were taken to a small sitting room and given hot sweet tea.

In due course, Dr. O'Connor arrived. The look on his face was grave. Was that concern about his patient or something more? They placed their teacups back on the table. Grainne's world stopped again, and everything became very quiet as she heard Dr. O'Connor say, "Your friend, Mr. Doherty, suffered a massive heart attack on the bridge today. He passed away peacefully looking at the beautiful Swan River." Grainne slumped. Mrs. Finnerty sat still then thanked the doctor and asked if Fiona Hannon was available. He replied, "Yes, I'm sure she is. She may even be in the building. If not, we will get hold of her at Dr. Owens." Leaning towards Mrs. Finnerty, he asked, "How are you?"

Mrs. Finnerty introduced Grainne, "This is my friend, Grainne, from Kelly's. When we first met, she changed my outlook on life completely. It's good for me that she is with me today." She looked at the slumped Grainne and, squeezing her hand, continued, "She helped Mr. Doherty on the bridge today. Those first few seconds were the most important, and she was there." Grainne slumped even more and now the tears came. Mrs. Finnerty continued, "Doctor, I would like to keep to the plan we made this morning about my operation. You know I'm anxious to get this over with."

"I want to run one or two more tests, following today's event. You feel strong, I know, these tests are for my peace of mind, okay?" he added. "If all is well, I would like to admit you now, give you a mild sedative, and order bed rest for the remainder of the day. Tomorrow we can do the bowel preparation, and you will be ready for Wednesday morning. By the weekend, you will have earned a few days of pampering at the Rehab Centre if needed. What do you say?" One more nod. "Starting the search for Fiona now," he said as he went through the door.

CHAPTER 33

Leaving the hospital on Sunday evening was unbearable for Tony Coughlan. Amy burst into tears and clung to Angela. Caroline clung to her own inner survivor.

Up to that point, there had not been much time to dwell on the inevitable. Dr. Myers and Amy formed a great bond over the handwashing and the fancy headdress. Amy voiced strong opinions on both. The doctor listened in amusement. The parents and sister observed from the sidelines, not really sure who this woman was. Amy soon cleared that up. The business of the admission started in earnest. "The reports and scans from Baybridge give us a great picture of where we stand," explained Dr. Myers once they were settled in Angela's room.

The main corridor through the unit from front door to pirate ship was called Happy Street. As expected, the unit mascot was a penguin. Whether pirates cared for penguins or not was never questioned. The rooms on Happy Street resembled small row houses with brightly painted doors flanked on either side by two small curtained windows. A home away from home. Each contained the usual hospital equipment, but colourful bedspreads, pillowcases, curtains, and the ever-popular blue chaise lounge served as a distraction. Along one wall, a cushioned bench beckoned the weary visitor to sit and conveniently became a bed when the time was right for sleep. All furnishings were either washable or wipeable. This was not apparent without close scrutiny. Angela and her mother moved into number four. The penguin was sitting on the chaise. Her house had the only yellow door.

"Angela, your friend the bone doctor did his homework," continued Dr. Myers. "I knew he would. Now, I would like to have a wee look at you myself, he wouldn't be very pleased if I missed anything." A flicker of anxiety passed across Angela's face, a look not lost on Caroline. She quietly opened the book bag, selected *Make Way for the Ducklings,* and placed it on the bed beside her. Noticing the reassuring glance from the doctor, Angela slid the book halfway under her pillow.

When the exam was finished, Dr. Myers asked, "Is that your duckling book?"

Angela just nodded, sliding the book a little closer. Both doctor and mother recognised anxiety at work. The doctor continued, "Is it okay if I sit on your bed and take a peek at this famous book? It is famous, you know, and so are you. Dr. Alan told us all about you and how you use your books to explain your thoughts. We've never had anybody stay with us before that knew how to do that."

Angela retrieved the book from under her pillow. Turning the pages, she found what she was looking for and read aloud to Dr. Myers: "And when night falls, they swim to their little island and go to sleep."

She closed the book and put it back under her pillow. "I see," said the doctor, smiling. "I like your plan, so let's get started." Within an hour, a central intravenous line had been placed, a chest x-ray was done, and blood samples were already in the lab. The ducklings had spoken.

The first round of chemotherapy was scheduled to start the next day at ten am and infuse over forty-eight hours. Other drugs would overlap with this, and fluids to prevent dehydration would also be included. On a scale of one to ten, easy to hard, this regimen rated fifteen. The side effects included nausea and vomiting, hair loss, fatigue, and mouth sores, to say the least. Fatigue fails miserably to describe the feeling associated with this treatment. Frequent blood tests were required to monitor for infection and anemia. Angela and Dr. Owens had agreed that if at all possible he would monitor her at home. Angela's plan was to be home by the weekend.

Dr. Myers was astonished by this ten-year-old girl. She had seen grit and courage in many instances over the years. This child's management of her own treatment was what left Dr. Myers in awe and singled her out from the rest. The use of the story book to convey her inner feelings was beyond most people's capability.

Tony recalled now how Angela had produced *The Wonderful Things You Will Be* from the book bag. It was very difficult for Amy to leave her sister. He could not see a resolution until Angela read aloud to her young sister,

When nights are black and
When days are gray—
You'll be brave and be bright
So no shadows can stay.

She wrote the quotation on a piece of paper and asked her dad if he would put it up on the wall in the bedroom at home. By the time they reached the outskirts of the city, Amy was calm.

It was agreed at the Garda Station that Sergeant Coughlan would work flexi hours while Amy was at school. He did not arrive at the station until late morning because he decided to update the headmistress and get more information about Wednesday's mass. As he was entering from the rear of the building, four or five police officers rushed past him. "Morning, Sarge!" was echoed from each without explanation. The reason for the scurrying was the sudden death of a man on the bridge. Tony immediately left the station and went to the hospital. A young Garda, notebook in hand, approached Tony. "Sir, the man has been identified as Nathaniel Doherty, aged sixty-eight, of Number 4, Shadow Ridge Avenue, Baybridge. No relative or next of kin identified. Gardaí are at the residence now, sir. Personal possessions consist of a wallet and a set of car keys. Should we canvass the neighbors yet?"

"Get an update first. Location of the car?"

"Not known, sir. Apparently not a patient here."

"Mm," came the muffled sound from the sergeant as he looked around the department. He saw the starched Sister O'Brien approach.

He knew her well from his many visits to Casualty. The starch melted on contact.

"Good morning, Sergeant," said Sister.

"Sister," said Tony in fake formality.

"A word in my office, please."

"Yes, Sister." As a young Garda, Tony had learned the secret of success. Always respect and follow Sister, be she a nun or a nurse, or God forbid, both! Once inside the office door, Sergeant Coughlan learned that Mr. Nathaniel Doherty had been Mrs. Finnerty's friend. He had driven her today to the Medical Centre for an appointment. He was waiting for her on the bridge when he suffered a massive heart attack and collapsed. This was a great shock to Mrs. Finnerty. As she was scheduled for an operation on Wednesday, Dr. O'Connor had decided to admit her. She was now asking for Fiona Hannon.

CHAPTER 34

Mrs. Murry was on duty at Baybridge Rehabilitation Centre when her daughter Carmel called her from Kelly's. She could hear in her voice that something was wrong. "Carmel, what is it? Are you all right? Is Maura—"

Carmel interrupted, "I'm okay, I'm okay, and Maura is too. We're at Kelly's by the river."

"What! Are you not back at school? Why are you at Kelly's?"

"Mammy, listen. A man collapsed on the bridge when we were just walking past on our lunch break. Grainne from Kelly's ran out to him. We followed her, and when she said no pulse no breathing, Maura and myself started CPR. When the ambulance came, they took over. They continued CPR on the trolley as they took him to the ambulance.

"Carmel, you did CPR with your sister? On the bridge? Oh my gosh, I'm so proud of you! You're great girls, you really are. Who's there with you at Kelly's? Is Mrs. Kavanagh, you know, the manager, is she there?" It was a real struggle for Mrs. Murry to keep her voice calm, considering what she was just told.

"Yes, she is. She gave us tea. Mam, Maura wants to say something." Carmel handed the phone to her sister.

"Mammy, can you find out how the man is? We don't think he did well at all."

"Oh Maura, you're worried about the man? You poor pet. I'll try. Even though I'm on the staff, I won't be told too much. Tell Mrs. Kavanagh I'm on my way."

Mrs. Murry prepared herself to share the limited information she had just received from Sister O'Brien over the phone with her twin daughters. She drove very carefully to the other side of Baybridge, all the while thinking how she was going to alleviate the girls' guilt at the news of the man's death. Then there was the added complication of his friendship with Mrs. Finnerty and her subsequent hospital admission.

Maura and Carmel were surprisingly calm about the unsuccessful CPR. Though they lived in the same community as Mr. Doherty, he was not known to them They suspected on the bridge the man was already dead. They were saddened by that and despite advice to the contrary, both from their mother and Mrs. Kavanagh, they insisted on going straight to the hospital to check on Mrs. Finnerty. Thanking the restaurant manager, mother and daughters left Kelly's, crossed the bridge, and made their way up the steep cobbled hill. They did not notice the Garda checking a parked car outside the old church at the top of the lane.

Fiona Hannon was in a small country house about twenty miles outside Baybridge when she was summoned. The occupant of the small country house was a Mr. Cawley. He lived alone and was doing well with his heart condition until he developed a leg ulcer. Fiona was there today with the district nurse, hoping to convince this fiercely independent eighty-eight-year-old to spend a few days in hospital. She was doing well, quietly making the case, eliciting the occasional nod from the patient. Then her pager went off. That was the end of the coaxing for Mr. Cawley. "All that noise, pinging, beeping, and ringing. I'll never get a wink of sleep. I have to have quiet, you see how it is here," he explained.

Fiona did. The small two-room house was set back from the road. Surrounded by overgrown bushes and shrubs, it had the appearance of a precious stone set deep in the center of a piece of jewelry. Wild roses randomly blooming, white wash yellowing around the windows, and red paint peeling in spots on the front door added an antique element to this jewel. Inside was neat and tidy. Cups of tea were welcomed by all who visited here without hesitation. The cups were spotless. It was the sort of place you were sad to leave.

Mr. Cawley felt that way. Fiona left him in the capable hands of the district nurse who knew from the start what the outcome would be. Back at the office, Dr. Owens didn't hold out much hope either.

Brenda decided not to share any of the details with Fiona when she answered the page. "Sister O'Brien needs a word—can you call in?" was all she said. She was aware that Fiona had over twenty miles yet to drive back into town. No need to worry her right now. She had enough on her plate. Angela was in Dublin starting her chemotherapy; Mrs. Finnerty would soon be having her surgery. Added to this was the sudden death of Mr. Doherty. Brenda was aware that all three of these people were friends of Fiona's.

Mrs. Quigley was not surprised when she saw the young Garda come into the shop. Police officers came in frequently on their way to and fro to pick up one of her sandwiches or homemade pie. She knew this young, friendly Garda. He was a fan of her pies. Today was different. He had a solemn look when he asked for a private word. She indicated for him to follow her along a narrow corridor leading away from the shop. It was a tight squeeze in the hallway as food-handling regulations prohibited them from entering the kitchen. "This is as private as it gets around here," offered Mrs. Quigley. "We could go round to the house if you prefer." The Quigley family lived on the premises and entered the living area via a separate entrance next to the shop.

"This will be fine, Mrs. Quigley," said the Garda. "Unfortunately, I have sad news about one of the neighbours, a Mr. Doherty. He had a heart attack today down by the river. He didn't make it, I'm afraid. I'm sorry." After a short pause, he continued, "He was waiting for his friend, Mrs. Finnerty to come out from an appointment at the hospital."

"Oh my god! This is so sad. He's dead, you say? Where is Mrs. Finnerty now?"

"She's in the hospital, she's okay just a bit shook up. How well did you know Mr. Doherty? You see, we are trying to locate his family. Maybe you can tell us a bit about him, how long he's been coming into the shop, where he's from. Customers often chat when they come in to shop."

It was Mrs. Quigley's turn to be shook up. "Oh my! This is really awful. Dead, you say. I knew he was taking Mrs. Finnerty to her appointment today. I can't believe it. He came in a few days ago and asked me if I could help with food for her after her operation. He said he would let me know the exact details today after the appointment. He explained his sister-in-law, who lives in Haymarket, had similar surgery two years ago. He remembered the dietary restrictions and knew Mrs. Finnerty could do with some of my home cooking during that period as she lived alone. The poor man even offered to pay in advance." She was tearful when she was telling him this.

The Garda, while feeling sorry for the lady, was glad his inquiries were productive. Emboldened by this, he ventured, "Is that the Haymarket over on the River Shannon?" She nodded, and he continued, "You don't happen to have the address, by any chance?"

Mrs. Quigley was about to say no, then she paused and said, "Wait a minute. I need to go to the house, come on over. I could murder a cup of tea, I'm sure you could too." On the way she explained that Tara Doherty was the widow of Mr. Doherty's youngest brother, James. She continued, "If I remember correctly, God rest his soul, he needed help at the time James died. I can't remember what, but he needed to post something to Tara. I think it was the wrapping I was helping with. Anyway, he gave me her address." She produced a piece of paper from a drawer. The Garda could not believe his luck. He respectfully declined the offer of tea, took his leave, and headed back to the station posthaste, forever grateful for all her help.

Mrs. Quigley put on her coat, begged a lift from her husband, and made her way to Baybridge Medical Centre.

Fiona stood in the open door to Mrs. Finnerty's hospital room. She studied the tableau that lay before her. Mrs. Finnerty sat in the armchair; Carmel Murry perched on one arm, her sister Maura on a footstool, Grainne leaning over the back of the chair, one hand on Mrs. Finnerty's shoulder; Mrs. Murry in her nurse's uniform standing near the bed; Sergeant Coughlan standing on one side of the large window; and Mrs. Quigley, tall, thin, and quiet, on the other. They resembled a pair of mismatched curtains.

Fiona stood still, tears in her eyes, feeling the full weight of her own clothesline while wondering what heavy items the others were trying to hang on theirs. One thing she was sure of, they were all handing clothes pegs to each other.

CHAPTER 35

Looking out their bedroom window before school, Amy and Angela often played this ever-changing story game. If they went out the back door of their house, leapt over the back fence in to Walsh's backyard, went in through their back door, passed through their front room (pausing to admire the new couch, of course), exited via their front door, crossed the road, and did the same again at Brennan's and Dunne's, they would find themselves looking into the playground of St. Paul's primary school. The story changed depending on what news the neighbours' children brought to school the day before. The Walsh's wouldn't mind showing off a new couch. As far as anyone knew, there was nothing new in Brennans or Dunnes to show off. All in all, going down Carter Hill, past Quigley's, and turning right at the bottom was the best way to go to school, they would decide.

Amy missed her sister and had mixed feelings about school today. It was Wednesday, and Angela's mass was at 10 o'clock. She wanted to go very much, but she didn't want the grownups to be all sad and saying things to her. She didn't feel sad and wondered if that was all right. She knew it would be difficult to explain if anybody asked her how she was doing or said, "Oh, you poor thing, it must be awful." It wasn't awful at all.

She need not have worried; the staff at the school was well aware of the many pitfalls on such a day. A large banner had been prepared with the words "joy," "love," "hope" inscribed in gold, each word entwined with the school colours of blue and white. The hymns were jaunty, the readings were light, and the mood among the children echoed that sentiment.

Amy was at ease as the sea of blue-and-white-clad children, banner held high, processed to the cathedral. This sight was not out of the ordinary once or twice a year on feast days. What was out of the ordinary on this day was the number of people at the school gate waiting to join the procession, including the students from the three other primary schools in Baybridge. As they proceeded towards the church, more and more people joined, thus causing a significant backup of traffic. Baybridge came to a complete standstill when the Gardaí joined the front of the procession and led the way into the Cathedral.

Not everyone got to go inside to the mass. Many people stood in the doorway and on the church grounds. Gardaí were evident here and there and mingled in with the crowd, in support of their sergeant's daughter. A low murmur of conversation could be heard from those farthest away from the church door. Mrs. Walsh was whispering to the woman on her right, "Of course, Caroline is staying above in Dublin with Angela. I was just saying to my Mick last night, apart from everything else, this is an expensive undertaking."

"I know what you mean. It's the little things that mount up and just catch a person unawares," replied the woman on the right. A silence followed. Then she said, "Are you thinking what I'm thinking?" After a brief pause, Mrs. Walsh opened her bag. "What! Now?" said the woman. "Do you think we should?"

"What better time?" came the enthusiastic reply. "Everybody is here now."

"Fiona Hannon is over there by the door, should we ask her?" offered the woman on the right.

Opening her handbag further, Mrs. Walsh rummaged around and produced a nicely folded tote bag. Everybody had one as there were no plastic bags in the stores anymore. "No need," she said. "We can ask her to give what we collect to the sergeant when we are done." With that, she opened her purse and put money in the tote. The woman on the right followed suit as did the woman on the left. Word spread, reminiscent of the miracle of the loaves and fishes. Quietly and discreetly, euros were dropped into Mrs. Walsh's shopping bag as the mass and private prayers continued. People handed money to each other in silence without hesitation, knowing that it would reach its intended destination. As the crowd began to disperse, those that had not yet contributed approached Mrs. Walsh and her tote bag, which was now being referred to as "Angela's Purse."

Fiona stood on tippy-toes in the cathedral door. Peering over the heads of the departing congregation, she wondered if she had missed Cate and Cara somehow. Ordinarily the schoolchildren would file out first. Today the crowd was so big, she thought they may have gone out the side door. She knew she was just going to get a wave from her daughter as she had her class to see to. Cara would be in line with her classmates so all she was expecting there was a discreet smile. Still, she lingered in hope.

Mrs. Walsh and her right-hand lady approached Fiona. "Mrs. Hannon, we did a bit of a whip round for Angela to help with the extra expenses. Would you be kind enough to give this to Sergeant Coughlan?" Looking at her friend as if for inspiration, she continued, "It's all here in my shopping bag, the one I always carry in my handbag. By the end it became known as Angela's Purse. Everybody put in a bit. We don't know how much it came to, but it might be some help. We hope they won't be insulted or anything, isn't that right, Madge? It's just that everybody wanted to chip in." Madge thrust the bulging bag stuffed to the brim with Euros against Fiona's chest. Fiona almost dropped it. She expected it to be heavier. It was very light. There were no coins.

Flabbergasted, all thoughts of Cara and Cate now vanished; she searched for a reply. No words came. Mrs. Walsh and Madge were crestfallen, thinking that they had done something wrong or worst still, illegal. Thanking God that Sergeant Coughlan was tall, she spotted him in the crowd. "Come with me, ladies," she said. The ladies were really worried now when they saw where they were heading. They reached him, and he greeted his neighbours. "Sergeant Coughlan, these fine ladies took up a collection today. They would like to give you this," announced Fiona, handing the bag she still carried back to Madge.

She, in turn, handed the bag back to Mrs. Walsh who, taking a deep breath, said, "We are all praying for Angela's recovery. Everybody at her mass today wishes her the best of good health. We all know that there is more to it than that, this is a costly journey. People want to help with some of the expenses. By the end of mass today, this bag was filled and is now known as Angela's Purse. It seems to myself and Madge that there must be some regulations about this sort of thing. Can you two help with that?"

Angela's dad shed his sergeant's persona in front of Mrs. Walsh and Madge and wept into their hugs. All was well with the ladies. They would take care of him. They found a secluded small space in the sacristy, and Fiona counted the money. She needed help. Tony counted it a second time. Such was the amount that they agreed they needed legal help, giving rise to a fundraising phenomenon the likes of which Baybridge had never seen.

CHAPTER 36

Mrs. Finnerty was drowsy but awake. "Welcome back," said the nurse with a smile. "You did very well, back in your room now with the big window. Dr. O'Connor will be in a bit later. Grainne is here with you. You can doze off again if you feel sleepy. Ladies, the call bell is right here."

When she left, Grainne pulled a chair up to the head of the bed. A closeness had developed between herself and this elegant lady. She could not fathom it. Her presence had stayed with her after she left Kelly's the day they first met. How did it happen that she responded the way she did the other day on the bridge? She was not given to flights of fancy, but there was a connection here beyond her understanding.

Working at Kelly's part-time enabled her to save extra money to fulfill the lifelong dream of owning her own beauty salon. She had an established reputation as a gifted hairstylist. She worked in an upscale salon but for somebody else. Now was the time to open her own business. She was more than ready. She lived in a flat out towards Three Peaks and came into town via Shadow Ridge Avenue. She moved out there about eighteen months ago and loved it. The mountains and the ocean were visible from her top-floor bedroom window.

On her way to work two weeks ago, she saw a "For Sale" sign in the window of a vacant shop diagonally across from Quigley's. She turned the car around, parked, and crossed the road to get a better look. It was perfect: large plateglass window, spacious but not rambling, clean and bright. Excitedly, she called the listed number right there on the street and got an appointment for later that day. It had just gone on the market, owned for years by a farmer who sold the meat from his farm there. He had recently retired, and the shop was for sale. Six and a half days later, her offer was accepted.

What Grainne did not know then was Mrs. Finnerty, the Murry twins, Sergeant Coughlan, Fiona Hannon, and the dearly departed Mr. Doherty all shared her new street address.

Angela was also doing well, all things considered. The vomiting was under control with medication, but every now and then a wave of nausea overtook her. Caroline was brilliant with her daughter, according to the nursing staff. Blood tests were frequent, but due to the presence of the Port-A-Cath, no painful procedure was needed. The fatigue was brutal, and Caroline soon developed a great appreciation for the mini chaise lounge favoured by Angela.

She rarely left her side. She was sitting watching the rise and fall of her daughter's little chest as she slept, when a gentle tap caught her attention. A small elderly man with a hat in his hand stood in the doorway. Dr. Myers stood behind him. Caroline stood up and met them halfway as they came towards her. "Caroline, I'm proud to introduce you to Sir James Butler, our distinguished paediatric oncologist. We are privileged that he still acts in a consultation capacity here at Park Edge. Sir James, this is Angela's mother, Caroline Coughlan."

"I believe we have met before," he whispered in reply, casting a glance towards the sleeping child, "on the train from Baybridge."

His hat caught Caroline's eye just in time for her to make the connection to the trilby-hat man. "Yes, yes, you were kind enough to share your table with Angela's dad," she answered.

"Small thing, but that leg needed a rest. How is she today?" he asked.

Dr. Myers was looking on, bewildered. This was Sir James, she reminded herself, nothing should be a surprise. He was a man devoid of airs and graces.

"The nausea waves can be harsh, but the vomiting is well under control. Still waiting for today's lab results.

"Good, good." He looked at Dr. Myers, forever the team player, and said, "Were you thinking of Friday for discharge, Dr. Myers?"

She replied, "That's the plan, Sir James. Dr. Owens, the primary care doctor, has agreed to do the home follow-up. Frequent contact with the team here is already set up. Dr. Moran is on board for the operation."

"Ah, the good Dr. Alan, is he still singing *Dem Bones*?" he asked with a chuckle. Not waiting for a reply, he continued, "I met him again in Baybridge a few days ago, spoke at a conference there. I met your Dr. Owens too, good bunch, the lot of them. Now, I know you will get lots of tips and advice before you leave here. No train this time, got to look out for infection. Handwashing, can't stress it enough. The next go round will be hard, very hard. Day at a time, day at a time. The whole cycle is thirty-five days. Home again to recover. Dr. Alan will do his magic a few weeks later. Dr. Myers here will keep me abreast of the progress. Tell the little girl the trilby-hat man called in." He left the room with a bow.

CHAPTER 37

Thursday was another busy day. Amy was up early. Since Mrs. Finnerty's admission, she had been given the responsible task of feeding Mrs. Miller. It wasn't a difficult assignment to carry out. Mrs. Miller, in her wisdom, was reacting to the absence of her owner and rarely left her spot on the windowsill in case she missed her return. Her food was in an airtight container at the side of the house beside the outdoor tap not yet attached to the hose. Rain showers were plentiful, thus no need for watering. Best not to mention getting clothes dry! Nevertheless, Amy took the task seriously and went so far as to record the cat's daily intake in a small notebook. Her father commended her on her diligence and answered two phone calls while Amy was feeding the cat. "Tony, good morning, how are things?" greeted Caroline as she made her first call of the day.

"Great here, Caroline, any bad news or anything?" Tony both dreaded and loved the twice-daily phone calls. His fear reflected in his voice, no matter how hard he tried to camouflage it.

"Actually, it's good news. We can come home tomorrow. Angela was so good with the treatment, no complaints at all. She weathered everything like the champion we know her to be. Only thing is the fatigue, she is wiped out, God love her. I just let her sleep. She loves those small wee couches better than the hospital bed, it's hard as a rock. Oh, you'll never guess—"

"Guess what?" cut in Tony, always on edge about the unknown.

"Relax, Tony, it's good." Caroline rattled on, "Remember the little elderly man, the trilby-hat man, the one on the train? Well, he came in yesterday to see Angela."

"What? Why?" Sergeant Coughlan asked, ever the policeman.

"He's a doctor, Sir James Butler, apparently a famous paediatric oncologist, and he's on Angela's case. He came in with Dr. Myers to go over the treatment and discharge plan. He had great praise for Dr. Alan and Dr. Owens. He was on his way back from speaking at a conference or something in Baybridge when we saw him on the train. Can you believe it? You shared a table with him too," explained his wife.

"Are you serious? I wondered ever since how he knew Angela needed to elevate her leg. What are the chances of such a man sitting in our booked seats? Wow, and he gave ye the okay to come home?" asked Tony.

"Yes, he did. He stressed the risk of infection big time. I went over all the precautions we have put at home with the nurses. We're okay, they say. I'm thinking Amy should come with you to Dublin, tomorrow," continued Caroline, "what do you think? I mentioned it to Mrs. Walsh—"

Tony cut in again, "No need, you are right, we will come together. It's important for her and Angela too. We'll bring a new batch of books."

"Oh, one more thing," added Caroline, "we got caught out. As Sir James was leaving the sleeping child, he said to tell the little girl that the trilby-hat man called in. Then he bowed and left."

Sergeant Coughlan bowed his head in mock shame.

"Call you tonight," concluded his wife.

Almost immediately the phone rang again, "Sergeant, it's Jack Hennessy, from Hennessy Motors," said a booming voice. "I have your number here from the time we had that break-in a few months back. Don't mean to intrude."

Although Tony was not feeling intruded upon, he was surprised at the call. When the owner of Hennessy Motors spoke, the wall echoed around him; when he laughed, the earth shook; and when he used the phone, nearby mountains took a sidestep. To say he was a big man would not conjure up the true image. To say he was generous would only scratch the surface. His discreet response to a need was felt far and wide. Only the recipient and bank manager knew anything about it. It was part of the pact, no names.

"Good morning, Mr. Hennessy," replied Tony. Best say no more now, more information would be coming. That's the way the man spoke, a little at a time.

"I heard about your young daughter. I'm sorry to hear it. The missus said to be sure to send you all her best. Her name is Dorothy, and her middle name is Angela." Soft voice over, he resumed his booming business tone: "Well now, Sergeant, would you be able to call down to the showroom at all this morning? I'd like you to take a look at something, not police work, more of a personal matter."

Nonplussed, Tony hesitated briefly, then replied, "I can be down after I drop Amy to school, if that works."

"Grand. I'll see you after a while," boomed the man. Then he was gone.

While he was pouring a cup of tea, he heard Amy come in. "Daddy, Mrs. Miller is in a bad mood, and she won't even come down from the windowsill. I petted her and coaxed her, but she wouldn't budge. I have nothing to put in my notebook. I'll have to check the dish after school. Daddy, would you try later?"

"Amy, cats are like that, especially her highness next door. She's just missing Mrs. Finnerty, we all are, not for much longer though. I'll check her dish later, okay?" Father and daughter hugged.

Hennessy's showroom was a sight to behold. It wasn't so much the brand-spanking-new cars, with the shine and the smell of leather, as it was the luxurious surroundings. The customer waiting room boasted soft leather oversized chairs, each equipped with outlets for laptops, mobile phones, and all manner of electronic devices. The aroma of freshly brewed coffee wafted towards the main doors, beckoning the passerby. No stale biscuits or doughnuts here, no, sir; freshly baked goods were delivered every morning from a nearby patisserie. Several copies of the major newspapers were scattered around; more than one reader might want a shot at today's crossword. Quality magazines for the news weary were also available and served as a pleasant distraction.

Sergeant Coughlan inhaled deeply, surveyed the luxury, and stepped forward to shake the outstretched hand of the owner. "Take a stroll out to the side with me before we sit down to a hot cup of coffee, if you have the time," said Mr. Hennessy. He ushered him through the enormous glass door, which opened automatically. They walked along towards the back of the building until they came to a metallic silver vehicle. To Tony, it had that brand-spanking-new look. It was what he understood to be a minivan. Mr. Hennessy pressed the remote, and the side doors slid open. The smell of fresh leather filled Tony's nostrils. "Plenty of space to stretch out there in the back seat," said the booming voice. "Sit in the driver's seat, get a feel for it."

If Tony was nonplussed on the phone, he didn't know what to do right now. He had no clue why he was looking at this luxurious, spacious vehicle. He found himself behaving as if this was a crime scene. He examined every detail, right down to the TV console in the back. Uncurling his long body, he stepped out of the vehicle and looked into Mr. Hennessy's face, his own facial expression conveying confusion and bewilderment.

"The missus and myself were having a chat, and she made a great point. She knows a fair bit about hospital visits, operations, and trips to doctors here in town and back and forth to Dublin. From her volunteering, she has seen many transportation problems and how hard a small car can be on everyone. It got me thinking. Then I remembered this beauty. When do you have to go to Dublin again?"

"Tomorrow morning," said Tony. "Angela can come home for a few weeks between treatments."

"Well, then, you're going to need a safe and comfortable vehicle to get her back and forth." Mr. Jack Hennessy knew that to get Tony to take the minivan was not going to be easy. He decided to break it down into stages. He said, "As far as I'm concerned, this vehicle is yours. The papers are already drawn up. I see your face, and I understand your surprise. How about this, take it to Dublin tomorrow, a sort of test drive. If it handles well, and little Angela can travel comfortably there in the back, we will finalise the paperwork on Monday. See what your missus thinks. That cup of coffee is calling my name. While we are drinking that, we'll get you legal for tomorrow, wouldn't look good for the sergeant to get pulled over on the Dublin road."

CHAPTER 38

Mrs. Finnerty was on her way back from physical therapy, walking steadily alongside her therapist. She had done well in her morning session, her sense of humour showing signs of reemergence, and her strength revealing some of her previous vim and vigour.

Waiting until the patient was safely seated in her room, one of the staff came to her door. Knocking gently, she said, "Mrs. Finnerty you have a lady visitor waiting in the lounge. She's been here about half an hour. Is it okay for her to come in?"

"Half an hour, oh my! Please bring her in" came the reply. A tall, dark-haired woman stood in the doorway. Her hair was cropped short, the highlighted tips creating a spiky effect. High cheekbones, dark eyes, and a fine jawline defined her face. A touch of blush and a pale lip gloss finished the look. She wore a tunic-length sweater over narrow jeans, and ankle boots with a hint of gold embellishment adorned her feet. From her bent arm dangled a two-toned Ana Faye leather handbag. Mrs. Finnerty did not know this woman.

Walking towards her, the visitor introduced herself as Tara Doherty, the sister-in-law of her good friend. Glad that she was sitting down, Mrs. Finnerty hoped against hope that her mouth wasn't gaping with her eyes appearing to pop out of her head at the shock. She did not know Mr. Doherty had a sister-in-law, certainly not a chic one. There was nothing chic about Mr. Doherty. "Pleased to meet you, Ms. Doherty," said the shocked patient, as she thought, *Does that mean there's a brother?*

"I would much rather we met in your lovely library than here in the hospital. Your house was the most-talked-about thing in *our* house since Nathaniel first mentioned you. The children nagged him to bring them over to choose a book too." When she finished, it took her a minute or two to interpret Mrs. Finnerty's reaction or lack thereof. Obviously, Nate hadn't mentioned them to her at all. She, on the other hand, was well-known to them through all the stories Nate had told them, even before the death of her husband. He was a bit of a dark horse, that Nathaniel.

They sat and talked for over an hour. Mary brought in a lovely tea tray from the kitchen, which included dainty slices of toast and a scone for the visitor. Mrs. Finnerty's diet was still advancing to normal but not there yet. They exchanged little nuggets about Mr. Doherty, general chitchat, nothing personal. Tara explained, "Mrs. Finnerty, the burial is in Haymarket on Monday. He will be laid to rest next to his brother, my husband, in the family plot. I want to thank you for your years of friendship with him. It's no surprise that you were together on that day. The family is glad of that. I also wish you a full recovery and your little neighbour, Angela, too." Tara stood up to leave.

"Thank you. It's a long road ahead for Angela. She's going to lose her beautiful hair. The least of the obstacles she will face, still, appearances do matter at that age." She told Tara about Angela's Tresses and Turbans, the foundation she intended to establish.

Taking her seat again, Tara said, "Mrs. Finnerty, I'm in the fashion business. I have two boutiques at home in Haymarket, one vintage, the other modern. I come across all sorts of pieces, garments, scarves, hats, miles of fabric, and the occasional turban. Would you be willing to collaborate? Would it help, do you think?"

"Oh, yes, it would. Indeed, it would. Mr. Shiva, the owner of our very lovely Indian restaurant here in Baybridge, shops in Haymarket for his spices. His cousin-in-law, who deals in Indian clothing and fabrics there, has also agreed to help. Mrs. Doherty—"

"Please call me Tara."

Mrs. Finnerty continued, "Tara, this project has to be bigger than Angela. She does not know yet what the plan is. When she hears of it, she will want hairstyles and turbans for every child in the country that loses their hair to chemotherapy."

Standing up again, punching the air with her fist, Tara cheered, "Consider it done!" Forgetting that she was still holding her handbag, she barely missed hitting Mrs. Finnerty in the head with her Ana Faye bag.

She stared after the visitor as she left. The thought crossed her mind that recovering from the surgery might be quicker than recovering from Tara's visit.

Before she could muster enough energy to decide, Dr. O'Connor appeared in her room. "Hello there, you seem a bit distracted, everything all right?" asked the surgeon.

"I'm fine," she replied and told him about the visitor.

"That must have been a surprise, but it's good she offered to help with your project. Now, as for you, you are making good progress. I thought when you asked to go to the Rehab Centre at first, it was a good idea. I still thought that after Mr. Doherty died. Knowing you are so motivated by your involvement with Angela has caused me to rethink. Staying in a medical facility puts the patient at high risk for infection. Weakened immune system, cross-contamination, antibiotic therapy, and a whole host of other factors put the patient at increased risk. If you were to get an infection of any kind, contact with Angela would be out of the question." Dr. O'Connor paused. Mrs. Finnerty gasped. "Now, now," he continued, "what if you went home on Saturday? The nurse will educate you on handwashing, cleaning objects, all that. You will be doing the same as Angela's family next door, putting up a barrier to block any infection. The oncology staff will have trained them well. It's a much-safer plan than staying here or in rehab."

She still looked a little lost until Dr. O'Connor explained that one of the nurses would be coming in later to discuss the discharge plan in detail. "You will not be abandoned. Your overnight babysitters will be a pleasant surprise. No chance of infection from those two, just ask their mother." On his cue, Carmel and Maura Murry entered the room. She felt she could not be in more capable hands.

CHAPTER 39

Fiona sat at her desk. She liked her little space tucked away in the back of Dr. Owens's office. She thought of it as a sort of container where she stored all the details of her work life and knew where to find them. Today she needed to access Angela's and Mrs. Finnerty's. Nowadays those two seemed to pop up in the same spot, as if their futures were inextricably linked. In Fiona's opinion, that wasn't a bad thing. Both households were good for each other. As she was solidifying that thought, Brenda buzzed. "Hi, Fiona, are you bogged down back there?" she inquired.

"No, just thinking" came the reply.

"Oh, you need to give that up, it's bad for your mental health. Anyway, Dr. Owens wondered if you can come over to his office to discuss the discharges, two, it seems."

"That's what I was just thinking about."

"Like I said—" started Brenda.

"Stop it!" ended Fiona. This banter got both through many a tough moment over the years. She made her way to Dr. Owens's office. He looked up with a wrinkled brow, causing Fiona to ask, "Something wrong?"

"No, I was just thinking," he replied.

"Well, don't let Brenda catch you," she warned.

"Oh, you're right. She doesn't go in for too much thinking, or so she'd have us believe," he added.

"We all know better than that, but it's good fun. She mentioned you had two discharges for the weekend."

"Two patients all right, Angela is coming home from Park Edge on Friday, and Dr. O'Connor is sending Mrs. Finnerty home on Saturday morning," explained Dr. Owens.

"So no rehabilitation-centre stay then, that sounds good," said Fiona.

"Apparently she made great progress these past few days. The procedure itself was straightforward. Her relationship with Angela changed his mind, reducing the risk of infection was paramount in his decision. Based on Dr. O'Connor's explanation as to the benefits of being out of hospital or rehab, she agreed. He sweetened the deal by throwing in Nurse Murry's two daughters to keep an eye for the first few days and nights. I was just digesting all this when you appeared. Brenda might be right about all that thinking, after all. The surgical staff did the discharge plan for Mrs. Finnerty, so that's all taken care of."

After a short pause, Fiona noticed a slight shift in his demeanor as he continued, "Angela tolerated the chemo well. The nausea persists but is diminishing. As expected, the fatigue is just wiping her out. Dr. Myers scanned the discharge plan just a few minutes ago. It's very specific, which is what we expect. District nursing is on board. Fiona, can you check who is on for Paediatric Oncology this weekend, and fill them in on the personal background, including Mrs. Finnerty's connection? The intake nurse thought it was Orla Higgins. If so, that would be great." Dr. Owens sat back in his chair.

"She is the best, for sure, though that whole department is amazing," said Fiona.

"I absolutely agree," said the doctor. "Angela's Port-A-Cath is still in place, so the district nurse can draw the labs too."

"If it's possible, I will coordinate with Oncology and make my visits while the nurse is there. Any special precautions like masks or anything?" asked Fiona.

"Handwashing. Handwashing. Handwashing."

"I hear from Dr. Myers that the family has the whole infection-control thing down pat. She personally trained Amy. She tells me she is in charge, so don't let her catch you missing a step," warned Dr. Owens.

"Doing so at my own peril, by all accounts," said Fiona, feigning fear.

"Could be barred," Dr. Owens threw in, escalating the consequences.

"I think I've got it, Dr. Owens."

"Good." Both became serious again. He summarised the plan, "You have your visit planned, Oncology will do labs, hydration, and cath care. I will leave my visit until Sunday, no need to overwhelm them. Fiona, if you feel there is something I need to know before then, call me immediately. Angela has about two weeks or so until she returns to Dublin for the toughest part of the first cycle. We need this time to be uneventful for her. Next time she is home, it will likely be a different Angela we see. We need to be prepared. Now we keep her in good spirits and infection-free. We monitor the blood count and let her rest."

Suddenly, Fiona's clothesline got very heavy.

CHAPTER 40

Baybridge had changed and so had its people. Sergeant Coughlan was known and respected far and wide. Now, so too was his daughter, Angela. As the citizens went about their daily lives, a sense of purpose and resolve filled them. Conversations opened between strangers. It was not gossip. The common theme consisted of "What can we do?" "How soon?" and "Can it be done without intruding on the Coughlans' wishes?" They were wholeheartedly behind this family.

Mrs. Walsh and Madge Costello were approached every time they went out and given donations for Angela's Purse. The public was not interested in designated donation sites or the bank and made their feelings about that quite clear.

"What a load of rubbish!"

"Never heard anything so daft!"

"Do they think we're all crooks?"

"You know best what to do with this."

They forced money on the original collectors. Angela's Purse grew fatter by the day.

Amy called the minivan the chariot from the first moment she saw it in the driveway after school. She did not ask any questions as to how it got there, merely hopping into it on Friday morning, bag of books and pillows in tow. Her mother reacted the same way in Dublin, only once casting a questioning glance in her husband's direction. Angela dozed her way to Baybridge, nestled in comfort on the back seat. Tony made up his mind on the way back from Dublin to accept Mr. Hennessy's gift. He would tell him and Caroline on Monday. No names, no strings.

It seemed to Mrs. Quigley that if the present trend continued, she would need to hire a delivery person. Increasingly, as a customer was at the checkout, they would say, "Mrs. Q, would you ever mind adding a few of your lovely sausage rolls to Coughlan's order when you're going over. Might tempt Angela. Just add them on there to my bill. Thanks, Mrs. Q, you're very good."

Another would add, "Just one slice of fresh apple pie."

Another, "A hot scone, just out of the oven," adding wistfully, "the smell might just whet her appetite a wee bit."

Smart ladies, all of them. This was their way of not intruding and overloading Caroline with food she could not possibly use. Yet some small morsel might be enjoyed by Angela. Mostly she would know that she was in their hearts.

Quigley's had a magazine-and-comic stand just inside the door. The staff were most impressed when children Amy's and Angela's age came in with their parents to get their weekly comic or coloring book and asked if they could get one for Angela too. Some thought Amy should have something in case she was sad. The example set by the adults was trickling down to their children. Usually one of the teenagers served these children and heaped praise on them for keeping the plastic cover intact to keep it very, very clean for Angela. They learned that chemotherapy children got infections very easily. The parents reported that kids were always washing their hands nowadays. Another lesson learned. Neither sadness, despair, nor despondency permeated the atmosphere. These people were about doing something.

Carmel and Maura were doing something too at Finnerty's when the doorbell rang. First visitor was Fiona. "Morning, girls! Not too early, I hope. I walked on the beach and caught the sunrise, well worth it," she said.

"Come on in, Mrs. Hannon," said Maura as she indicated the hand sanitizer strategically placed just inside the door. "Mrs. Finnerty was up with the birds anxious to get home," she added as they walked back towards the kitchen.

Just then, Mrs. Finnerty stepped out of the lift. Fiona now knew how Mrs. Finnerty got upstairs. Nobody would ever guess that the woman facing them had undergone abdominal surgery a few days ago. Dr. O'Connor was right, she was thriving. "Fiona, you look wind kissed, have you been running on the beach?" asked Mrs. Finnerty.

"It was glorious! You look radiant yourself. How are you?" Fiona asked as they gently embraced.

Mrs. Finnerty replied, "I'm ahead of myself, they tell me. Thanks to these two professionals here, I was able to come home. Girls, did you get some breakfast? What about Fiona? Cup of tea?"

"I'll get it," Carmel said.

"Thanks, I'd love one," said Fiona.

"Don't be late for work, girls," said Mrs. Finnerty.

Maura answered for them both, "We're going in at ten o'clock," doubt sounding in her voice.

Mrs. Finnerty reassured her, "I will be fine. One of the district nurses is expected and Mrs. Quigley is bringing up some food later." Addressing Fiona, she continued, "She told me how Mr. Doherty enlisted her help with the dietary restrictions after the operation. Oh, Fiona, he was a good friend. It's all so sad. I'm okay, girls, really, I am. Off you go, home to get ready, thank you both. I will see you this evening. Fiona will be here for a little while." She looked at Fiona, hoping for a yes.

"It's official business for me, anyway, so that works out perfectly," said Fiona. Mrs. Finnerty looked relieved.

"They didn't want to go, you know. I'm glad for their company, but they have their own young lives. It's good they have school on Monday. As they don't have exams this year, things are winding down. Soon, summer holidays will be here. Have you seen Angela yet?" inquired Mrs. Finnerty.

"No, that's my second visit, but not until later. I got fair warning about the handwashing and was advised that Amy is a stickler about it. No doubt you will get your in-service." They both laughed.

During the conversation that followed, Mrs. Finnerty filled Fiona in on meeting Tara Doherty and all she had learned from her visit. Fiona was fascinated to discover that Amy was the inspiration for Angela's Tresses and Turbans. Was it destiny that Mr. Shiva's cousin-in-law and Tara Doherty lived in the same town and were both going to play major roles in the foundation?

"Mrs. Finnerty, what do you make of it all?" asked Fiona.

"It's going to happen, absolutely, and it will change children's lives." She pronounced this with such confidence Fiona knew that it would.

CHAPTER 41

Caroline popped over to Mrs. Finnerty's just before ten in the morning. The Coughlans were surprised but delighted she was home. Contrary to what they expected, after traveling the day before, their whole household was up early. Amy sat on Angela's bed and listened, transfixed as her sister told her the story of the Dublin hospital. "It's a nice-enough place, but I didn't make any friends this time. We were mostly in our rooms. One girl is coming back the same time as me. Her name is Amelia. She's nice. I don't like the bed, it's too high, and it's very hard on your bum." They both chuckled and covered their mouths.

Amy asked, "Do they have a Nora's nook and hats?"

"I asked Dr. Myers about that. They have a Biddy's bed. I didn't see it, but Biddy doesn't stand up, she lies in a bed and can bend her elbows and knees," explained Angela.

"I like Nora better," announced Amy. "Anyway, Biddy can't have hats if she is lying down."

"They would keep falling off and the bed would be full of hats." Angela's contribution had them in fits of laughter, just like old times.

When they recovered, Amy asked, "Did the medicine make you very sick? Did Dr. Myers help you? She seemed very nice. Does she always wear the hat?"

"Dr. Myers did help, she gave me a different medicine to stop the vomiting. She has lovely hats and scarves on her head, not the same one every day. People wonder what she might be wearing before she comes in. Everybody loves them."

"She had a grand one on last week, all goldy and shiny," Amy added.

After what seemed a long silence, Angela hugged her sister to her. While still cradling her, she said, "Mammy was the best. Day and night, all week she was the best."

Amy looked up, hoping her sister was not crying, and asked, "Do you want to get her something nice, Angela?"

Angela nodded, her chin bobbing on her little sister's head. "I don't know how."

Baby sister to the rescue: "Daddy will know."

Before Caroline could knock on the door, Mrs. Finnerty opened it. They both stood looking at each other. Caroline stopped to clean her hands before stepping into her neighbour's arms. "You look great," Caroline said. "Are you sure they did the operation, or are you just lollygagging?"

"Oh, Caroline, I missed you. How are *you*? How did Angela weather it all? Tell me everything.

"She did well, very well, in fact. She's a trooper. The staff were phenomenal, I can't praise them enough. The ward is set up like a street with each patient's room like a little house, with a painted door and a number. You'd never believe it, the nurses' station is a pirate ship! I'm sure Angela will show it to you when it's the right time." Caroline's voice trailed off; she wondered when that time would be. Mrs. Finnerty watched her and recognised that Angela was just at the beginning of her very long journey. She wished with all her heart that somehow this young mother's anguish could be alleviated. Forcing herself back to the here and now, Caroline said, "I just heard last night about Mr. Doherty. What a thing to happen, what a shock, especially to you."

Mrs. Finnerty replied, "Yes, it was. He was a good friend to me over the years and softhearted under that gruff exterior. He knew about Angela and was all set to build her a set of bookshelves on wheels to go between our two houses. I think he wanted to paint Angela's library or something on it."

"He was going to do that for our Angela? I can't believe he intended to do that. How sad it all is." After a pause to complete her thought, Caroline blurted out, "Well, it's going to be built! We'll get a plaque made saying, 'Mr. Doherty's Gift,' that's what we'll do."

"Caroline, you're the best!" said Mrs. Finnerty. "If you have a few more minutes, there is another iron in the fire. I need your blessing before talking to Angela about an idea I have." An afternoon tea invitation was extended and accepted for 3 o'clock. During tea, Angela Coughlan gave formal consent for Angela's Tresses and Turbans to be registered as a Foundation.

CHAPTER 42

Mrs. Walsh was on a mission. She rummaged in her stationery drawer until she found the right-sized envelope. She carefully placed all the money in it without counting it; that was the bank's job.

Comfortable but stylish shoes on her feet, she headed into town. Each step brought her closer to doing what she wanted to do. She would only be deterred if it was illegal. Bank policy or best practice didn't interest her. As she expected, she collected more money on the way.

Madge and herself talked a fair bit over the past few days as to how best to proceed. Madge was adamant that Mrs. Walsh was the one for the job and assured her that she had her full confidence. With the majority vote of one, off she went.

Mr. Roberts, the bank manager, greeted her as she was shown into his office. He wasn't a stranger to her; she had known him for many a year. His reputation was that of a fair and kind man. She had no reason to think differently after dealing with him last Wednesday when they came to him with Angela's Purse. She sat down in the chair he offered to her, thinking he would sit in the impressive leather chair behind his desk. Instead, he sat beside her and turning towards her, asked, "Anything good in the bag, Mrs. Walsh?"

"Yes, indeed, Mr. Roberts," came the reply. Taking the manila envelope from her handbag, she continued, "I came to ask if it is permissible for me to give this money here, or any money, for that matter, directly to Angela's family." She sat straight up in the chair, not leaning forward to plead, not leaning back to assume.

Taking his cue from her direct approach, he answered, "It is permissible, no legal barriers. No declarations required."

"Good news for the casual donor. When the heart is in the giving, the more direct the route to the need, the better. It's what people want. Red tape is an obstacle to the sentiment," so stated Mrs. Walsh. "Before stopping by the Garda station to give this to Sergeant Coughlan, I would like it to be counted, please. Is there a way you can keep a record of what is given directly? It's best if it's official."

"No problem, just give us a few minutes. Would you like a statement to give to the sergeant, you can enclose it with the money," said Mr. Roberts.

"Thank you, that's a grand way for them to keep track of things." Mrs. Walsh kept her erect position in the chair until he returned with the counted money and the statement.

As he walked her to the door, he took out his wallet. He handed a sizeable donation to Mrs. Walsh, saying, "Add this to the envelope, if you please."

"Thank you. I presume you have included this in today's official tally." They parted with a silent nod and a broad smile.

Sergeant Coughlan was in at the moment she was told at the front desk. Could she wait a minute? There were people milling about all over the place. She took a few steps back to make a path for all the toing and froing. It was like a tennis match, not that Mrs. Walsh would know, she'd never been to one. After some delay, Tony appeared. Now that she was face-to-face with Sergeant Coughlan, she got cold feet. It was a sensitive issue after all, handing donated money in an ordinary envelope to the father of a sick child in a police station. Maybe she should have dealt with Caroline. She decided she would in the future but now was now. "Mrs. Walsh, they haven't arrested you again, have they?" Sergeant Coughlan said, leading her through a nearby door.

"Not yet, I'm just in for questioning," she replied, picking up on his sense of humour. She spoke immediately once they had privacy. It was obvious he was busy. She opened her handbag, took out the envelope, and handed it to him, explaining, "According to Mr. Roberts, it's okay to give some money from Angela's Purse directly to the family. Looks like I'm the messenger. Please take this from all the people who wish Angela and yourselves the very best. They have no time for banks and the like. They like to give to myself or Madge, and you can be sure it will continue. Caroline can call and let us know if there's anything specific needed at any time."

Tony was hanging on her every word, not sure how to respond. He spoke from the heart when he did: "I tried to explain what happened at Angela's mass and ever since to Caroline. How we now have an Angela's Purse, a separate bank account, and more spending money than we ever imagined we would need. We haven't mentioned it to Angela because we haven't fully grasped it ourselves. Would you help us and tell the girls how it was that day? Angela wants to treat her mother for her help in Dublin. I know a mother doesn't need that, but sometimes a child does. Can you do it? Maybe Madge too. The girls know and like you both."

Tears were welling up in Mrs. Walsh's eyes as she listened to Angela's dad. She couldn't wait to tell Madge of their new assignment.

Heads turned when she was escorted by a sergeant out of the police station still clutching an envelope full of money.

CHAPTER 43

At about the same time as Mrs. Walsh was making her way from the bank to the Garda Station sporting her comfortable stylish shoes, Fiona Hannon caught up with Dr. Owens. The usual Monday mayhem had made an earlier meeting of the minds impossible. Her report suggested that the Coughlans had some mayhem of their own on Saturday afternoon. "Busy day at Angela's on Saturday, Dr. Owens," she started. "All to the good, I might add. Amy and her sister got reacquainted and seemed to be conspiring, but nobody knew for sure. Margo Watters opened Angela's case for Oncology. You may recall she's one of the supervisors. We managed to coordinate our visits. You can rest assured that the care plan was scrutinised like a spy's discovery in an espionage novel! In my opinion as a social worker, the prevailing atmosphere in the home is one of excitement, rather than fear or sadness. That is not to understate their understanding of what's to come, not at all. This family dwells on the good of the moment, rather than anticipating what is to come."

"I agree, Fiona, they all have that knack. Would that more of us could react that way," said Dr. Owens.

While Fiona and Nurse Watters were there, Caroline announced that Mrs. Finnerty was invited to tea at three o'clock and wouldn't it be a nice idea for them to put on a frock or something? Fiona and Dr. Owens had a good laugh at the word, *frock*, as the Coughlan girls had when their mother used it earlier.

Fiona continued her report, "That's what I mean, enjoying the fun when it presents itself. Mrs. Finnerty's visit had less to do with tea than a vision she has for Angela's future. A chance remark from little Amy started the whole thing. There is a plan afoot..."

"Fiona, I have to stop you there, I'm in on it. On Sunday, after we got the medical update out of the way, oh, by the way, labs are good, I heard the plan for the turbans. I assumed it was influenced by Dr. Myers, but you are right, it was Amy."

"How did Angela take to the idea? What did she tell you?" Fiona had to know.

She took one of her books out of a beautiful soft cloth bag, she turned a few pages of *The Wonderful Things You Will Be* and read aloud,

I know you'll be kind
And clever and bold
And the bigger your heart
The more it will hold.

Amy clapped, spun around, and shouted, "Goldy, shiny hats for all the children!" Then he added, "So there you have it, we're all in this together. Do you suppose our houses will be overrun by goldy, shiny cloth?" asked the doctor as he took a step towards his office.

"More than likely," said Fiona as she took a step in the opposite direction.

Mrs. Walsh did not go immediately to Madge. She had to gather her own thoughts first. Walking home at a leisurely pace gave her an opportunity to relive last Wednesday from a ten-year-old's point of view. She had to start by telling her about the crowds, the procession, the Gardaí, how there was no space in the cathedral, so the people had to stand outside, and that's how the collection started. It was a simple thing. She would tell her about the shopping bag and how it got stuffed with money and how some man was looking for Angela's purse, so he could put money in it. He must have heard someone mention a bag and thought, purse. That's men for you! That's how it became Angela's Purse. It wouldn't be a hard thing, at all, to tell a little girl that the people cared so much about her and her family, that they wanted to pay for a few things for them. She would have to explain how Madge passed the bag to the first person, and that's how it all started.

By the time she convinced herself that she and Madge could handle this task, she was on Shadow Ridge Avenue. She saw some activity at the old butcher shop. Wondering if they were going to get something new on the avenue, she crossed over. She really got a surprise when Grainne, from Kelly's, greeted her. She was standing out in front of the shop looking up, as if admiring the building. Spotting the new arrival, she said, "Mrs. Walsh, don't tell me you're my neighbour!"

"Grainne, are you telling me this is yours? The one you've been dreaming about? How many scones and cups of tea have I consumed in Kelly's waiting for this moment? Tell me more," urged Mrs. Walsh.

"Ta-da!" heralded Grainne with a tap dance and a dramatic gesture towards the showboard. It simply read, *Wisps.*

"Your very own beauty salon. I love the name and the elegant décor. When do you open?" asked Mrs. Walsh.

"8 o'clock Saturday morning," announced Grainne. "I intend to interrupt the Saturday flow to Baybridge.

"Do you have any appointments open?" Mrs. Walsh asked.

The feigned urgency in her voice not lost on Grainne. "Yes, as luck would have it," came the reply.

The perfect gift for Angela's mother was just across the street.

CHAPTER 44

Confident as all get out, the designer-clad Tara Doherty walked through Harbour Market. She loved it. Passing each stall without stopping required the ultimate in self-control. This was not the place to shop if you just needed a few spuds for the dinner. No, sir! That was for the corner shop. Harbour Market took the shopper on a trip, one that needed preparation and time. The sounds, smells, colours, languages, and exotic offerings both transfixed and transported. Halfway down the first lane, the tantalizing spice odours assailed the nostrils. Large open bins brimming over with ground cumin, ginger, turmeric, cloves, nutmeg, cinnamon, and all manner of things unknown promised the unsuspecting home cook, a plethora of delights. Professional chefs' reputations depended on them. One deep breath through the nose, and you fancied yourself shopping in Marrakesh.

Resisting temptation, Tara continued on her quest. Soon she found the stall she was looking for. Bold as brass, extending her outstretched hand towards Mrs. Shiva, she introduced herself, "My Name is Tara Doherty and it seems we have a mutual friend in Baybridge, a Mrs. Finnerty."

Mrs. Shiva remained unshaken by this abrupt arrival. Mrs. Doherty was known to most of the traders. She had her favourite haunts, mingling with the bric-a-brac or the antique merchants, always in search of an unusual piece for one of her stores. She would spend hours browsing vintage items. "I'm pleased to meet you, Mrs. Doherty, I've seen you around here from time to time. I like *your* shops. Find anything interesting today on your way?" asked Mrs. Shiva.

"I forced myself not to even look. Now that I'm here, though, I like that fabric there on your stool, brilliant colors," remarked Tara Doherty.

"Good eye, good eye," came the reserved reply, "it's for a special order."

"Lucky customer, and please call me Tara. I came to see you today because Mrs. Finnerty in Baybridge told me about the fantastic idea to make headdresses for children who lose their hair due to chemo treatment. She and my late brother-in-law were good friends. He died suddenly very recently. I went to meet her. She's a very impressive lady and totally committed to this project. I offered to help, and I understand, so did you. Can we do it together? With a bit of planning, we could, couldn't we?"

Mrs. Shiva took a minute before answering. There was something abrupt about this woman. She had that reputation in the market and indeed in the town. Maybe the direct, no-nonsense approach was what this project needed. Considering who their clients were, the less-emotional approach would be more productive, and she needed the help. Tara Doherty had skill, experience, staff, two premises, and contacts. "Yes, I think together we can make quite a difference," decided Mrs. Shiva. "Let me show you something." She reached under the fabric display table and produced a perfect glittering child's turban and handed it to Tara who turned it every which way.

"It's perfect," she concluded. "This is your sample, the special order."

Mrs. Shiva nodded. "Is it what we're looking for?" she asked.

"Oh, yes, but where did you get that material?" she asked, running a corner of the fabric on the stool through her fingers.

"Mrs. Finnerty brought it back from India. She asked me to take it and try it out when we met at my husband's cousin's house. It worked, it's holding its shape. Our turbans won't need wrapping. We need to make turban hats."

By now, both the ladies were discussing the minute details of the construction of a turban hat. "You can get all the fabric we need?" asked Tara.

"Yes, I import it from India. Let's also see what materials we can use from other sources. The construction is key. I think we're in the hat business. Mrs. Finnerty has plans for us to cover lots of little heads in style."

"Can you come to Dublin with me on Thursday?" asked Tara.

Without missing a beat, Mrs. Shiva said, "Yes, and call me Ame, please. Where are we going?"

"A hat factory," replied Tara, dramatically running her fingers through her perfectly coifed bob.

CHAPTER 45

Mrs. Miller had a bird's eye view from her perch on the windowsill. Birds! She never had an interest in them, not ever. She failed to understand what other cats got out of chasing one of them. What good would it do to get her white fur all muddy, lying in wait for what? The bird merely flew higher, rested on a tree limb or a high wall, and outwaited the cat. If the purpose was to scare the bird, it seemed mean-spirited to Mrs. Miller. After all, she wasn't a savage or an animal!

Anyway, today she had to really focus on the humans. Between her own house and next door, there was a lot going on. It was good that the lady of the house was home again. It seemed she needed a bit of looking after because the twins stayed at night. An extra lady, wearing a name tag and carrying a bag, visited already. Home she may be, but things weren't normal. She supposed it was good that none of them seemed sad or worried.

Just about then, the front door opened, and Mrs. Finnerty stepped out. Stroking Mrs. Miller's head, she said, "Good afternoon, lady, you have the best spot as always." Shielding her eyes from the sun, she disengaged from the cat and continued down the driveway. *Where can she be going?* purred Mrs. Miller to herself, no cardigan, no handbag, no helper, and no keys. She elegantly slid down from her perch and, hugging the hedge, followed at a safe distance. *Now what?* she thought, as Mrs. Finnerty turned into the Coughlans' driveway and made her way to their front door. It was ajar. That meant she was expected. But why? It could mean that someone in Coughlans needed help, or the lady of the house was in some distress and needed help herself. Mrs. Miller wished for more details but with none forthcoming decided to stay close at hand, just in case. You just never knew when you might be needed. She settled in under the hedge with a clear view of the front door, not a bird in sight.

"It's me!" announced Mrs. Finnerty as Amy came running into her arms. Bracing her abdomen for the squeeze, Mrs. Finnerty kissed the top of Amy's head. The stitches were due to be removed on Friday. Although her own house had been drastically remodeled, this house felt familiar to her.

"Come in," called Caroline from somewhere inside the house. Amy took her by the hand and led her back to the huge welcoming kitchen. If she were to have any regrets about the changes she made in her own house, it would be the forfeiture of the kitchen. She enjoyed the Coughlans' kitchen, she realised, because of the people in it. Back in her own house, she knew that her presence alone would not have the same effect. No regrets, her magic was in her books.

Her attention was immediately drawn to two ladies seated at the kitchen table. She vaguely remembered seeing them in the past. She did not know their names. Caroline came forward to save the day: "Mrs. Finnerty, this is Mrs. Kitty Walsh, she lives directly behind us, we share the back fence. Mrs. Madge Costello here, she prefers to be called Madge, lives one street further down, nearer to the school. Their children are a wee bit older than our two. Ladies, this is Mrs. Finnerty, my good neighbour from right next door." Indicating the vacant chair next to Mrs. Walsh, Caroline continued. "Take a seat here now, and I'll get you a nice fresh cup of tea. "The ladies shuffled their chairs as a symbol of welcome for the newcomer.

Then followed the usual litany of "Nice to meet you at last," "I've seen you out walking many times," and "I'm sure we've met in Quigley's." When the icebreakers were exhausted, they settled in to a normal neighbourly exchange. Soon, as often happens, the awkwardness wore off, and they spoke as if they had known each other all their lives. Mrs. Finnerty explained that her lack of agility was due to a recent operation. Madge accounted for her casual attire on account of being invited at short notice. Mrs. Walsh was gulping her tea due to being fierce thirsty after walking the length and breadth of Baybridge this morning. As they were forgiving each other for not being perfect, Mrs. Finnerty noticed Angela's absence.

Caroline explained, "Angela is taking a wee nap right now, and Amy has gone up to change out of her uniform. The girls have been listening to the ladies explain an extraordinary thing that started at Angela's mass and now has spread all over the place. Tony and myself are at a loss to understand it all. Why don't I just let Mrs. Walsh and Madge tell you what's going on? Angela wanted you to know."

Mrs. Finnerty was having another one of those Tara Doherty moments while trying to erase the bewildered look from her face. She was getting a lot of practice with that these days. Mrs. Walsh told the story of Angela's Purse, down to the last legal detail. Madge nodded her unsolicited approval at every opportunity. Mrs. Walsh drained the last drop of her now-tepid tea when she finished.

Instinctively, Mrs. Finnerty knew why Angela wanted her to know from Mrs. Walsh directly. Angela was very astute for her age. She wasn't certain that Caroline saw the danger of Mrs. Walsh feeling slighted at her response. This was a conversational minefield. The next move was monumental. Talk of Angela's Tresses and Turbans did not belong in this conversation. Mrs. Finnerty spoke sincerely when she said, "I get a clear picture just by listening to your account of that day, how a selfless gesture by both of you, one made straight from the heart, resulted in such an outpouring of generosity in others. I don't think it would have been so in any other hands. Congratulations."

Madge stole a glance at Mrs. Walsh, who, sitting straighter in her chair, simply said, "Thank you, Mrs. Finnerty."

Mrs. Miller was relieved to see the lady of the house appear in the doorway. Scampering ahead of her, she was back on the window-sill before Mrs. Finnerty reached the end of their driveway. No need for her to know that she had been followed. After all, Mrs. Miller wasn't a stalker! Just a concerned cat.

Mrs. Finnerty was so engrossed in thought about the Angela's Purse revelation, that she almost shut her front door in Mrs. Walsh's face. She neither saw nor heard her approach. "Oh, my goodness, I'm so sorry, I didn't see you there," explained Mrs. Finnerty.

"No, no, not your fault at all. I'm actually sneaking," whispered Mrs. Walsh. "I don't want Caroline to see me. I just need a quick word. Can I just step into the hall?" Mrs. Walsh was making a poor attempt at being sneaky. Mrs. Miller raised the one eyebrow and reached the conclusion that they had all lost their minds.

Mrs. Finnerty ushered Mrs. Walsh into her house. There was no hall. Mrs. Walsh stood among the volumes and tomes. Without commenting on them, she said, "Part of the reason Madge and myself called in next door today was to help Angela do something special for her mother. The sergeant brought it up when we were talking about Angela's Purse. He said Caroline would not expect any such thing, but he felt the little girl really wanted to. When I was walking home today, I was so surprised to see the old butcher's shop had been converted into a hairdresser's. The new owner is Grainne from Kelly's, no less. Can you imagine? She has it done up really nice, and she opens on Saturday morning, brand-spanking new. Do you think treating Caroline to a new do would be a good gift?"

Mrs. Finnerty noticed that all this had been spoken in a measured, even tone, no sign of breathlessness or undue excitement. She, on the other hand, needed to sit down just on hearing it. She invited her guest to take the other chair in the reader's corner just inside the door where they were standing. Still no comment on the books as Mrs. Walsh continued, "I couldn't ask Caroline this without letting the cat out of the bag, so I said to Madge, Mrs. Finnerty will know. Angela's hair will start to get thin in the next few weeks, and she also cannot go into public for fear of infection. Am I on the right track?" Mrs. Finnerty nodded. "What if Angela, Amy, and their mother all got their hair done on Saturday morning? No risk of infection as the place is brand-new. That would be a nice treat for them all. I told Grainne to keep the first appointments open, and I would come back to confirm. We laughed as she pretended to be booked up already. It would be great for her too. So what do you think?"

Mrs. Finnerty was so taken by this woman, she had to compose herself before answering, "Mrs. Walsh, you're absolutely on the right track. It's the perfect package."

"Oh, I knew you would know! I think Grainne would be happy to have the Coughlans as her very first customers. I'm off now to tell her and officially make the appointments." Mrs. Walsh stood up, hesitating as she gathered her handbag, while adding, "Wouldn't it be grand if Grainne's appointment book had a few more names in it? Make it a busy sort of first day. I know my hair could do with a tidy up, and Mage always has to be dragged to get hers done." Casting a questioning glance at Mrs. Finnerty, much like Mrs. Miller often did, she waited.

Mrs. Finnerty got the message. "I'm sure the recent surgery did nothing for my mop, so count me in."

"Oh, I didn't mean to imply—"

"You would be right, though," interrupted Mrs. Finnerty. "Apart from that, I know Grainne and I'm really excited for her and her new place. This is another of your good ideas, Mrs. Walsh. Do you mind if I walk over with you? I'd love to see her."

Much to Mrs. Miller's dismay, the two ladies left the house and crossed Shadow Ridge Avenue together.

CHAPTER 46

Mrs. Finnerty felt good on Friday morning. Meeting Grainne at her own beauty salon had brought her great joy. She remembered their kind and reassuring encounter at Kelly's after a previous visit to see Dr. O'Connor. She will hold Grainne forever in her heart since the death of Mr. Doherty, and truly believed she deserved her success. It warmed Mrs. Finnerty's spirit to witness the success of the young, always had.

Today was a big day for her. Having the stiches removed signified not only the healing of her belly, but also the restoration of her healthy strong self. She looked upon her recent medical issues as an obstacle to her relationship with Angela and her family. The death of Mr. Doherty laid heavily on her, always going back to the single futile question: what if he hadn't come with her that day? The world was full of unanswered what-ifs. No more of that! The stiches were coming out, the future awaited, and she had things to do.

No sooner had she had that all sorted when the doorbell rang. Without waiting for her to open the door, the twins bounced in. The pinging of the doorbell was just out of courtesy; they had a key. "It's just us two," came the chorus from the front of the house. Carmel and Maura appeared and stood looking down at Mrs. Finnerty sitting in the tiny kitchen. "Well, girls, I just brewed a small pot of coffee. Did you smell it from the street?"

"We did, but we knew you would anyway," answered Carmel. "Lovely."

"I ordered Jimmy's taxi to take us to the doctor. You have time for a cup each before he comes. No scones! I have a surprise for us after the doctor's."

The twins smiled at her as she spoke. Concerns about returning the house key now vanished. They could sleep at home tonight. Mrs. Finnerty was back.

Fiona Hannon was in Baybridge Medical Centre on Friday Morning visiting a new admission. Mr. Cawley's leg ulcer had deteriorated, causing him to swap his quiet oasis in the country for a bustling ward in the hospital. Despite his unease, he remained the gentleman, and Fiona was glad to see him.

Knowing Mrs. Finnerty's appointment was at half past eleven, she made her way to Dr. O'Connor's outpatients. As usual, it was wall-to-wall people, no surprise there. No surprise either at Mrs. Finnerty's perfectly healed abdomen and her discharge back to Dr. Owen's care. Maura and Carmel were proud of their healthy patient. Fiona expected this good outcome.

As they prepared to leave, Mrs. Finnerty had a thought and, taking a chance, said, "Fiona, I am taking the girls to Pepper's for lunch. I know Cate can't be with us, but if you could join us, it could be a celebration like we talked about the last time we were there."

Memories of that day at Pepper flooded back to Fiona. It seemed so long ago, and so much had happened since. Checking her watch, she realised that Dr. Owen's office was closed for lunch, and her only remaining visit today was with Angela. Shocking herself, the girl most unlikely too said yes.

The twins had never been to Pepper. After they all piled into Fiona's car, the sound of juvenile gloating could be heard from the back seat, as they talked to their mother on the mobile. "Yes, Pepper, that's what I said, Pepper." The two ladies in front glanced at each other and smiled.

When they arrived, the welcome equaled that of the Prodigal Son. All but the fatted calf was offered. They sat at the same table as before, and Mr. Shiva prepared the dainty box of laddu in anticipation of their departure. There was no sign of a bill.

Fiona drove everyone home, parked at her own house, and walked back up to Coughlans. Things seemed very quiet to her as she approached the house. Reaching for the doorbell, Caroline appeared in the doorway. "Fiona, come in," she said, closing the door quietly. They made their way back to the kitchen as Caroline whispered an update to Fiona. "Angela is sleeping. Dr. Owens called and said yesterday's blood count was low. He wants to start treatment to give the white cells a boost. Orla Higgins is on her way. We love Orla, but I am so glad to see you right now."

When they both finished giving their hands a good scrub, Caroline went upstairs to check on her daughter. Fiona absentmindedly plopped into a kitchen chair and stared at the wall. Within minutes, Orla arrived. Fiona let her in and directed her straight upstairs to join Caroline in Angela's room. She returned to the kitchen and made a fresh pot of tea. When Caroline joined her there, her eyes were wearing a weak smile—weak it might have been but a smile nevertheless. Fiona stood up, and they walked into each other's hugs.

"No temperature and her lungs are clear, Thank God, no infection. Orla is starting the medicine now, so she will be upstairs for a while." Glancing at the cooker, she asked, "Is that fresh tea?" Not waiting for an answer, she produced two mugs. The tea tasted so good.

Orla popped her head around the kitchen door and accepted Caroline's invitation to come in. She declined a cup of tea, instead saying, "Angela is doing fine, back to sleep, which is good. I just finished giving the report to Dr. Owens. He recommends that Angela return to Park Edge tomorrow. He talked with Dr. Myers, and the thinking is that it is best to get ahead of any possible infection. It's a precaution. He is coming this evening to give her a good checkup, as another precaution. At that time, you will have a chance to talk things over with him more fully. Mrs. Coughlan, just be assured that this is forward planning, no major setback as of now, and that is the way we want it to stay."

As Orla let herself out, her last thought was *I have had better days.*

CHAPTER 47

Tony Coughlan and Amy arrived home both in a cheerful mood. Fiona and Caroline were in the kitchen, and he knew by them that something had changed. Fiona got the measure of things immediately. Remembering Mrs. Finnerty's gift box from Pepper, she addressed Amy. "How are you, Amy?" You get bigger every time I see you. Shocked them all with how much you knew at school today, did you?

"Mrs. Hannon, I did not. I got a gold star on my spelling test on Monday," she offered with a grin.

"There now, I knew it. I know someone else who would like to know too, Mrs. Finnerty. If it is okay with Mammy and Daddy, we can go next door and tell her. I think she may have some news for you as well."

"Can I, Mammy?" came the plea.

With relief and gratitude in their voices, they said yes. Halfway to the front door, still wearing her school uniform, Amy stopped and ran back to the kitchen. "Is anything wrong with Angela?" she asked.

"She got a new medicine today. She fell asleep while Orla was giving it to her. Dr. Owens is coming later to check that it is working."

"We'll let her sleep so," said Amy. She ran back to join Fiona.

In the Coughlans' house, Caroline was bringing Tony up-to-date. Going to Dublin was not such a big deal. It was just a few days earlier than planned. They had talked during the last few days about Tony staying at Park Edge this time, knowing she and Angela would need him. The issue at hand was the care of Amy. They had relatives in various parts of the country but none whose ages or circumstances allowed them to uproot themselves and come to Baybridge indefinitely. It would not be an option for Amy to go to any of them. They looked at each other, remembering where Amy was right now and, without saying anything, wondered if that was a possibility.

Mrs. Finnerty could hardly believe her eyes when she saw her visitors. "Come in, come in. I was trying to think of a way to see you and here you are," beamed Amy's favourite neighbour. Inside the door they performed their handwashing routine lest they forget, not that Amy would allow that to happen. Mrs. Finnerty led them through the library to the patio outside. "I was just sitting here in need of good company, and you arrived, both of you. How lucky am I?"

"Amy has news for you from school. We decided to come and tell you while her mammy and daddy were having a chat," explained Fiona.

Mrs. Finnerty understood immediately. "I am glad you did. Tell me," she urged.

"Well, I got a gold star for my spelling on Monday." Taking the usual breathless pause of an eight-year-old, she continued. "Angela got a new medicine today from Orla, and she fell asleep, and Dr. Owens is coming to check her. Could you mind me for a few days if Dr. Owen's says she is sick? Mrs. Finnerty, I don't think you are sick anymore. Are you?"

With that Amy hopped up on the patio chair, straightened her uniform pinafore, and waited for the answer. Mrs. Finnerty replied: "You are right, Amy, I am quite well now, well enough for minding people. The doctor said so today. He told me to go away and not come back for another year. I said okay. Mrs. Hannon, the twins, and myself went to *Pepper* and brought you back…"

"Laddu!" screeched Amy.

"Indeed, we did, would you like one?" asked Mrs. Finnerty.

Amy was about to say yes, she really wanted one. Instead she said, "I think I'll wait for Angela.

"That's a good idea. It's nice when all four pieces are in the little box. I brought some for me too, would you like one of mine for your gold star?"

Amy's eyes widened. "Yes, please," she said.

"Okay, wait right there. I think a glass of milk would wash it down nicely. Maybe a piece of cheese on the side would add a nice touch."

Fiona sat beside Amy, totally enthralled by the relationship between these two. If it became necessary for Tony and Caroline to leave Amy in Baybridge, it seems the arrangements were already made.

Dr. Owens's visit was uneventful. He confirmed Orla's findings. He found no sign of infection. "Dr. Meyers recommends that Angela return to them a few days early to avoid any delay in completing this chemo cycle. Angela may experience some joint or muscle pain because of today's treatment. It can take a day or two for the white-cell count to rise significantly. Best be on the unit while all this is going on," the doctor explained.

"It makes sense. We can see now that you have explained everything Caroline said." She hesitated before continuing. "The next matter may seem trivial, but it is very important to Angela because it's a gift from her to me. She got help in arranging appointments at the new hairdressers across the street for us all tomorrow morning. We will be the first customers. Does this pose any risk to Angela?"

The doctor thought about it for a moment or two then answered: "If Angela feels up to it in the morning, I see no risks. Her emotional well-being is as important as her physical. It may even be good for her."

His last comment before going through the front door was "I hear a new hairdo does wonders for you ladies."

CHAPTER 48

Angela was sitting comfortably in an armchair in the front room when Amy returned from Mrs. Finnerty's. Handwashing completed, she ran to her sister and, using the safe method taught to her by Dr. Meyers, hugged her. Fiona and Mrs. Finnerty rejoined Caroline in the kitchen.

From her position on the footstool, Amy looked up and asked, "Are you sick, Angela? Do you have to go to Dublin?"

"They are afraid I might get sick because my blood count has dropped. I could get an infection. Nurse Orla gave an injection today. It didn't hurt because she put it in the port. She is very nice to me and sat with me until it was all finished. I fell asleep. Dr. Meyers told Dr. Owens it's best if I go back tomorrow while I am still okay. I need to be ready for the rest of the chemo medicine. Dr. Alan wants the lump to shrink before the operation."

"Shrink? Does he mean like your old school jumper?" asked Amy.

Both girls burst out laughing, to the delight of the adults in the kitchen. "Smaller, I hope," said Angela.

"This small?" Amy asked, creating a small space between her index finger and her thumb.

"Yes, that's why I have to be well enough to take the chemo medicine."

"That's the one that makes you sick? Right?"

Angela simply nodded.

"Mrs. Hannon took me over to Mrs. Finnerty's when Mammy and Daddy were talking. I know they were trying to make a plan.

Daddy wants to be with you and Mammy in Dublin this time. That's good. I already asked Mrs. Finnerty to mind me in her house. I can mind Mrs. Miller. She will eat this time because Mrs. Finnerty is at home. It's all settled now, Angela, so you don't have to worry." Having said all that, the girls sat, holding hands in silence. Neither noticed the light fade.

Earlier when Mrs. Walsh told Caroline quietly about Angela's plan to treat her to a hairdo, she was overcome. Regarding her friend through tears, Caroline knew she had made this happen. Mrs. Walsh was reading much more into today's developments. She deduced that Angela's return to Dublin was about to be brought forward. Based on that belief, Angela's Purse was opened wide enough to pay Grainne and generously cover the expenses in Dublin. Taking care to depart before an onslaught of thank-yous, Mrs. Kitty Walsh walked briskly down the driveway and headed for home. She would get her own crying done as she walked.

When the Walsh's phone rang later that day, Michael Walsh, the youngest son, answered it. His voice filled the house as he shouted from the hall. "Mrs. Coughlan, for your mam." Then the house was filled with silence. Fear gripped his mother as she took the phone from his outstretched hand. A weak hello from Mrs. Walsh was followed by a more robust voice on the other end. Once it became clear the conversation was about hair appointments, Mrs. Walsh resumed normal breathing. Her offer to alert Grainne about the uncertainty of the morning hair appointments was graciously accepted by Caroline. Knowing that there was still work to be done at the salon, she decided that Grainne would be there. The best course of action was to just go there and work out a new schedule with her. Between them, they had it fixed in no time. Mrs. Coughlan should keep her eight o'clock. Grainne suggested she then go back to the house and attend to Angela there. She would take an unopened pack of smocks, gloves, brush, comb, and the other tricks of the trade with her. Leaving them there in Angela's room for further use was the safest. She had done this before with other chemo patients. Mrs. Finnerty and Amy would come to the salon after the family had set off for Dublin. Mrs. Walsh and Madge continued as planned.

The new timetables worked well on Saturday morning. Dr. Owens was right about hairdo(s) being good for the ladies. Angela was in good spirits and feeling pretty. Grainne helped choose an outfit for the trip. Angela's reflection in the full-length mirror confirmed she was indeed pretty. "Quite beautiful" offered Grainne, as she stood behind her, hands gently placed on her slender shoulders. "Very stylish indeed."

Fiona came to help Caroline pack. Amy had put her things together the night before. Caroline opted not to fuss over Amy's choices. Mrs. Finnerty had a key to their house. They could go back and forth between the two houses as needed. All the talk about shampoos and haircuts prompted Fiona to call Cate, and before anyone knew it, three more people were added to Grainne's appointment book: Fiona, Cate, and Cara.

Just after noon the chariot was packed and ready for the road. As the assembly of well-wishers, now including Madge and Mrs. Walsh, stood waving along the driveway, a loud "*Stop!*" erupted from Amy. *Poor child*, everyone thought, *she doesn't want to be left behind.* All eyes were on her as they noticed her tugging at Mrs. Finnerty, who bent down to hear her whisper. Quickly she ran back into her own house and, returning, handed something to the child. Tony stopped the chariot and slid open the side door. Amy reached in, handing the small box from Pepper to Angela, explaining, "I kept all four pieces together. The extra one is for you."

Her dad slid the door shut, trapping the kiss his precious young daughter blew into the vehicle. They took it with them all the way to Angela's room on Happy Street, their address for at least the next week.

CHAPTER 49

Silence prevailed in the Coughlans' driveway as each well-wisher sorted the events of the day, deciding in which order they would be hung on today's clothesline.

Fiona was the first to speak. "It's a beautiful sunny day. Angela and her parents got on the road in good time, thanks to everyone pitching in. That little girl is going to get the best care in Dublin. She will come back soon, and we will all pitch in again to get her ready for her operation. We have Amy all to ourselves for a few days, that's if Mrs. Finnerty shares." The stony silence began to crack a little as Fiona continued. "I suggest a celebration is what's called for. How about everybody meet at my house after Grainne has worked her magic. I believe Mrs. Finnerty and Miss Amy are next. I am off to see Mrs. Quigley now before it's our turn. How about five or half past at Hannon's?" The spell was broken, the mood had lightened. It got even lighter as Fiona added, "Come one, come all. No need to be making a meal at home tonight. Plenty for everyone." Fiona knew extending the invitation to include family would ease the pressure on Madge and Mrs. Walsh, both of whom had a house full of kids

Fiona made her way to Quigley's as sounds of gratitude echoed in her ears. Mrs. Quigley was aware that Angela and her parents had left for Dublin. Caroline has been in the shop earlier getting supplies for the trip. Not a lot of words passed between Fiona and the shopkeeper on that matter. No need for words. Instead Mrs. Quigley did what she did best, assembling an array of fresh foods the likes of which would outdo anything supplied by the best establishments. Without missing a beat, she promised to have it delivered to Hannon's by quarter to five. Jonathon would not only deliver the food but also set it out, ready for serving. Anyone who did not know Mrs. Quigley would be surprised by this. Fiona was not surprised. This was Mrs.'s Q's contribution.

She called Mark at the club. There were no major matches today, so things were quiet. "Hi, Mark, it's me."

"Hi yourself. Did the Coughlans get away okay? No hitches? Are you okay?"

"I'm okay," she replied. "Everybody did their bit, no hitches. Amy stayed with Mrs. Finnerty. I hope you don't mind, I asked everyone to come to our house for a bite between 5:00 and half past. Mrs. Quigley did the honors as usual, and her young Jonathon is going to set up. Can you get home, do you think?"

"That was quick thinking there, Fiona, lighten the mood a bit. And it's a great evening for a get-together. Yeah, I can be home. Do I need to pick up drinks or anything?"

"You're a great support, Mark. We could do with some drinks. I can't remember if I told you, Cate and Cara are getting their hair done with me. Colm with probably come up with Matthew later," explained Fiona.

"You did mention that about the hairdresser. I'm sure Colm will be up," said Mark.

"Good. Thanks again, Mark," replied Fiona and added quietly, "I love you."

"I know," came the cheeky reply. All was well with the Hannons.

The party was a blast, kids running wild, *oohs* and *aahs* about the hairstyles, and about how big the children were now. The food was delicious and plentiful. Mrs. Quigley got all the credit.

Mrs. Finnerty noticed Mark doing a woodwork project with some of the younger boys. She wandered over to get a closer look. They were making a small stool. As she stooped down to admire it, Mr. Doherty and his mobile library popped into her mind. She suddenly felt very sad. Fiona approached her and noticed she was crying. This was a shock to Fiona as Mrs. Finnerty wasn't prone to emotional displays. She led her away to a quiet corner but not before Mark also noticed her crying.

Later when everything had returned to normal and Mrs. Finnerty was back in the middle of the festivities, Fiona had a chance to explain to Mark the reason for her sadness: Mr. Doherty's plan to build the bookcase for Angela. "Oh, that is sad, all right," said Mark, "Mr. Doherty had some surprising soft spots it seems." He paused for a moment before adding, "I could come up with something like that for Angela's books if she still wants it made. Colm would help I'm sure. It's not a big job."

Now it was Fiona's turn to tear up. She nodded and said, "She wants 'Mr. Doherty's Gift' painted on it."

"Grand, let me find Colm," he said as he headed down towards the shed. He found his son-in-law along the way. The project had already started.

CHAPTER 50

The party at Hannon's was an enormous success. Sunday was a day of rest. Amy and Mrs. Finnerty puttered about, at ease in each other's company. Later in the day, they ventured next door to pick up Amy's schoolbag and uniform.

Monday started a week of action on many fronts. Mark bought the supplies for Angela's mobile library. The plan was to have it completed in time for her return from Dublin. Mrs. Finnerty took Amy to school and continued into Baybridge for a 10 o'clock appointment with her bank manager. Papers had been previously exchanged between the bank and the solicitors. Today the documents were complete. All that was required now was Mrs. Finnerty's signature. With the final transfer of money, Angela's Tresses and Turbans foundation was registered and operational. A momentous day for Mrs. Finnerty. She found herself wishing she could call in to Mr. Doherty on her way home and tell him. She sent up a silent prayer instead.

Tara Doherty and Ame Shiva learned a great deal about hat making in the Dublin factory. Between them they had completed six no-wrap turbans. Showing them to Mrs. Finnerty was the next step. Amy Coughlan would have the final say. It was decided, as Tara had business in Baybridge connected to her brother in laws property, that Ame Shiva would travel with her and meet with Mrs. Finnerty and Amy.

"Amy, Amy, over here," Mrs. Finnerty called out, waving enthusiastically as Amy appeared in the doorway of the school. The smiling child ran to her with equal enthusiasm. "You had wonderful day at school, didn't you?" she asked. Amy, still smiling, just nodded. On the walk home, Mrs. Finnerty reminded Amy of the day they found the fabric in the guestroom. Amy was using that room now.

"It was lovely and shiny," Amy replied.

"You said it would make a beautiful scarf or hat, do you remember? I said you were a genius because you gave me an amazing idea. After that I spoke with a few ladies about what you said. They agreed with you. Amy, when you were in Park Edge, you met Dr. Meyers. You noticed she was wearing colorful hats, and you and Angela admired them. Covering her hair is her way of supporting children all over who lose their hair when they take the chemo medicine." Mrs. Finnerty paused and then suggested they walk through the nearby park before going home. Sitting on a swing, her legs dangling, the swing still for now, Amy said, "The hats are going to be made, aren't they?"

"Yes they are, my clever pet, yes, they are," came the joyous reply.

Tara Doherty and Ame Shiva arrived in Baybridge on Wednesday morning. Neither shop nor office were yet open. Ame visited Mr. Shiva and his family. Tara Doherty had breakfast with Mrs. Finnerty and Amy. Not shy to admire the house, Tara took herself on a tour and admitted to being beyond jealous about the library and the lift. She was left alone to browse through the books while Amy was taken to school. By the time Mrs. Finnerty returned, Ame Shiva had arrived, bringing with her the turbans for inspection. The joy felt by the three women examining the headwear was palpable. Amy would be delighted. Finally, Ame Shiva sheepishly produced one more sample from her basket. Tara was taken by surprise; while all the others were suitable for girls, this one was different. It had a more rigid structure brought together higher in the front, sporting a jewel at its apex. It resembled the headdress of a maharaja. "It's for a *boy!*" both the onlookers said in unison.

"While I was sewing one evening, my son, Previn, asked me, were we making any for boys?"

"Goodness me," replied Mrs. Finnerty. "We would have nothing at all if it wasn't for the children."

After the business side of things was explained and accepted, Mrs. Finnerty sent the ladies off to increase and multiply the product. It was settled that production headquarters would be in Haymarket. Financial arrangements were in place to cover materials, staff, and a workshop. Both Tara and Ame felt that because of their networking these costs would be minimal. Mrs. Finnerty would promote the foundation in Baybridge.

Amy wore the first turban to school on Thursday. By Monday, half the children in the school wanted one. Teachers and mothers wondered if they come in adult sizes. As the wave of interest grew, Mrs. Finnerty was forced to call a meeting. The school offered their assembly room. Once again, the children did the work. Angela's Tresses and Turbans was well and truly launched in Baybridge.

CHAPTER 51

The report from Dr. Meyers was good. Dr. Owens relaxed. When Angela left for Dublin he was not sure if she escaped without infection. It seemed she had. According to Dr. Meyers, his intervention was timely. Chemo had started as per schedule. As expected, this current regimen was brutal. Nausea and vomiting, though eased with medication, persisted. The inside of Angela's mouth was raw and sore and was further irritated by the vomiting. These side effects, though expected, were upsetting to see in a child.

Caroline and Tony's hearts ached at seeing their young daughter in such a state, but being together helped. Tony knew he had made the right decision to be with them. Angela's hair was thinning, but it was the least of her worries. She hardly noticed. When the symptoms allowed, she slept. On one of those days, Tony encouraged Caroline to take a day trip back to Baybridge. He knew all too well that she was pining for Amy. Mrs. Finnerty has reassured her on the daily phone calls. Nevertheless, nothing substituted for holding her young daughter. Indecision haunted her. She sat looking back and forth between Angela and her husband, her thoughts moving in tandem with her eyes. Sir James Butler stole into the room following a light knock on the door. It was his second visit since they returned. Tony enjoyed meeting him earlier in the week. They had a man-to-man chuckle about the train encounter. Today he came bearing good news. "She is doing well," he said, indicating that Caroline should remain where she was sitting. Tony stood up and took a step towards the doctor. "As Dr. Meyer explained yesterday, current labs and tests are good. We will however remain vigilant. The next several days are crucial. Methotrexate is a bear but an effective one. Twenty-four hours after the last dose, we will deactivate the residual. Its work will be done. Now, is there anything at all we can do for you both?"

"Thank you, Dr. Butler," said Tony, moving closer to Caroline's chair. "My wife is missing Amy, our youngest. We were mulling over whether a day trip might be a good idea."

"Is the little girl with someone she loves and loves her?" asked Dr. Butler. "These circumstances are often a recipe for some spoiling."

"Oh yes," came the joint reply.

Caroline continued, "It's the lady next door, and they are best of friends."

"It's a very common dilemma we face around here. We're of the same opinion as the Beatles, *all you need is love.* Nothing beats a short simple phone call just after tea to look forward to."

Sir Robert continued his rounds. Caroline Coughlan, the haunting indecision over, stayed in Park Edge. Amy was thrilled with the evening phone calls where she got the chance to tell all the news to her mammy and daddy. The whole phone call was just for her.

Fiona met Dr. Owens in the corridor. Discreetly, he brought her up-to-date on Angela's condition. There was nothing surprising in the report. "I am planning to check on Amy and Mrs. Finnerty after school today," said Fiona. Dr. Owens nodded in acknowledgement as he continued his way.

The report from Mrs. Finnerty was also good with no surprises. Amy had adjusted well to her new accommodation. In fact, she was quite enjoying herself next door. The tiny kitchen intrigued her, and the lift fostered the notion that this was like a hotel. A social worker's dream report. They did need to discuss another matter with her if she had a moment. While Amy went upstairs to retrieve the turbans, Mrs. Finnerty explained, "Our first collection of turbans has been delivered. Amy and I are so excited." She paused as Amy returned with the basket, her hair stunningly wrapped in shimmering colorful fabric. As she turned towards the two adults, they noticed her eyes glistening with unshed tears. For what seemed an age, nobody moved. Then Amy opened the basket and began modeling the contents. Fiona was as speechless as the first day she entered this house.

"Thank you, Amy," continued Mrs. Finnerty. "Now show Mrs. Hannon the surprise." On command, the maharaja sample appeared. Fiona recovered her power of speech with the words "It's for a *boy*," words familiar to Mrs. Finnerty's ears.

"Yes, it's for a boy. Mrs. Shiva's son in Haymarket requested the boys be considered too. This is exhibit A. She and Tara Doherty are managing a talented team there, and apparently production is well underway. The turbans will be made in Haymarket but distributed far and wide to any child, boy or girl, who wants one. We have a lot of support already at Angela's school, don't we, Amy?"

"I wore mine to school the other day. Mrs. Finnerty had to come to the assembly room to explain we cover our hair to support chemo children like Angela, not because it's a nice hat. Everybody said they *knew* that. Anyway, they wanted to wear a turban for Angela, and their mothers gave Ms. Flynn in the office money for the turban fund. They were very nice." Amy sat down.

"Out of the mouths of babes," said Mrs. Finnerty. "Now, Mrs. Hannon, we need your help with two things in particular. Right, Amy?"

Amy was busy packing up the remaining turbans and simply looked over her shoulder. She did not speak. She picked up the basket and came to stand by Mrs. Finnerty still wearing her turban. She placed the basket on the floor and inched her way onto Mrs. Finnerty's lap. Quietly she said it would be nice if Dr. Myers had one of Angela's turbans. Mrs. Finnerty replied with a hug filled with love and admiration. She made the phone call to Haymarket later. Fiona observed her, tender feelings welling up inside her. She found herself recalling feelings of her own, right under her ribs. They still plagued her. She pondered over what items might be hanging on Amy's little clothesline today.

CHAPTER 52

Kitty Walsh was trying to work out the best use of Angela's Purse to help Angela and her family. She looked around her: schoolbags on the chairs, today's used school lunchboxes neither in nor out of the sink, one football boot by the door, and the other still outside. "I'll be back," she said loudly to anyone who could hear her as she stepped over the stray boot outside the back door.

It was a late afternoon with perfect weather for walking. She decided to head towards the town, take the left turn, head up Carter Hill, and return home passing Quigley's. By that time, something had better come to her, or she was the wrong man for the job. To tell the truth, she didn't give Angela's Purse much thought for the first mile or so. Instead, surrendering herself to the sights and smells of the neighborhood as she eased on down the road.

She was suddenly reminded of the purpose of the walk by a van parked outside one of the large houses on Carter Hill. It was a medium-sized vehicle, and its boot was open. Visible to the passing eye were all sorts of spray bottles, spray cans, mops, and brooms. It was dark blue in color with *Nuala's Cleaning Services* ornately painted on the side. Now with a clear mission, Mrs. Walsh steadily walked until she reached Quigley's shop. "Mrs. Walsh," said the shopkeeper as she was beckoned to the side by a discreet nod and a slight shift of the eyes. Mrs. Quigley left the customers to her teenage assistant and followed the newcomer outside. Not one to beat about the bush, Mrs. Walsh said, "I know it's teatime rush, so I won't keep you. What do you know of Nuala's Cleaning Services?"

She looked up at the tall lady, expecting her to know and to share this information with her. The answer came calmly and quietly.

"There're fairly new but good and reliable. Owned by a young couple who take it very seriously. They have a catering company too, run by Nuala's husband. An original innovative idea if you ask me."

"I *am* asking you," said Kitty Walsh, "and for a very good reason. Do you think this kind of service would help Caroline?"

She waited still looking up as if into the eyes of a sage.

"Of course, what a relief that would be to her," reassured Mrs. Quigley.

"You wouldn't mind about the food part. I mean—"

Mrs. Quigley cut in, "Not at all, it's a whole different thing altogether."

"Thank you, thank you," whispered Mrs. Walsh as she set off home where neither the stray boot nor the lunchboxes mattered. She rang Mrs. Finnerty, who agreed with Mrs. Quigley. It was settled then. Mrs. Walsh would make the arrangements, and during the next phone conversation between Caroline and Mrs. Finnerty, a casual mention would be thrown in about the house getting the once over prior to Angela's return. No need for details.

The first task given to Fiona by Mrs. Finnerty and Amy was to find out if anybody was going to Park Edge in the next few days. Yes, three Baybridge patients had appointments there on Thursday, and the first patient Fiona asked considered it a privilege to take Angela's turban to her. Problem solved. The second task was not that simple. The issue was how to identify and target those who might appreciate a turban or need hairstyling as their hair thinned. "Could social services help in this area?" Mrs. Finnerty had asked that day. The answer was yes. Fiona went on to explain.

"All these patients have assigned social workers. We coordinate with each other, various departments and services as a matter of course. Some hospitals are already liaising with hairstylists and wig makers. I will research what is already available and see how Angela's Tresses and Turbans can enhance what is currently in place. Give me a day or two."

She did indeed do her research. She was surprised at the overwhelming response to the turbans. Following two returned phone calls, she contacted Mrs. Finnerty with an order for ten, including one for a seven-year-old boy, the first of Angela's maharajas. He lived in Baybridge. It was likely that the boy's hair would need cutting. Mrs. Finnerty enlisted Grainne's help as she had offered her services to the foundation previously. Grainne visited the boy in his home, cut his hair before showing him how to wear the turban. She left a very proud, happy little boy waving to her as she returned to her car that afternoon. Whatever else he had hung on his little clothesline that day, his last item made him smile.

CHAPTER 53

Dr. Owens kept Dr. Alan Moran informed about Angela's condition. He also received periodic updates and results from Dr. Meyers. His phone rang, and assuming the voice and persona of a Eurovision song contest announcer he answered, "Hello from Baybridge, come in, Dublin."

"Here are the results from Dublin," answered Dr. Meyers, playing along, "and the winner is, Angela Coughlan."

"Good job, Dublin," came the congratulatory reply.

"We have rewarded her a well-earned ten out of ten." Casting aside the fake role, Dr. Meyers continued. "Oh, Alan, she is such a brave girl. The poor wee thing has had a grueling week. It was made all the worst by her sore mouth. That's resolving now that the chemo is complete. On rounds this morning, she reported her breakfast tasted good, which indicated she can tolerate food orally. Failing to suppress that smile of hers, she slid your duckling book from under the pillow and read her go-to line aloud.

"'*And when the night falls, they swim to their little island and go to sleep.*'

"She then produced the most elaborate turban and coyly placed it on her head. Slightly tilting to the side, she threw her arms in the air and said, 'Ta-da.' I told her she was a star."

"Wow, that duckling book has come in handy to let us know her wishes. Dr. Owens mentioned something about turbans the other day. Is that kind of what you wear?"

"Oh, mine are rags in comparison to this," she answered. "Apparently her neighbor Mrs. Finnerty has set up a foundation in

Angela's name. She used to live in India, and all the turbans are made from Indian fabric. This week's patients from Baybridge brought one for Angela and a few extra. Plenty more for units all over the country in the works. It's great. I hope they can make one for me. Alan, I think our star has given us notice up here and will soon be heading your way. You had better hone your skills, Mr. Bone Doctor."

"All honed and ready, keep us posted," he said, adding, "you're the *star*."

"Aww," said Dr. Meyers as she hung up.

Angela sat silently when Dr. Meyers left earlier. Her parents noticed her withdrawal while resisting the urge to ask questions. "I'm just going down to check on the chariot," Tony said, using it as an excuse to give mother and daughter some time alone. "Want anything from the cafeteria or the dreaded snack machine?" He took the silence that followed as a no. Caroline moved to the chair beside the bed and continued leafing through the pages of her glossy magazine. Angela spoke when she was ready.

"Amelia needs a turban. I won't wear mine until she gets one. Mammy, can I talk to Mrs. Finnerty? Can we ring her now? I just must find out if there are any more made yet. I could give Amelia this one, but I know we can't share things. Please, Mammy, can we just ask Mrs. Finnerty?" She was pleading now. Caroline sat quietly, listening to her daughter, and was not at all surprised at her selfless generosity and concern for her friend two rooms down.

"I think it would be a great treat for Mrs. Finnerty to hear your voice. If we hurry, we might catch Amy before school too." She punched in the number as she spoke. She knew that Amelia would get her turban this morning. Mrs. Finnerty deserved the chance to tell Angela that herself.

Marion Duffy, the unit social worker, popped her head around the yellow door of Number Four Happy Street. "Amelia says thank you for the special turban," she quietly said into the room as Angela put her own back on her head.

CHAPTER 54

Amy was so excited after Angela's phone call that she skipped ahead of Mrs. Finnerty all the way to school, schoolbag bobbing up and down on her slim shoulders. Other children skipped down the road, knowing that in less than two weeks school would close and the summer holidays would begin. She had an added bounce in her step because there was a hint, somewhere in that phone call, that Angela was coming home soon. This time she would be home for ages because Dr. Alan was going to get rid of the lump. It must be really small by now, she decided, hardly a lump at all. Hurray!

Mrs. Finnerty, though very happy about Angela's progress, was unnerved by the call. Thank God they had more than one turban to send to Park Edge when they sent Angela's. Fat lot of good that was as nobody thought to tell her, notably Mrs. Finnerty herself. Once again, it was the child who pointed out the flaws in the current system. Spurred into action Mrs. Finnerty called Tara Doherty again. "Hello, Tara? Not too early?"

"Don't be daft, I have a day's work done. How are things in Baybridge?" Tara asked.

"It's not Baybridge so much that's the problem, it's the rest of the country. I just got off the phone with Angela, and I am ashamed to admit that without realizing it she highlighted the flaws in our system. That is, even if we have a system," replied Mrs. Finnerty. She went on to explain how Amelia needed a turban and how upset Angela was to the point of not wearing her own because she didn't have one for her. "The social worker had the extra turbans we sent, but Angela did not know that." Getting more worked up, she continued, "Tara, this was a poor attempt on my part, inept at best. It took a call from a child's hospital bed to wake me up to that fact. It is Angela's foundation after all, and it must meet her standards."

Silence. Tara poured another cup of tea and waited. With the dead air ringing in her ears, she announced, "Simple business practice, Mrs. Finnerty, supply and demand. A change to a business model is what's needed. It's obvious that a turban here and a turban there is not what we are dealing with. An increase in production is what is called for, which will require more staff and, ultimately, an effective delivery system."

"The train service is reliable between Baybridge, through Haymarket, and onto Dublin," offered Mrs. Finnerty.

"It is on that route. It's a start and worth a try. Now storage is the next hurdle," added Tara.

The more they spoke, the more it became apparent that this could not be fixed in one phone call. Mrs. Finnerty suggested a meeting in Haymarket. "Grand," replied Tara. "Bring Amy, take her out of school for a day. By the way, your special order is almost ready to ship. Brilliant idea from Amy.

"Without Amy, we wouldn't be making turbans at all. Now go buy a computer and look for a small factory for us."

Amy was still in high spirits as she ate her after-school snack. Mrs. Finnerty spent the afternoon mulling the business over and over in her mind. While watching Amy savor Mrs. Quigley's delights, she suddenly remembered something from her last visit to the football field. An impulsive invite to take a walk up there was accepted by Amy with enthusiasm. Mrs. Miller, sitting in her usual spot, gave them both the raised-eyebrow treatment as they giggled past her. She just couldn't keep up with them all anymore. Having made that decision, she lowered the eyebrow, closed both eyes against the early evening sun, and resumed purring.

Mrs. Finnerty saw it from the end of the road that led up to the club, a white-washed two-storied structure situated a short distance from the road they were now on. An overgrown path seemed to lead to the front door. Old but sturdy was Mrs. Finnerty's impression. Amy didn't seem to notice it at all and skipped ahead. By now the noise of Gaelic football filled their ears as they hurried to Mrs. Finnerty's spot on the bench. She took a deep cleansing breath as she sat. It had rained earlier, the last drops still wet and glistening like small diamonds on the grass in the evening sun. By now Amy had sought out Cara and Matthew, who attempted to kick a ball like the team players in the wet grass.

Mrs. Finnerty looked around for Mark or Fiona. She didn't see them. Sitting there, she began to plan a future for that forgotten white house. She laid it out clearly in her mind. If no obstacles presented themselves, she would buy it, renovate it, convert it into an office with meeting space and a conference room. Above its humble front door, a sign would say: "*Welcome to Angela's Tresses and Turbans.*"

That was the evening Mrs. Finnerty had her first dizzy spell.

CHAPTER 55

Amy gave Mrs. Walsh a tour of their house prior to the arrival of Nuala and her cleaning crew. Mrs. Walsh was adamant that Angela's parents' privacy be respected. Mrs. Finnerty agreed. Amy's job was to point out the areas upstairs used by herself and her sister. The downstairs was easier to figure out. When Caroline came home, she and Nuala would come to their own arrangement. For now, they were expected weekly. "Don't forget to tell them about the handwashing and how Angela can't get an infection," instructed Amy as they came downstairs.

Mrs. Walsh replied, "I will not, Amy, isn't that why I asked for your help today, to make sure nothing important was left out?"

"We use a lot of towels. Will they wash towels, do you think?" inquired Amy.

"I'll ask them," came the reply. By now they had reached the front door. "Thanks to you, Amy, I have a much-better idea of what is needed in the house. You go on over to Mrs. Finnerty's now, take the key with you. I will stay and lock the door behind me when the job is done. Good girl, Amy."

The phone rang. Mrs. Finnerty was surprised to hear Mark Hannon's voice. "Evening, Mrs. Finnerty," he greeted. "All is well with you and Amy, I trust? The mobile library is ready to roll, looks good too. I was wondering if you wanted me to hang on to it or bring it up? I know Angela is still in Dublin."

"That's quick work, Mark, thank you," she said. "Would you mind bringing it here? Amy will want to stock it before we roll it over to her house. Angela is expected home in a day or two. Oh, Mark, it's so good of you and Colm to get it done in time. I can't wait to see it."

"Now is as good a time as any, if it's okay," said Mark.

"It is, it is," she replied excitedly.

"What is?" asked Amy as she came into the room.

"You'll see," she said, taking her by the hand. They stood in the open doorway as jittery as two small children. Mark was right. It was a beautiful piece of furniture. It rolled easily on two casters on either end. Inside sat two sturdy bookshelves. A pair of doors opened out and, when closed, were secured by a brass locking latch. As Amy stepped closer, she exclaimed, "It's got 'Mr. Doherty's Gift' painted on the top." Without the slightest hint of shyness, she sprang at Mark and hugged his legs. "Did he ask you to make it for Angela?" she asked. Mark shot a questioning glance at Mrs. Finnerty. Without hesitation, she nodded.

"He did," came the reply. "Cara's dad painted his name on there to remind us. Mr. Doherty would be very pleased that you like it."

Mark showed Amy how to open the doors. Soon she was sitting on the floor surrounded by books. Choosing was hard. If Mark noticed the layout of this house, he made no comment. "Could I take one more minute of your time?" Mrs. Finnerty asked as they moved closer to the still-open front door. In fact, they had barely moved into the room at all. It was reminiscent of the first day Mrs. Walsh had called to the house.

"Of course," he said.

She shared with him her interest in the white house. She discovered that it did not belong to the club, but to a private citizen, a Mr. Foley. Mark didn't know much more about it. Some said it had been a gate house back in the day left to the present owner by his uncle. Nobody knew for sure. "Do you want me to make a few inquiries for you, Mrs. Finnerty?"

"Mark, you have done enough, and you are a busy man. I have business in town in the next few days. I'll ask Mr. Leech to do the leg work," she said. As Mark headed down the driveway to his car, he looked back to find her standing in the doorway, wearing that eager determined look. Feeling absolutely sure that the house would be hers, he shouted, "Welcome to the white house!"

Inspired by Mark's remark, she called Mr. Leech's office on the off chance that either he or one of his two sons would still be there. One of Mr. Leech's boys answered. It was Martin Leech, the youngest son. She explained her interest in the house and her plan for the its future.

"Well, Mrs. Finnerty, that's a fine idea I must say. The gentleman who owns that property is a bit sentimental about it. It goes back a long way in his family, you see. He has kept it in good condition and remains attached to it. For that reason, he has resisted parting with it over the years. He is a wealthy man and does not need to sell. I would like to put your proposal to him and see how he feels. I think this project might just hit the right note with him. As soon as I get his reaction, I will be in touch. Thank you, Mrs. Finnerty. Enjoy the rest of the evening," concluded young Martin Leech.

Mrs. Finnerty was beside herself with anticipation. No wet heavy items on her clothesline today, no sir.

CHAPTER 56

Ms. Flynn sent word with Amy that she needed Mrs. Finnerty to call into the school office at her earliest convenience. After Amy went into class the following morning, Mrs. Finnerty walked down to see Ms. Flynn. She shared an office with four others. In the interest of privacy, they met in a small empty classroom. Sitting at a desk, legs tucked, and knees squashed, Mrs. Finnerty was amused. It had been quite a while since she had been in a classroom. She could not recall ever having sat at a desk, but she must have.

"It's a matter of the turban fund," began Ms. Flynn. She was a tall young woman in her midtwenties. Coiled up, she sat at the desk opposite Mrs. Finnerty. Despite the first impression of intensity, she was pleasant and jovial. Her long dark hair swept back in a ponytail reveled a heart-melting smile. "The contributions have been generous, more than generous, and not everybody who paid into the fund requested a turban. Twenty-two children and seven adults did, however."

"Seven adults you say, are any of them men?" Mrs. Finnerty asked.

"One male adult," explained Ms. Flynn. "He is the teacher's assistant. He often helps in Angela's class. Seven of the children are boys. I have an envelope full of money here, and with school closing soon, I thought it best that you should have it and place the order for the turbans."

"Ms. Flynn, it seems I have made a lot of work for you, and I had no intention of burdening you with this responsibility. To be honest, I did not expect this level of response. Shame on me for not judging our community correctly," said Mrs. Finnerty.

"Oh, I didn't mean it was a bother, no way. I loved doing it. Being part of this community has taught me a lot. I will be sad to leave at the end of the term. I got this assignment through my university as part of my Master's in Social Work program. Nobody, least of all my teachers, expected me to have exposure to such an enlightening endeavor. I hope to find something equally rewarding when school closes. By the way, my name is Una. I think the Ms. Flynn thing was just for the children."

Looking across the desk with absolute confidence, Mrs. Finnerty uttered the words "Ms. Una Flynn, how would you like to continue with Angela's Tresses and Turbans in an administrative capacity? We will soon be opening our offices just around the corner."

"I can't think of anything I would like more," said Una Flynn, the confidence in her voice matching that of Mrs. Finnerty. "I will keep this envelope until our office opens. We do need to order the turbans, however."

Martin Leech called Mrs. Finnerty later that day. He had spoken to Mr. Foley, who confessed that subconsciously he was holding on to the white house for a moment such as this. He had promised his late uncle that he would not sell. In keeping with the spirit of that promise, he would donate the property to the foundation. He admired Mrs. Finnerty's instincts and would be forever grateful to her for making a dream he wasn't aware of come true. Mrs. Finnerty admired Mr. Foley for his recognition of the foundation and its mission. Having the head office in that location, right in the middle of the community where Angela and her supporters lived, made a dream she wasn't aware of come true. Mr. Leech Jr. stated that per Mr. Foley's request she was to be given the keys immediately. Anyone who was prepared to buy a property sight unseen for such a cause deserved the opportunity to proceed unhindered by documents and signatures.

Mrs. Finnerty asked Mark Hannon to accompany her on the maiden voyage to the house. He was excited to be asked. They met at her house and walked up together. The keys had been dropped off earlier by a young man from Leech's office. "You know this house comes with a parcel of land? It abuts the club's property line on two sides. I don't know how far it extends to the main road," chatted Mark as they walked.

"Outdoor space is precious around any building, a place to picnic, play, and enjoy being outside. I would not be in favour of any deviation from that. I see it as an extension of the football club. The white house has been part of this landscape forever. We need to keep it as close to that as possible." As she finished speaking, Mark was turning the key in the lock.

It was unexpectedly bright inside, with high ceilings and exquisite original wood floors. A polished staircase rose up to the left of the entrance, its sturdy carved bannister reassuring the climber. A knotty wood-paneled door opened into a sparsely furnished parlor on the right. A bright hallway led back to the huge kitchen running along the entire width of the building. A window following the line traced the kitchen, drawing it outside, as if relocating it to the foot of the mountain. They both turned to each other in disbelief. It was hard to tear themselves away from the view and mount the stairs. The upstairs was traditionally laid out with all three bedrooms offering the same draw to the mountain through large windows. Without speaking, they returned to the ground floor and walked outside. To say that the house was amazing exceeding all expectations; a gem and a substantial gift only scratch the surface of its significance. They walked home in happy silence, each deep in their own thoughts. Mark wondered how it was possible that he passed this treasure as often and for as long as he did without any interest. Mrs. Finnerty, unaware of what Mark was thinking, knew exactly why that house had never been sold. It was Angela's.

CHAPTER 57

Amy and Mrs. Finnerty were laying out an after-school outfit when the doorbell rang. Eager to take an extra spin in the lift, Amy offered to answer it. Mrs. Walsh hovered on the doorstep. Sure of what she should do, Amy asked her in. Unsure of what she should do, Mrs. Walsh continued to hover. She changed her handbag from one arm to the other a couple of times before being put somewhat more at ease by the arrival of Mrs. Finnerty.

"Mrs. Walsh, come in, fresh tea in the pot, just made. Come on back." Halfway through the library, she realised she was alone. Looking back over her shoulder, she saw Amy staring at Mrs. Walsh, who was staring at the room. She recognised the trance and, knowing that it would last a while, she proceeded to the kitchen, poured a cup of tea, and took it back to the visitor who was close enough to sit down at the table in the reader's corner. Amy was dispatched to finish the task of deciding what to wear for Angela's homecoming. Mrs. Finnerty sat down minus her own cup of tea. She wondered if the recovery would take long as it was almost time for school. When the guest remembered that it was her habit not to comment on other people's décor, she said, "Nice books." Daintily sipping, she continued, "I need to pop in with some new towels next door. Amy was saying that they use a lot. Can't have enough towels, I find, not in any house. Nuala rang asking if we knew yet when the Coughlans were coming home. They need to cook and stock the fridge." One more dainty sip, and the cup was back on the saucer. No evidence remained of the shock the poor woman suffered earlier.

"Later today, we just heard last night. Oh my! is that short notice for the food? I am sorry. I didn't think about that. I was pre-occupied preparing Amy for this evening," confessed Mrs. Finnerty.

"No bother," came the easy reply. "That's why I called into you early in case you had word. They are doing simple popular dishes until they get to know the family's tastes. The fridge is spotless and will be stocked with staples today," Mrs. Finnerty went on to explain.

"That was a brilliant idea of yours, Mrs. Walsh, to engage Nuala and her husband. Otherwise, I would be running around in a scramble this afternoon, seeing as food was the farthest thing from my mind. I am trying to time it right. Amy must be fed, showered, and put into clean clothes before they arrive. Can't have her hugging Angela still wearing her school uniform. We don't know if they are even on the road yet."

Is it my imagination, or is Mrs. Finnerty a bit flustered? thought Mrs. Kitty Walsh.

"It'll be fine. They will probably give you a ring when they are on the road. It's not a quick thing getting out of the hospital, you know. I'll put in a call to Nuala when I go next door. Good thing I thought to wash the towels." Then she was gone. In less than a minute, she was back. Mrs. Finnerty held up the Coughlans key when she caught sight of her. Reaching to take it, Mrs. Walsh said, "We're a right pair." Mrs. Finnerty agreed.

"Yes, we are indeed, we are a right pair. Speaking of pair, I want you to look at something with me, maybe when you finish next door."

"Right so. I'll be done there by the time you drop Amy. Remind me to return the key." They separated, smiling.

With another key in hand, both ladies went for a walk. Small talk filled the space between them as Mrs. Finnerty took Mrs. Walsh to the white house. A matter-of-fact atmosphere prevailed as they stood inside the front door. Without comment, together they toured the house as Mark and Mrs. Finnerty had done. They finally settled in the spacious sunlit kitchen. Mrs. Finnerty produced two scones and two small coffees from the bag she carried. It would not be possible for an onlooker to distinguish hostess from guest as they ate. Equal would be the verdict.

The silence was finally broken by Mrs. Finnerty as she addressed her friend. "Asking Grainne to do everybody's hair was nothing short of genius. As you know, hair is an issue for chemo patients. Unknown to you at the time I was giving that a lot of thought due to a chance remark made by Amy. She saw a piece of Indian fabric at my house one day. Admiring it, she suggested it would make a nice hat. Right there, kneeling on the floor, studying the material, the turban idea came to me, and thus, a Foundation known as Angela's Tresses and Turbans was born. Grainne and others already served chemo patients. They welcomed the opportunity to network and expand those services That's the Tresses part of the foundation."

Mrs. Walsh raised her paper cup from its midair position to her mouth and took a long sip before asking, "Did Jim Foley give this house to the foundation?"

Nodding, Mrs. Finnerty answered, "Yes, and the land."

"At last, his uncle's home found a home." Kitty Walsh's eyes sparkled. Mrs. Finnerty continued without comment on the relationship between the Walshes and the Foleys.

"We are having the first cuppa in what is to be the head office. As you said, we're a right pair." They clinked their paper cups in a toast to each other. "You are managing Angela's purse with such skill and imagination, it astounds me. Your ability to sense the Coughlans' needs is uncanny, and you have fire and determination in meeting them. I know it's your priority currently, and I have no wish to pry. The foundation is a distinct and independent entity. You have an honest way with people, compassionate in a practical way, and you understand money. The foundation needs a treasurer." Mrs. Finnerty paused, took a sip of cold coffee, and picked at the edges of her scone. She waited. Kitty Walsh stood up and walked to the window. She felt like she was halfway up the mountain in that effortless walk. She shared her thoughts with its majestic apex.

"This is a good thing you are doing, and Jim Foley knows it. The work will go on forever. Angela's Purse is for now. It's a way to ease the burden on Angela and her family. People stop me all the time with their donations. Giving helps them too. It is bigger than Angela. With God's help, she will heal and grow and fulfill her dreams. The people who contributed will remember their small part in her success. The purse is a temporary vehicle, the foundation is permanent. It would be a privilege to be a part of that."

Mrs. Finnerty joined her at the window; they looked so solemn, that they might have been praying.

"Then we had better get over to Haymarket and find out how the production team is spending your money. That's where the turbans are made. Right now, Tara Doherty is out shopping for a factory. We'll take Amy with us." Mrs. Finnerty had spoken!

Did either of them notice that they just spent time in a spacious kitchen, not exactly what you'd expect for a boardroom in the head office of a foundation? Nah! Both their clotheslines boasted silk and lace today. Why go looking for a wet blanket?

CHAPTER 58

Amy sat on the footstool, her summer dress and turban matching. She noticed Angela's pink tracksuit. It was new. Amy thought how lovely her sister looked in pink. Her turban had some of the same shade in it. They were admiring the mobile bookcase. ""Do you want to put the books from your bag on the shelves?" asked Amy.

"Oh yeah, except the duckling book, I'll keep that one with me" came the quiet reply. Angela's voice betrayed her fatigue.

"Well I know that, silly," said Amy. As she stood to open the door of the bookcase, she asked, "Have you seen what's written on the top?"

"Written? Did somebody write on it?" questioned her sister.

"I mean painted," Amy explained. "Did nobody show you?"

"There was such fussing going on when we arrived, nobody had the time. Some people were here talking about cleaning and food. I just sat in here to wait for you and Mrs. Finnerty. What does it say?"

"It says 'Mr. Doherty's Gift,'" declared Amy. Mrs. Finnerty said he wanted to make it for you before...you know. So Mr. Hannon and Cara's dad made it instead. Cara's dad painted that, so we wouldn't forget."

"I didn't even know him, and he wanted me to have a mobile library. I bet Mrs. Finnerty had a hand in that. Can I see?" Angela said, easing herself to a standing position.

"She did," Amy replied, pushing the bookshelves closer.

"It's lovely," said Angela, using it for support. "Why is everyone so kind to me? There are lots of sick kids."

"Yeah, but you're *our* sick kid, and everyone wants you better soon," answered Amy. A sadness came over Angela. Amy, quick to fix that, asked, "Aren't you wondering how we got it into the house before you got home? It wasn't easy, you know. Mr. Hannon brought it to Mrs. Finnerty's first. Today after school I pushed it towards the front door, and she walked backways."

"Backways?" interrupted Angela. "Backways?"

"Yes," explained Amy. I was walking front ways and she was walking backways. I was pushing, and she was pulling."

"Backwards, you mean. She had her back to the door," Angela said through a smile.

"That's what I said silly, until we came to the top step. Then we were stuck." No holding back now! Angela let out a loud laugh, which meant Amy did too. Through their familiar sputters, Angela asked.

"What did ye do?"

"I said, why don't we go out the side door and go around the house like Mrs. Miller does? That's what we did, and that's how we came into our house too."

"So now *you* had to go backways." Too much, the outburst of laughter brought Caroline and Mrs. Finnerty to the front room. Tissues were needed for tears of laughter. Once the reason for the jocularity was made known, her good, friendly neighbour feigned hurt, saying, "Oh, I could have fallen backways out my own front door." she wailed, tickled pink at the word, *backways*. Caroline had to quiet them, including Mrs. Finnerty. She caught her breath, let the girls settle, then said, "My goodness, you two are a right pair. Angela, the demand for the turbans has grown a lot in recent days. I am so sorry I made the mistake of not telling you about the extra turbans we sent to Park Edge. That caused you to worry unnecessarily about Amelia. You made me realize I was approaching this as an amateur. I have since been advised that it needs to be handled like a business. So progress has been made along those lines but not yet finalised. I hope to have lots of news about your foundation in a few days. Mrs. Walsh is helping us now. She and I are another right pair. We are going over to Haymarket where the turbans are made. We need more space, we need a factory. Amy, your mammy said you came with us if you like."

Amy stood up and went to stand behind Angela's chair. Placing her hands gently on her sister's shoulders, she lowered her chin to rest on the top of her turban, thus stacking their two turbans, which framed their beautiful faces. The adults beheld a tableau of youthful strength and resolve. Then Amy said, "No, thank you, if it's all the same. When Angela is well enough to travel, we will go together to the factory and see her turbans being made. The two of us will go with you then." She bent down and kissed the side of her sister's turban as close as she could to her cheek. In an instance, Amy made it clear that this was Angela's foundation.

"That a much-better idea," replied Mrs. Finnerty. The effort to be casual was almost too much for her, Caroline noticed.

"Girls, we let our tea get cold running up to you two scoundrels. Come on, time to brew a fresh pot." She ushered her friend back along the hallway and urged her to sit when they reached the table.

"You have two extraordinary daughters. Congratulations to you and Tony," said the now-recovered friend.

"They can knock the socks off a person, I'll give you that. They are like two wise auld grannies and two giggling kids all at the same time. I don't know where they get it from," said Caroline. By now the fresh tea was made, and a few biscuits appeared. Before either of them got a chance to continue their conversation, both the girls appeared in the kitchen door. Angela took the nearest chair while, as before, Amy stood behind.

Angela asked, "Would it be hard to put a duckling on each turban, like a sign it was from our foundation?" Stunned silence followed before Mrs. Finnerty replied.

"You mean a logo?"

"I told you that's what is was called, Angela," Amy whispered around the back of the chair. "A logo."

"Mrs. Shiva in Haymarket can do anything. She is the designer. Dr. Myers is getting a special grown-up turban by special messenger, she may have it already She even made one turban for a boy. It's a bit different, more like the headwear worn by an Indian maharaja. Mrs. Hannon told us of a boy here in Baybridge who needed it. Grainne took it to him, and it made him smile. His name is Marty, and he is seven years old. That's what your turbans do, Angela, they make the children smile. The duckling will make their eyes sparkle."

CHAPTER 59

The day before the trip to Haymarket, Fiona was at her desk. "You called, your highness?" she said, picking up the phone. Brenda answered, "I'm glad you remembered your place." Her attempt at sounding regal felt short, so she gave up. "I have a Mrs. Garvey here, wondering if you are in. Are you in?"

"I'm in. Any idea what it's about?" asked Fiona.

"She didn't say, only asked if you were in," replied Brenda.

"Okay, I'll be right there," said Fiona, adding, "is the conference room free?"

"All yours," confirmed Brenda.

Fiona ushered the visitor into the conference room. They both sat on the nearest chairs clustered together at one corner of the long mahogany table. As close as they were, Mrs. Garvey leaned towards Fiona as she spoke. She was casually dressed in a floral maxi dress and chic sandals, her recent visit to the beauty salon evident by the manicured toenails. Not so with her hair. Her head was a mass of unruly ringlet curls, brazenly advancing down one side of her face. Any attempt to tame the mass, futile. Nevertheless, their natural beauty was an eye-catcher. "My name is Sammy Garvey, Samantha, but nobody calls me that. Anyway, I live on the Hill, two doors down from wee Marty McKenna. I heard that it was through you that he got his lovely little turban. You have no idea what a change has come over him since then." She paused for a breath, one hand making a brave effort to clear the curly mop from her face. Fiona knew where she lived, not because of Marty, but because she said she lived on the Hill. It was a housing development at the top of a hill on the opposite side of town. The houses were set out in a horseshoe shape surrounding a patch of green grass where children played. Those who lived there came into their shop when she was a child. Their children and grandchildren still lived there. The women of the Hill were the reason she was sitting here today wearing a social worker's name tag. Sammy Garvey's mother and grandmother were regular customers. They, like so many others, worked hard to keep their homes together, to clothe, feed, and nurture large families with dignity. Her mother was part of that. So too was Fiona. Sammy Garvey continued, "A few of us were admiring Marty's turban. He took it off, so we could get a closer look at how it was made. Four of us are good dressmakers, we learned out of necessity, I suppose. My grandmother taught me when I was a wee nipper. I took to it straight away. She made clothes for the neighbours and their kids, very good she was too. Sometimes people paid her, but if they couldn't, it didn't stop her."

"I knew your grandmother, she came into our shop once or twice a week," said Fiona.

"She was great friends with your mother. I remember your father too. One time he fixed our Stevie's bike. He was a holy terror on that bike. Your father showed him how to fix it for the next time. After that he was always showing off that he knew all about bikes," Sammy said.

"Daddy was good with bikes, all right. We would have been lost without them growing up, that's for sure," added Fiona. They talked a while longer about old times. Sammy then explained the reason for the visit.

"Four of us would like to offer our services in the making of the turbans. We studied Marty's, and we feel it's within our grasp. I came on their behalf to find out how to go about it." Those unfamiliar with the women of the Hill would have been astonished at this offer. Not Fiona. She knew them well, knew their raw generosity. Those that had shared with those in need today. They fully understood that their turn would come tomorrow. They bore witness to the well-known adage "There go I but for the grace of God."

Fiona made a phone call. Mrs. Finnerty met Sammy Garvey for the first time over the phone. Sammy Garvey made her first visit to Haymarket the very next day. Mrs. Walsh was delighted with the addition. On the way there, the right pair became a threesome. There was one condition, Sammy was not to be called Mrs. Garvey, a request that endeared the newcomer to them.

They arrived late morning and parked by the river. Though some tourists were apparent with their colorfully framed sunglasses and cameras, the town was relatively quiet. Soon school would be out, and Haymarket would be assaulted. Parking where they now parked was a mere pipe dream, and walking three abreast along the river path, impossible. Boats, barges, yachts, and all manner of cabin vessels were about to arrive and obscure the view of the water by their sheer numbers. Most importantly, the chance of getting a pot of tea, toast, scone, and jam all made on the premises of the most famous café in all of Ireland was nil.

Not so today. Sitting there savoring the smell of baking bread and tasting the scones and jam, Mrs. Finnerty brought the others up-to-date. "When I spoke with Tara yesterday to confirm we were coming today, she had two pieces of news. All the turbans for Angela's school are ready, we can bring them back with us. They chose the school colors for the fabric. She found our factory. "It's a surprise," she said. "I can hardly wait. Tara's idea of a surprise in not everyone's, so brace yourselves. I told her we had a few surprises of our own. She and Mrs. Shiva will need to brace themselves. They may have found a factory, we were given a white house with a beautiful ready-made work space."

Visions of light colorful fabric draped over clotheslines filled their minds as they scooped up the last of their jam-covered scones.

CHAPTER 60

The clear view of the river from this vantage point, undulating like a silk scarf through green banks, took their breath away. The space was an enormous sunlight loft recently vacated by an artist. Reminders of that lingered. Splashes of paint on long narrow tables, spattered wood floors, doorknobs with permanent colorful fingerprints, and a few abandoned easels against one wall. To say that you could smell the drying canvases was not an exaggeration. It provoked their creativity, inspired their artistic spirits, and initiated a new attitude. Their turbans were works of art individually crafted by hand. The children wearing them would react as if owning a painting by an old master, their souls elevated with hope. Angela's Tresses and Turbans in an instant became a school of artists. Tara Doherty did not fail to surprise. The surprise would also be on her if she knew the depth of what she had awakened.

Exhilarated and hungry, they accepted Mrs. Shiva's invitation to lunch at her house. The Baybridge visitors followed Tara as she and Mrs. Shiva traveled together. Tara was driving today because she and Mrs. Finnerty had planned to visit Mr. Doherty's grave later in the day. Silence prevailed in the Baybridge car. Each thought the other was admiring the town, glancing out the window at something of interest. Not so. All three were reliving their experience in the loft, stretching that realization of being artists far into the future. Mrs. Walsh did not yet know the extent of the budget. She wondered if it would support the ideas that were chasing around in her head at this moment.

As they arrived at a beautiful house close to the river, Sammy had to put her Baybridge plans aside for now. She knew exactly what she and her three friends were going to do. The budget never entered her mind. "Welcome, make yourselves at home," Mrs. Shiva said. The earlier silence gave way to an outburst of chatter. Mrs. Walsh was first to speak, thus breaking her cardinal rule of not commenting on people's houses or their décor.

"Your house is beautiful, Mrs. Shiva, so bright. Oh, just look at the back garden. There's the river," she added, peering out a nearby bay window. Nobody answered. She didn't notice they too were talking and pointing and stepping on each other's words. It was verbal chaos for the first few minutes.

"Here are the turbans for Angela's school, two extras in the school colors for the girls," Tara interjected. Silence as all eyes focused on the boxes. Soon the verbal chaos started again. Sammy was focusing on the smaller of the two boxes. It contained the maharaja's turbans. She picked up the adult's size, a broad smile on her face, as she carefully examined it. Mrs. Shiva noticed.

"I think we can sit outside today, it's lovely with a nice breeze from the river. Lunch is set out so just help yourselves," she said. An array of salads, fresh bread, cold meats, and fruits for the less-adventurous. A selection of delicate Indian dishes, naan bread, and chutneys for the brave. Sammy was the last the join the others on the patio. It took her by surprise to discover the outdoors was an extension of the indoors, separated by fully retractable glass-panel doors. A smaller version of the kitchen, complete with a built-in brick barbeque, met her eyes. The others were milling around, choosing and praising food. She knew she was from the Hill. Some might say to her, "'Tis far from this you were reared." That was true. She also knew in her heart these words would never pass the lips of anyone in this group of women. She confidently joined the others and shared lunch with them in comfortable ease. Mrs. Finnerty was now ready to share her news from Baybridge. It was a working lunch.

"Ladies, first, Angela is doing well, she's resting now and recovering from the chemo. In a few weeks she will be ready for her operation. Both girls love their turbans and wear them proudly. We invited

Amy to come with us today. She was quite adamant about this being Angela's project and said they would come together when the time was right. Angela had one request, a logo, a duckling on each turban. She uses a book about ducklings searching for a home to communicate with the doctors. The surgeon who is doing the operation lent it to her when they first met. I don't think it's on loan anymore. I assured her that our designer Mrs. Shiva could do anything. Am I right?" A pause in eating and drinking as they focused on the speaker. There was no doubt as to who their fearless leader was. "Can you do anything, Mrs. Designer?" A round of applause concluded in Mrs. Shiva accepting the position of design director. Their fearless leader continued. "Mrs. Doherty, congratulations on the loft. It's perfect, just perfect. More of that in a moment. We already refer to you as the production manager. That all right with you?" Another round of applause and a curtsy from Tara. "Now let me introduce Mrs. Walsh to you. She is successfully managing Angela's Purse, distributing locally donated funds to the Coughlan family, helping defray their extra expenses currently. Mrs. Walsh agreed to be our treasurer as Angela's Purse, God willing, has an expiry date." Applause and a wave from Mrs. Walsh concluded that bit of business. "Now the big news. Sammy, brace yourself. Mr. Foley, a generous and kind man, gifted the white house near the football club to the foundation. Mrs. Walsh and I spent some time there a few days ago. When we entered the loft today we had a similar experience. Both spaces are flooded with light, bringing the outdoors in. In Baybridge the sheep grazing on the nearby mountain seemed close enough to touch. The view from the loft leads one to believe they are sailing the river. We have found our creative spaces. We have also found our office space in the white house. Una Flynn, who currently works in Angela's school, will be joining us as administrator when her term there ends. Her placement at the school was part of her training as a social worker. Her diligent attention to our cause launched the school turban project She is excited to be continuing that work. Sammy, Baybridge needs a production branch. The sunny room in the white house is the perfect place and you are the perfect person to manage it." Sammy was stunned, sitting there in silence, until a burst of applause and cheers urged her acceptance. Without any sign of reluctance, she addressed Mrs. Shiva.

"One of the girls in our group, Kitsy Kelly, draws a lot. She's very good. If Angela could let her see the duckling book, she could do a few sketches, and Angela can make her choice for the logo. We could make them in Baybridge and then send them to Haymarket. I think we would be very good at making the maharaja turbans too."

Sammy did know exactly what she and her friends were going to do.

CHAPTER 61

The journey back to Baybridge was beckoning Mrs. Finnerty. Afternoon sunshine illuminating the landscape, partnered with a gentle breeze, soothed her. No doubt it had been a wonderful day. To witness a bond forming effortlessly between the ladies was a gift to her. Angela's foundation sat on solid ground. Still, she had to admit to being tired. A dizzy spell at the top of Mrs. Shiva's stairs causing her to grip the bannister alarmed her at the time. Now that the three of them were settled comfortably in Mrs. Walsh's car, she put that episode down to tiredness. Oh! And all that talking.

Remembering the visit to Mr. Doherty's grave surprisingly comforted her. She did not discuss Sammy's ideas with her; instead, she allowed the image of Kitsy Kelly—a person she had not yet met, poring over the duckling book and subsequent sketches with Angela and Amy—to germinate in her mind. The scene progressed like a favourite movie clip. Her fellow passengers smiled at the sound of her snoring. Their fearless leader was fast asleep. Once again, a silence lulled by Mrs. Finnerty's breathing prevailed in the car.

A few more miles and they would be home. The spire of the old church near the medical centre looming above the city came into view. Then the soothing rhythm in the car was replaced by a sort of moist grunting. Mrs. Walsh glanced over at Mrs. Finnerty and then to the back seat. Sammy leaned forward. Without the need for conversation Mrs. Walsh pulled the car over. Sammy was out of the car and at the passenger seat in one step. Gently nudging her, she said, "Mrs. Finnerty, Mrs. Finnerty, we're home, it's time to wake up." Silently she prayed for a response. A slight flicker of one eyelid and a futile attempt at stirring was what she got. "That's good Mrs. Finnerty, that's good. We need to make a wee stop on the way, just a bit of a detour." While saying this, she noticed Mrs. Finnerty's right arm laying limp as if it no longer belonged to her. Her mouth drooped at one corner. Mrs. Walsh understood the detour reference. Sammy now in the back seat continued her calm reassurances. They made their way past the most visible church in Baybridge, the one where Mr. Doherty had once parked his car, and went straight to the ambulance ramp at the Casualty Department. Sammy ran in and made no bones about the urgency of the situation. Sister O'Brian appeared. Mrs. Walsh explained what had happened in the car just a few minutes ago. All was now under control.

Mrs. Walsh and Sammy sat in the waiting room. They had been a threesome for less than a day. How was that possible? The anguish they suffered sitting there was that of a family member or lifelong friend. Mrs. Walsh spoke first when the obvious questions occurred to her. "Sammy, they won't tell us anything you know. They can't. Should we be calling someone? Will they know who to call?"

"They will, it will be in her medical chart. We will wait though, she might come out of it," answered Sammy.

"Oh, please, God, please, God, she does," prayed Mrs. Walsh.

She did. At Mrs. Finnerty's request, Sister O'Brian came to get them later. At first glance, Mrs. Finnerty looked the worse for wear; her right arm lay as if it couldn't be bothered. Her smile, through twinkling eyes, made one side of her mouth droop like it couldn't be bothered either. While Mrs. Finnerty smiled, her visitors cried. When Sister O'Brian assured them, their quick response had made a good outcome more than likely, they cried even more. "As with all things Mrs. Finnerty, we now call Fiona Hannon," Sister O'Brian said as she chuckled and winked at the visitors.

They left the hospital, made their way to the car, now in a regular parking spot. It was laden down with turbans in St. Paul's school colours, bales and bales of fabric for future creations, and the memory of Mrs. Finnerty's breathing.

Today's clothesline had winter jumpers, swimsuits, and a soaking-wet blanket all mixed together. Some of that stuff might never dry.

CHAPTER 62

Mrs. Hennessy kissed her husband goodbye on the doorstep. He proudly drove in his posh car to his luxurious showroom. She was equally proud of her old banger, which took her to Baybridge Medical Centre where she volunteered several times a week. Before marrying Mrs. Hennessy, she worked as a social worker in Dublin. They met at a fund-raiser, a whirlwind long-distance courtship ensued, resulting in the wedding of the century in Baybridge, then the volunteering and fund raising began in earnest.

First stop was at Admissions where a list of new patients awaited her. "Good morning, Margo," greeted Dorthey Hennessy. Being in the presence of Margo from Admissions wasn't always easy. Unawares, she had the ability to unnerve the calmest of peoples. It's important to point out that Margo, despite her title, did not interact with the general public; hers was purely an inside job. She oversaw all records, written and electronic. The introduction of the latter served only to enhance her anxious demeanor. Mrs. Hennessy loved Margo, explaining that there was just something about her, when asked why.

"Oh, is it that time already?" she said. It was more of a discovery statement that an actual question. Mrs. Hennessy didn't answer, just waited. "Here's your list, Mrs. Hennessy, six for you this morning." She spoke as if she was personally responsible for the fate of the listed people. The mixture of compassion for those admitted and her efficiency for tracking them kept Margo in employment all these years.

Mrs. Hennessy's pen hovered over the page as she completed the Volunteer Visit Sheet for each new patient. The name under the stalled pen was Mrs. Rebecca Finnerty. Though they were not fast friends, their paths crossed at Baybridge Literary Society meetings. She was also a generous donor. Because of the location of her unit in relation to the other admissions. she would be the last visit. *Good,* thought Mrs. Hennessy.

Sitting in an armchair, Mrs. Finnerty smiled in recognition of her visitor. She did not need the name tag or the volunteer jacket to help her. A good sign following a stroke. Her speech was clear, although her mouth drooped as she said, "Dorothy, how lovely. It's your visiting day."

"Rebecca, let me have a look at you, sitting up in your chair. How do you feel this morning?"

"Well, I think. They say I am doing well so I had better believe them. This arm of mine has gone a bit astray" came the surprisingly witty answer."

"That's the spirit, Rebecca, let the staff worry about the arm. Those therapists can do wonders especially with a fighter like you with a rogue arm."

"So they tell me. I am due to see them sometime today. Dorothy, please sit over here beside me. Mrs. Walsh and a new lady, Sammy, came with me to Haymarket yesterday. We had a wonderful day. You know we are making turbans for the children." Dorothy Hennessy did know and nodded reassuringly, as Mrs. Finnerty expressed her concerns. "I am unclear as to how we left things. The children in Angela's class need those turbans. I think Mrs. Walsh has them." As if by divine intervention, Fiona Hannon appeared in the doorway. Entering the room, she said, "Morning, ladies, what a treat to see you both." Dorothy, glad as always to see Fiona framed in the doorway of a patient's room, returned the greeting.

"Rebecca was bringing me up-to-date on her trip to get the turbans for Angela's school," explained Dorothy.

"Yes, I hear you filled all the positions over lunch and gave a good accounting of the progress to date," said Fiona. "Mrs. Walsh took the turbans to Una Flynn at the school yesterday. Apparently, the plan is for Angela's class to wear theirs as they parade out on sports day tomorrow. Best bit of news is that the Baybridge Star is covering that event as usual. This year they are also doing an editorial piece on Angela and the foundation. I didn't say a word to Declan I promise. You know my brother when it comes to a local story. According to Cate, he has been looking for an angle for a while now. The sports day was the perfect opportunity."

"Your brother will give us a good boost, his editorials are hand-picked. We are lucky but not surprised. He has always advocated for cancer patients," said Dorothy.

By now Fiona and Dorothy were sitting on opposite sides of the armchair. She looked directly at Dorothy, her eyes clearly indicating that her help would be needed in dealing with the next matter. Dorothy's demeanor said yes. Fiona continued, "Angela and Amy will need their new turbans for tomorrow. Word has it that Angela is going to surprise her friends by sitting on the bench on the far side of the playground away from the crowd. Ms. Flynn intends to walk the class down to her all wearing St. Paul's turbans. It would be best if Dorothy and Mrs. Walsh went to the Coughlins today while Amy is at school. Dorothy can explain how well you are doing resting in hospital. The new turbans and sports day plans will be a distraction for the girls when Amy gets home. Would you both be okay with that plan?"

"I know that nobody can replace you Rebecca. Your relationship with the Coughlin's has no equal. Angela's foundation is part of your core forever. Your leadership will sustain it for many, many years to come. Right now, that energy and love of yours is needed for your own healing. One week from today, you will be well on your way to recovery, and all this will be just a blur. Let me stand in for you for a while. No decision other than where to put a box will be made without your permission." Dorothy's pleading ended.

Mrs. Finnerty attempted to raise her hand in reply. She nodded instead. Her right arm slipped over the side of the armchair. She looked at it. As she looked back to Fiona and Dorothy, her expression was that of someone caught drinking a glass of wine with their cornflakes or not wearing any underwear or caught eating a giant bar of Cadbury's Chocolate one square at a time. It was shame. Dorothy repositioned her arm. Mrs. Finnerty fell asleep in the armchair, crying and feeling ashamed. Two kind nurses put her back to bed. Shame signaled the first step in Mrs. Finnerty's recovery.

CHAPTER 63

Madge Costello, the original donor to Angela's purse, was deeply upset about Mrs. Finnerty's stroke. It had nothing to do with the things she did. For Madge, it was the woman herself. In her opinion, this lady now lying in a hospital bed was the finest human being she had ever met. Madge hatched a plan.

She attended the sports day at St. Paul's. Her children by now had grown out of that school. She captured the spirit and sights of the day with her camera. She clicked away through Mrs. Finnerty's eyes, recording that which would be of interest to her. Kitsy Kelly spent a whole morning with Angela and Amy sketching and choosing the duckling logo. Madge was there transmitting the drawing, the erasing, the faces, the frowns, the smiles, the laughter, and ultimately the final choice though the camera to Mrs. Finnerty. Caroline Coughlan was so pleased with Nuala's cleaning services at her house, that she hired them to do a massive spring clean at the white house. Madge was there with the camera to record their efforts. She managed to gain access to Nora's nook on the day Angela had her appointment with Dr. Alan to discuss surgical options and set the date for the operation. Angela placed a turban ceremoniously on Nora's head. She was invited by Grainne to accompany her when she went to style another little boy's hair, capturing the moment he first donned the maharaja's turban. His smile was transformative. The last photo before she took her camera to the photography shop in town was Sammy arranging bales of fabric in the clean bright work space overlooking the mountain at the rear of the white house. Sammy wanted to know if Mrs. Finnerty would agree to it being called the Bright

House. Madge agreed to ask. She stopped at the Baybridge Star office and as prearranged picked up the pristine copy of the paper containing the sports day photos and the editorial. The marvelous photography man at the shop praised the captions she had composed for each photo. The album would be ready in two days.

Unaware of visitor restrictions for Mrs. Finnerty, Madge approached a nurse with unassuming confidence. Something about the charm of Madge's request to see Mrs. Finnerty resulted in her being ushered to the bedside without question. Madge approached, not knowing she was the only nonstaff person to gain entry since the patience's admission. At first Madge thought she had strayed into a section of the botanical gardens. Mrs. Finnerty, by no means a small woman, was dwarfed by the surrounding foliage. Peeing above a monster vase of roses, she exclaimed in delight, "Mrs. Costello, you broke in, good for you." Madge took this to be about the array of flowers and replied, "I did, I thought for a minute there I was in the hospital greenhouse."

"Might as well be," answered her friend with a lopsided smile. "Not for long, though. Marian, the young volunteer, will distribute them wherever she sees a need, children's ward, hospice, or just to someone feeling a bit lonely. She knows best. She gathers up the cards and helps do the thank-you notes for me. There's a pile in the drawer there right now. It's time-consuming with everything else she must do. Anyway, make your way around here and sit by me."

When Madge presented Mrs. Finnerty with a pictorial record of recent events, she had a moment of doubt. She wondered if she had made a big mistake. The silence in the room was deafening. This was her project, hers alone. Her tribute to a woman like no other. She waited, hardly breathing, for a response. Mrs. Finnerty went back to the first page of the album and read each caption aloud, adding her own commentary. The smile on her face, though a little off centre, broadened, highlighting her twinkling eyes. All was well. They pored over every detail more than once. They concluded there was no favourite photo. When they came to the pictures of Sammy and the bales of fabric, an overwhelming yes was elicited to naming the white house the Bright House. Not wishing to crumple the newspaper, they decided waiting to spread it on a table was the best way to go. Madge said, "I could iron it for you," causing Mrs. Finnerty to do a sort of heehaw laugh, which made them both laugh even more. Before leaving, she added, "I will come in the mornings after the kids go to school. We will make a start on your thank-you cards. I can address the envelopes while you go to physio if we run over. I will let the nurse know."

Still unaware of visitor restrictions, Madge announced the plan to the nurse as she left. No objections were raised.

Mrs. Finnerty slid the album under her pillow. Wherever and whenever she slept, it would remain under her pillow for the rest of her life.

CHAPTER 64

Dr. Alan glanced at Dr. Owens when Angela asked the question. The appointment today at Nora's Nook, as Dr. Allen's office was now called, was to discuss the final arrangements for the operation. Dr. Owens was present to reinforce his part in the postoperative plan and to reassure and support Caroline and Tony. Mostly he was there because he wanted to be. "Mammy said to ask if it was okay to visit Mrs. Finnerty?" Angela asked again filling the silence caused by the two doctors glancing at each other, a glance not missed on Angela. "I have a note to give her. Amy made her a card, so can I?" The surgeon's attention returned as he snapped back to the present and brightly answered.

"I see no harm in a short visit Angela. We'll check to make sure she is not at rehab. Kathleen, call the ward and ask if Mrs. Finnerty is in, to receive a VIP."

"A VIP, is it?" said her dad. He wanted to pull her close to his aching chest, hoping that would quell his pain. Instead, he patted the top of her head. Caroline by now had plenty of practice at mastering the art of not falling asunder.

As they made their way to the lift, Caroline was nervous. She did not know Mrs. Finnerty's current condition. Although unspoken, she felt that part of nurse Kathleen's mission was to check out that very thing. She did know her daughter. Leaving without seeing Mrs. Finnerty was not an option. Her nervousness dissipated as soon as they stood in the doorway of the private room. There sat their wonderful, generous neighbour surrounded by a new batch of flowers, wearing her best frock, and both arms outstretched towards

Angela. Shame may have been the catalyst that triggered her recovery; pride was evident today in those outstretched arms. Caroline's lack of mastering her emotions was almost revealed. "Come, let me look at you?" she addressed her young visitor. Remaining in the background, Tony and Caroline watched them embrace.

"Amy made you a card, and I wrote you a note. Dr. Alan said it was okay to give them to you," Angela explained. "The operation is all set now, and soon the lump will be out. Afterwards, Dr. Alan said there are lots of exercises I must do. They said you must do exercises too. Do you?"

Mrs. Finnerty affirmed. "I do. I just finished before you came. I had to put on this frock by myself to help strengthen my arm. I suppose you will be strengthening your mended leg too. Between us we're worth an arm and a leg."

Turning towards her parents, she said, "That's funny." As usual, Mrs. Finnerty had lightened the moment. "Dr. Alan said when I get home, I will go every day to the rehab centre near us and get stronger," continued Angela. "Will you do that too?"

"Oh yes, I must. Isn't that marvelous? Maybe we can be there at the same time. I really hope so. Now, you must not stay too long, but I have something to show you before you go."

Reaching under her pillow, she produced her album. Angela stared as she was reminded of her own duckling book under her pillow. Caroline and Tony gathered round as Angela turned each page slowly without comment.

"Will you always keep it under your pillow?" she asked at the last photo.

"I always will," came the reply.

"So I will always be with you," deduced Angela.

"Always," affirmed Mrs. Finnerty.

Later when everything was quiet, there was time to read the card from Amy.

Mrs. Miller is not fussy about her food anymore. She misses you. So do I. Love Amy.

Angela's note read:

We are both sharing the same island. Sleep well. Love Angela

Retrieving the album, Mrs. Finnerty tucked the card and the note into the pocket of the back cover. She replaced it under the pillow and slept very well.

Between having her blood pressure taken at six in the morning and the arrival of breakfast at 8:00, the well-rested Mrs. Finnerty studied her album. It didn't take her long to realise that the foundation was marching on. She however, was a few steps behind. That would never do. Fiona Hannon and Dorothy Hennessey were summoned. Delighted as they were at her remarkable recovery it was clear that work lay ahead for the both of them. "Ladies, you're here, good. We have a lot to arrange." She was propped up in bed, which enhanced the aura of authority surrounding her. "I made a list and you need to see this." She produced the album from under the pillow and searched for the list while they looked through it. "As you can see a lot has been going on. Unfortunately, I did not have an opportunity to put things in place for the work to continue. We decided in Haymarket who would be responsible for what. This…this…medical event prevented me from legalizing those positions. Mrs. Walsh is treasurer, but the poor woman has no money, not a penny." Mrs. Finnerty signed. Fiona and Dorothy Hennessey looked at each other. Taking in the Queen Victoria vision in the bed, they howled with laugher. The occupant of the pillow throne looked around, saw the humour of it all, and joined them. When the young girl came to clear away the breakfast tray, she thought it best to call a nurse. A fake frown and a wagging finger from the nurse quieted them. "Oh, stop it. You two have to help me," pleaded the *queen*.

"Let's have a look at that list," Dorothy said. It was a list of names. It included those who met in Haymarket and their titles. Also listed was Mrs. Hennessey, CEO; Mark Hannon, general manager; Fiona Hannon, social services director; Madge Costello public relations; and Una Flynn, administration.

"Well," said Mrs. Hennessey.

"Well indeed," echoed Fiona.

"Any objections?" inquired the *queen*.

With all due deference to her majesty, Fiona and Dorothy said "none" in unison as they curtseyed.

Two days later, the bank manager Mr. Roberts, the solicitor Mr. Leech, the board members, and Mrs. Finnerty, the benefactor, assembled in one of the two family sitting rooms on the first floor of the Baybridge Medical Centre. Multiple papers were signed, sealed, and delivered. Foundation credit cards were issued appropriately, Madge captured it all on camera, and Fiona and Dorothy knew now how the album came to be.

Mrs. Finnerty had a quiet word with Una Flynn. "I know you had to vacate your flat when the position at school ended. Have you found other accommodations yet?"

"Not yet. I have a few days left. I am getting a bit desperate," Una explained.

Mrs. Finnerty continued, "Would you consider sharing with someone not quite your peer? My house is in need of human contact right now. I will be staying at the rehab centre for a while after I leave the hospital. I hope to return home then. I could do with the company and a cup of tea occasionally. Mrs. Miller the cat needs a bowl of food daily, but she lives outside. I have a good library you might enjoy. You would have the house to yourself for a while.

Una said yes quickly in case she fainted before doing so.

Today's clothesline boasted a mixture of fabrics. All would dry easy in the gentle breeze.

CHAPTER 65

The flurry of activity as witnessed in the vicinity of the Bright House resembled a movie set. Getting the green light from Mrs. Finnerty was akin to a director roaring *action*. Money was not the issue; the promise not to change anything had been the holdup. No more. Cobwebbed ladders were dragged out of sheds, dungarees were rescued from indefinite hibernation and unfurled, brushes were readied for the numerous cans of paint, some bought, most donated. Grainne had two large tins of white and two small tins of red not used in the recent decorating of her salon. She mentioned that the red might make a nice trim somewhere. It did. She also had a pack of brushes, assorted sizes, unopened. Nuala's crew pronounced the wood floors in remarkable condition, no sanding, just buffing required. "Good news," declared Mrs. Walsh, "saves us a lot time not having to wait for floors to dry." More good news when Sammy informed her the curtains that did not match her new couch were a perfect fit for the bay window in Una Flynn's office. "Thank you, Sammy, never thought my colour blindness would be an asset. It's an ill wind that favours nobody," replied Mrs. Walsh as she fell over a desk parked right in her path. A guilty look passed over Mark Hannon's face as he looked across the desk at the tottering lady.

"Oh sorry," Mark offered.

To release him from his unease, she said, "Lovely piece of furniture you have there, Mark."

"It is," he explained. "Fiona has been falling over it in the corner of her gym room ever since the kids moved out. To save any more accidents, it's time it had a place of its own. According to my measurements, it will fit perfectly in the front office. Looks like it was made for Una Flynn."

His son-in-law popped up behind him. "Colm is here to give me a hand." Together the men moved the desk, enabling the trapped lady to escape. She peeped through the bay window from the outside. She decided it looked quite quaint and would indeed suit Una.

She was just a short distance from the house when she met the twins, Carmel and Maura. "Mrs. Walsh, is it true about Mrs. Finnerty. We were on our holidays at Auntie Jean's. We just heard the news. Is she all right?" Carmel spoke apolitically, explaining why they were absent until now. Her sister stood close, wide-eyed, and head nodding. Mrs. Walsh felt sorry for them. Giving them both a hug, she reassured them.

"Yes, girls, she is in hospital. We were in the car when her breathing changed, so we took her directly to the medical centre. She was attended to immediately and continued to improve daily. Really, she is doing very well. No visitor for another day or two. Then she will transfer to the rehab centre, and you can see her every day." The girls looked relieved and smiled at each other.

"We work two extra days in the summer at the Saturday job. The rest of the time we will be at the centre with Mammy." Maura felt the need to clarify that.

"Mrs. Finnerty will thrive with you two around, no doubt about it," declared Mrs. Walsh. With broad smiles, the girls appreciated the vote of confidence and offered to go now and help at the Bright House.

Looking back at them as they walked with a new spring in their step, she noticed her husband on top of one ladder. His friend from work atop another. She was proud to take in the sight of their eldest son standing guard at the base of his dad's ladder. He shifted his position slightly, revealing the two bright earbuds on either side of his head. He was listening to music! All she could do was pray that neither of the men shouted for help from their lofty position. Still she remained proud of her son. After all, he could be at home sprawled on the new couch, two big-sneakered feet on the coffee table. Shrugging, she made her way to the Coughlans'.

The activity at the Bright House was dizzying. Sammy, Kitsy, and her girls toiled away undisturbed. Their work space did not need painting. Not much wall there, mostly window. Kitsy's duckling logos got rave reviews, old penny-sized discs made from reinforced fabric that were embroidered with a little duckling whose wing bore the letters *ATT.*

Everybody wanted one. All requests were denied. If on a rare occasion a mistake occurred, the disc was destroyed. No point in rummaging in Kitsy's bin! Above the door leading to this bright space, Kitsy painted the logo and the words *Hill Hands.* This became the focal point once you entered the building.

Then, as if the pause button had been pressed, it all stopped. The entire cast dwelt in the space between the diving board and the water. It was the day of Angela's operation.

CHAPTER 66

When news of Ms. Flynn's plan to move in next door reached Amy, she was at once excited and worried. "Ms. Flynn is very nice when you have to go the school office for anything. She was very good with the turbans. I am worried Mrs. Miller will make a fuss about her food again, and the house is different with no stairs or anything. I must show her where Mrs. Finnerty keeps things." She rambled on with her list of concerns. Caroline and Mrs. Walsh listened intently.

"You certainly have a point there, Amy," agreed Mrs. Walsh. "I wouldn't know where things were."

"It's a bit of a problem, all right," affirmed Caroline. She gave a go ahead nod to Mrs. Walsh.

"I'm thinking we're are in need of your expertise, seeing as you are the only one familiar with the layout next door."

Amy, aware of the truth of that statement, answered.

"I'll go out and wait for her so. She will need help for the first new nights too while you and Daddy are at the hospital." The two adults swiveled simultaneously and watched this amazing child walk out the front door.

She sat on Mrs. Finnerty's doorstep. Tony Coughlan paused to drink her in before approaching. "I heard you were on the Ms. Flynn case," he stated using his Garda tone as he sat down beside her, his long legs stretched out before him.

"Daddy," she yelped. She kissed him on the cheek. Then a frown crossed her brow. "Does she have a key?" she inquired

"Yes, she does, pet, Mrs. Finnerty gave her one. I think it's great that a young lady from your school will be right here. You like her, don't you?" asked her dad.

"I do like her, Daddy. I think she is going to get a bit of a shock when she sees all the books. I don't know what will happen when she finds out there's no stairs," mused Amy.

"Sure won't you be here to help her with all that? Lucky Ms. Flynn," reassured her dad. He patted her head as he stretched to his full height. He left her on the steps contemplating her responsibilities.

Marry Poppins crossed Amy's mind as Ms. Flynn approached. She was carrying an old-fashioned suitcase; her clothes were dark and her smile bright. Amy looked up, saying, "Ms. Flynn, I am going to help you find things."

"Amy, that's great news. I was a little worried about not knowing the place. I hear you are no stranger to this house." Una approached as she spoke. She put her bag down and sat beside Amy on the step. Closer, Amy could see that Ms. Flynn's luggage was an expensive leather carryall. It just looked like a suitcase. She wore black jeans with a tailored jacket cropped at the waist. Not a bit like Mary Poppins, except for the smile. They chatted for a while as Caroline kept watch from a discreet spot in her garden. Ms. Flynn did not fail to surprise with her excited reactions to all that Amy showed her.

Mrs. Miller watched all the comings and goings from the windowsill and vowed not to be put off her food by any of it.

Amy and Una sat on the fluffy quilt atop the bed in the guestroom. First, they read aloud to each other. At intervals they stared at the ceiling as they exchanged past stories of their own and future dreams. They fell asleep, Amy almost across the bed, Una scrunched in a corner. The folding camp bed meant for Amy stayed folded. The next morning, they packed Angela's ornate book bag for the hospital and replenished Mr. Doherty's Gift bookcase for when she came home. Una was fascinated by Amy's explanation as to how both of these items had come about.

Madge was in the waiting room with Caroline and Tony on the morning of Angela's operation. It was her usual time with Mrs. Finnerty. This morning she served as the news bearer on Angeles's progress. Caroline was glad of her presence. She sat quietly. Tony was flanked by a senior collogue. They didn't lose track of time they just weren't tracking it. At this point they were the only people in the waiting room. A tea cart stood in one corner, bearing small sandwiches, sliced bread for the toaster, and an electric kettle to make tea. On a small table in the opposite table sat a phone connected directly to the inside of the operating theater, enabling the staff inside to update a designated person in the waiting room. Tony was that person. Caroline thought whoever put this in place ought to be canonised. The phone rang. Stillness in the room as Tony approached to answer it. He recited aloud what he was hearing exactly as it was being told to him.

"The knee joint is not affected. The edges of the shinbone remaining after the removal of the tumour is healthy. Doctor Alan can proceed now with the graft. It's good news, Sergeant, good news indeed. Angela is tolerating the procedure well. Have a cup of tea now and eat something." Tony was staring straight at his wife as he spoke. Madge captured the moment with her camera from the tea corner and then made some tea. Caroline collapsed into her husband's arms. Madge went to tell Mrs. Finnerty, who, in turn, collapsed into Madge's arms.

Several cups of tea later, Dr. Alan appeared in the door of the waiting room. He indicated that they should stay seated. They did not. "It went well. The knee joint is unaffected which as you know was a major concern. The tumour itself was lower down the shinbone than we first thought, small and contained. The tests done during the operation showed the ends of the remaining bone was clear of cancer. The prosthesis attached well, and we are very hopeful. Complex and lengthy as it was, each step was uneventful." He was emotional as he finished speaking. His eyes were brimming tears. Caroline stepped forward with a tissue.

"Dr. Alan, I thought they mopped the surgeon's brow in there," she said through her own tears. Madge captured this precious moment for posterity.

"Must have been the cheap swabs today," he said. He touched her shoulder and left them. A nurse replaced him to give further instructions.

Caroline stayed with the sleeping Angela when she returned to the ward from the recovery room. Tony went home to give the news to everybody, returning later to spend the night in the hospital.

Action! The painting and the hammering at the Bright House resumed in earnest the next morning. They had a new deadline. Everything had to be in shipshape by the time Angela and Mrs. Finnerty were discharged from hospital.

CHAPTER 67

The morning after Angela's operation, Una and Amy walked to Quigley's. Much as Una Flynn told Amy to please call her Una, she just couldn't. Instead, she started to call her Ms. Una. Very American she was told. That settled it. Ms. Una it was.

Mrs. Quigley was not surprised to see the two of them together. It appeared as though they were expected. A box of mini sausage rolls, two small raisin scones, a container of mixed berries, and a single-sized carton of local milk awaited them. "Breakfast is served," announced Mrs. Quigley. She placed the box on the counter and continued, "Ms. Flynn, your favourite coffee is coming right up. I also have an envelope here with donations to Angela's purse. Will you give it to Mrs. Walsh for me before it bursts at the seams. I'm going to need something a bit sturdier if this keeps up. Maybe she has some ideas." She put her two elbows on the counter to bring her closer to Amy, and then she whispered, "Congratulations on the wonderful news, give Angela a wee kiss from me." Amy's broad smile said yes. Straightening up to the tall thin space she usually occupied, Mrs. Quigley handed Una her cup of coffee. "Enjoy," she called as they went through the shop door.

They headed back towards Mrs. Finnerty's. Amy stopped. "Ms. Una, can we go to the park? I never had a picnic breakfast. Have you ever had a picnic breakfast?" Una stopped, put a finger to her chin, seemed to be in deep thought, and then answered.

"I don't remember if I ever did. I will remember our picnic breakfast, though."

They turned around, entered the park, and walked a little bit. The smell of the sausage rolls soon put a stop to the walking. The nearest bench beckoned them. They savored the food in the morning sun and were the envy of all the joggers. Mothers with prams smiled as they walked past, recognizing Mrs. Quigley's picnic box. Una continued. "Amy, Angela is probably going to be very sleepy when we visit. She had a very big day yesterday and will need time to recover. She might be drowsy for the next few days because the nurses will give her medicine to stop the new leg from hurting. The good thing is she can hear everything your say and is smiling inside. Just talk away as usual. We won't stay too long. Okay?" Amy finished her sip of milk before explaining.

"Angela has to teach her new leg how to talk to her brain, so she can walk. That hurts and takes a long time. I'm going to be her helper." She finished the rest of the milk. Una sat in silence. No parent, no teacher, no tutor, no professor had ever made her feel as inadequate as Amy's simple explanation did at this moment. A reply was not needed.

They piled into Ms. Una's red mini, ornate bag of books on the back seat. They sang along to the car radio on the way. It didn't' matter that neither of them knew the words. Round and round the car park they went until finally a space opened.

Angela was drowsy but awake. She and her sister huddled close, making their own plans. Caroline brought Una up-to-date. Dr. Alan and Dr. Owens made rounds earlier. Both were happy with the progress. Caroline and Tony were educated on how to access Angela's pain level. Adequate pain management was key for the next several days. Passive exercises at first would advance to active, requiring Angela to participate. Pain control was necessary to optimise the outcome. The hope was that in a week or ten days, Angela would go home and continue her rehabilitation therapy daily at the centre near their home. "Ms. Flynn, we can't thank you enough for taking care of Amy. She just hoisted herself on you. Is that okay?" Caroline added.

"Actually, I have been renamed. I am Ms. Una now and loving every minute spent with my new friend. Please relax here with Angela. Do not squander a single second worrying about us. We intend to go to help at the Bright House this afternoon if you have no objections. She tells me she wants to see my office and spend time with Kitsy and Sammy." No objections. Amy retrieved the duckling book from under Angela's pillow. Quietly, she read it to Angela.

While Amy and Ms. Una were at the Bright House, Sergeant Coughlan drove Mrs. Finnerty to the Baybridge rehabilitation centre in the chariot. That afternoon she started the rigorous work required by the therapists to progress from the clinical wing to a room in the manor. Eight days later, she was joined by Angela, who started her daily outpatient sessions. When the first session was over on day one, she joined the book club, reestablished by the twins and Mrs. Finnerty. Ms. Una restarted the book club at Mrs. Finnerty's house. Amy was joined by Cara and a few of Sammy's friends from the Hill.

As part of the rehabilitation program, a therapist accompanied the patient on a home visit. As both their homes were known to be safe by the therapists, the Bright House was chosen for their outing instead. The welcome for Angela and Mrs. Finnerty as they arrived together was legend. Tara and Ame were overcome when they saw them alight from the rehabilitation vehicle, helping each other walk towards the entrance. It took Mr. Shiva all his time not to step forward to assist. No need, they made it together. Mrs. Finnerty being the more able with of the two at this point was Angela's support. Madge had prepared a brag wall along the main hallway. A photo of Mr. Foley flanked by Mrs. Finnerty's dominated the center. The image of Caroline Coughlin mopping Dr. Alan's brow held everyone spellbound.

Two weeks later, Fiona woke to the bright sunshine filling her room. She sat upright in bed, knowing something was different. She lay back on her pillows then sat bolt upright. She realised the gnawing feeling of apprehension under her ribs there for so long had gone. "It's gone," she sang aloud. "It's completely gone." She didn't care, rather loved talking to herself.

Without a doubt, she knew that her clothesline for today would be draped in her best finery. The very finest item would be added later when she stood on the sand dunes and told the oceans.

CHAPTER 68

Dr. Angela Coughlin, paediatric oncologist, adjusted her turban before stepping through the doors of Happy Street. Her hair was lighter now than when she was a child, with a slight wave. She stopped for a split-second when she passed her old room. However busy she was or how fast she was walking, her head turned involuntarily towards the yellow door. It was Friday, late morning. She was not on call this weekend and planned to be on the road to Wicklow by one o'clock. Her parents and sister were coming for the weekend. One last check on a new patient's labs would put her mind at ease if they were within normal range. Jonathon, an eight-year-old and current resident of her old yellow-doored room, was reclining on the small chaise proudly wearing his maharaja turban. At first glance he appeared to be sitting on a throne in the lotus position. One leg was crossed in front of him; the other had been amputated. He was not wearing his prosthetic limp, thus revealing a white gauze dressing applied to the stump. "Hello again, Jonathon. Thought you'd seen the last of me today. I promise to leave you alone if these last tests are good." She approached the pirate ship, where she was met by his nurse. They checked the results together. No sign of infection. "You are right as rain, my dear fellow," she said to Jonathon as she passed his throne. "Keep an eye on them all until I get back."

"I will so, Dr. Ange," came the reply. He found himself looking at her cane as she walked away from him. He remembered what she told him about her own journey, how she needed three operations in all as she grew. He took solace in that and loved her for sharing with him. The story about the turbans intrigued him. Jonathon had plans of his own.

Her car was packed. She stayed in rooms on the grounds of Park Edge Hospital when she was on duty. She drove the hour-plus journey to Wicklow when she did not. Today she was leaving till noon on Monday. Bliss! As she drove home, she found herself reflecting on how she came to live in Wicklow in a beautiful house overlooking the River Vartry. It reminded her so much of Baybridge. This was all due to Mrs. Finnerty. Everything seemed to be. Two months after her last chemo treatment when she was ten years old this extraordinary woman died peacefully in her sleep in her own extraordinary home, Madge's photo album tucked safely under her pillow. She did not dwell on the weeks that followed. She could not. Not even now.

Mr. Leach came to see her parents and informed them that Angela had inherited Mrs. Finnerty's parents' house in Wicklow. It had been rented out until a month before her death. Amy inherited Mrs. Finnerty's house in Baybridge. Angela never once attempted to explain to anyone what this generosity meant to her. She could not meet that challenge today if her life depended on it.

Before going home, she had one stop to make, a detour of one and half miles to where Mrs. Finnerty was buried next to her parents. Today was the anniversary of her death. Angela patted the box on the passenger seat beside her, just checking.

Taking the box with her, she walked to the grave. Close to the gravestone sat a glass dome encasing a turban. Angela removed it and replaced it with a new one. The old turban was put in the box and taken home. Angela had put a new turban on Mrs. Finnerty's grave every year since her death. The vividness of the turbans faded over time. It was important to Angela to revive the glory of the fabric each year with a new turban. Equally important to Hill Hands was that it be made by them in the Bright House. Bending her head, she read the inscription on the tombstone aloud. *And when night falls, they swim to their little island and go to sleep.*

She parked in the driveway of her beautiful old Wicklow house and walked towards the door. She heard him before she opened it. "Mamma, Mamma!" screamed her three-year-old son, Finn, as he leapt into her arms. She could see, lying on the play table behind him, the book he always had close, his very own duckling book. Hers was under her pillow.

Today was sure to be the perfect drying day!

DEDICATION

To my parents, John and Bridget Finn.

ACKNOWLEDGEMENTS

My husband Paul Loving
Norma Donato my typist
My sisters Brid Keaveney and Mary Pattison
Michele Stanco my chemotherapy adviser
Mary Simpson and Mary Braun from church

ABOUT THE AUTHOR

Eileen Finn Loving was born in Sligo, Ireland, a place she returns to often. She moved to London to pursue a career in nursing. She worked there as a registered nurse until Paul, a young man in the United States Navy, swept her off her feet. After their marriage, they were deployed to the San Francisco area where their two sons were born, then to Rota, Spain, back to London, and finally to the Pentagon. They settled in Northern Virginia where four lively young grandsons keep them on their toes.

april 2020.

To Kim,

my covid-19.
leader and
neighbour.!

Best wishes

Eileen Finn Loving

CPSIA information can be obtained
at www.ICGtesting.com
Printed in the USA
LVHW051134130919
630971LV00005B/110

9 781644 24764